S0-APO-728

TWO COMPLETE WESTERNS FOR ONE LOW PRICE!

HAMMERHEAD RANGE

Suddenly Curt Lawrence's brows drew down and gave him a predatory look. "Do you know Jack Perry?"

Buck played ignorant. "Never heard of Jack Perry."

"Seems to me Jack Perry boasted about a couple of drifters coming into this area to side with him."

A stiffness had gone through the riders. Hard eyes were on Buck and Tortilla Joe. Lawrence's right hand, big and thick-knuckled, rested on his gun's grip.

"You two gunhands comin' in to side with Sam Perry?"

Buck shook his head.

"Okay," Lawrence said, but Buck knew the matter was not ended.

THE TALL TEXAN

"Don't be in such a rush, sodbuster!"

Jim's only hope was to make a good fight of it. And his right, arcing up, slammed into Nelson's jaw.

From the corner of his eye, Jim saw the other two gunmen leave the hitchrack. They came in like wolves pulling down a young steer. Hard fisted, ruthless, they made a punching bag of him. He remembered staggering from one to the other, rocking under their blows. Blood was salty in his mouth.

His lips were cut, his nose bleeding.

Then something hard crashed across Jim's skull.

And he slipped into blackness.

HAMMERHEAD RANGE/
THE TALL TEXAN

LEE FLOREN

LEISURE BOOKS   NEW YORK CITY

A LEISURE BOOK®

January 1993

Published by

Dorchester Publishing Co., Inc.
276 Fifth Avenue
New York, NY 10001

If you purchased this book without a cover you should be aware that this book is stolen property. It was reported as "unsold and destroyed" to the publisher and neither the author nor the publisher has received any payment for this "stripped book."

HAMMERHEAD RANGE Copyright © MCMLV by Arcadia House
Copyright © renewed MCMLXXXIII by Lee Floren

THE TALL TEXAN Copyright © MCMLXXXVII by Lee Floren

All rights reserved. No part of this book may be reproduced or transmitted in any form or by any electronic or mechanical means, including photocopying, recording or by any information storage and retrieval system, without the written permission of the Publisher, except where permitted by law.

The name "Leisure Books" and the stylized "L" with design are trademarks of Dorchester Publishing Co., Inc.

Printed in the United States of America.

HAMMERHEAD RANGE

CHAPTER ONE

The wind howled across the Arizona desert. It bent mesquite and sagebrush, and it made an eerie sound as it whistled through desert willows. Even ghost trees had to bow before the demands of the hard wind. Head bowed, Buck McKee, the tall Texan, rode into the wind, with his partner, Tortilla Joe, the Mexican, taking the lead. Their weary horses plodded forward, hoofs shuffling on sand.

They were rounding the toe of a small hummock when suddenly a rider roared out of nowhere. He rode in wild haste and, because of the thick sandstorm, he did not see Tortilla Joe's horse until the two broncs had collided. The rider's horse hit that of the fat Mexican head on.

"What een the heck ees thees—?"

Tortilla Joe's startled yelp jerked up Buck McKee's head. Hurriedly the lanky Texan reined his horse to one side, thereby escaping the kicking entanglement of horseflesh.

Because the wind had been blowing in the wrong direction neither partner had heard the rider approach. Tortilla Joe's horse lay on his right side, kicking like a wounded jackrabbit. The fat Mexican sat on the sand, his thick jowls showing a wild, startled look.

Buck McKee looked at the other rider, and surprise touched his high-cheekboned, suntanned face. This rider also sat on the sand, about ten feet away from where Tortilla Joe sat. The rider's mount—a sweat-streaked sorrel gelding—had painfully staggered to his feet. Now he stood with his off foreleg lifted, plainly in pain. But Buck was not interested in the lamed saddler. He had all his interest focused on the strange rider.

For the rider was not a man. The rider was a young woman—and a lovely one, at that. Her hat, hanging by the jaw trap, lay on her back, exposing a mass of black, shiny hair. Her face was small, and right now it showed anger.

Buck saw a rather thin face, and the mouth seemed rather severe for one so young, but he blamed this on the duress of the moment. She tugged at her buckskin riding skirt, for it had slipped above her knees. She had very nicelooking knees, Buckshot McKee noticed instantly.

"Quit gawking at my knees, you long-eared baboon!"

Buck grinned. She had a temper, too. Quickly he went out of saddle. Three strides of his long legs, and he was beside her. He winked at Tortilla Joe, still sitting on the sand, and the girl did not see the wink.

"Did you skin your knee, miss?"

She tugged at her riding skirt and hid her knees. "Keep your hands off my person!" she warned. Again she jerked at her dress. "And I can get up alone, too! If you two galoots had only watched where you were going— Oh, my ankle!"

Buck had her by both elbows. He was still grinning like a monkey who had just discovered an open paint can.

"Maybe it's busted," he said.

"You sound hopeful," she said hurriedly. "I got to take the trail again. They're chasing me."

"But you just got here," Buck joked. "We like your company, don't me, Tortilla Joe?"

The Mexican nodded. "We sure does, mees—"

She did not give her name, though. She hobbled a little, getting her ankle in shape to hold her weight. Buck stood, hands on his hips, and watched, a satanic grin on his wide mouth.

"You sprained your nigh leg. Your bronc has sprained his off leg. You two should have worked together and sprained legs on the same side. And by the way, miss—who is chasin' you, and why?"

"Oh, close your big mouth!"

Buck smiled wider. Tortilla Joe grinned, but he remained sitting. He seemed to be so lazy he did not want to get to his feet.

Buck said, "A frosty little girl, eh? Tortilla, you down for the day—or do you figure to walk again?"

Laboriously the fat Mexican got to his feet. He seemed to be all right; the shock had passed, and his dark face was smiling. The girl almost fell, and again Buck McKee got her by both elbows.

"Get your hands off me—"

Buck said, "I'll give the matter proper thought. You got a nice set of elbows, miss. They're soft and feel good, and they sure are tanned and well-formed— Ouch!"

She swung a right hand, intending to slap him. Buck ducked hurriedly and stepped back, and she almost fell. Buck kept on grinning and she spat at him. Then she hobbled over to a granite boulder. She had tears in her eyes. Buck wondered whether they were caused by pain or by anger.

He decided to stop teasing her. Her ankle might even be broken. Anyway, it was sprained

—and sometimes a sprain was as bad as a break, if not worse. Buck therefore said nothing.

Tortilla Joe looked at his horse which, by this time, had struggled to his feet. The bronc had all four hoofs on the ground and he stood in apparently good shape.

"My *caballo,* he ees all right, Buckshots," the Latin said. He panted his words. "But the weend—she ees steel knocked out from under my ribs." Suddenly he cocked his dark, heavy head and seemed to be listening to something which Buck had not yet heard.

"What do you hear, Tortilla Joe?"

The Mexican wet his thick bottom lip. "First, I hears the weend—all the time, the weend. Then I hears something else, Buckshots?"

"What is it?"

"Somewhere I hear riders an' they come thees way—and they come at a fast pace. You heard them now, no?"

"I hear them," Buck said.

Suddenly the pain left the girl's face. She was on her feet, her limp completely gone now.

"Riders coming?" she demanded.

"I hear them," Buck said. "Sounds like quite a bunch of them. This sandstorm hides them. Hey, where you going, young lady?"

"I got to get away from them!" The young girl panted her words. "If they catch me— I got to get to Cinchring camp. I got to get help for Jack. They'll lynch him unless I get help!"

Buck stared at her. The hoofs of the horses came closer; they rode at a hard pace, breasting the sandstorm. Tortilla Joe stared, tongue idle on his bottom lip.

"Who they lynch named Jack?" the Mexican asked.

"You two don't know him; you're strangers here. I know every man on this range—you two don't fit in. . . . But I'll tell you, and then I got to get out fast. They aim to lynch Jack Perry!"

Buck said, "Jack Perry. . . . Now who aims to hang Perry, and for what reason, woman?"

But he got no answer. Unexpectedly she darted toward Buck's horse. Despite her lame ankle, she moved like a frightened antelope. Tortilla Joe, guessing at her idea, tried to grab her. He might just as well have grabbed for a hunk of the wind. Buck caught his partner by a wide shoulder.

"Let her go, Tortilla!"

"Buck, she ees goin' to steal your horse, no!"

"Let her go!"

She was already in saddle. The stirrups, stretched out to fit Buck's long legs, were too long for her; therefore she put her feet in the leathers, using these for stirrups. Her quirt rose and fell and the startled horse roared away, with her words whipping back over her shoulder.

"Thanks for the use of your bronc! I'll bring him back when I get done with him."

Then she was gone around a sand hummock. And Buck McKee looked thoughtfully at solemn Tortilla Joe, who in turn gazed back at his partner.

"Always," the Mexican said slowly, "there ees the troubles for us, Buckshots. When our troubles they weel end?"

"When we're both dead, I reckon. Did she say Jack Perry?"

"That name she deed say, Buckshots. And what ees the more, she ees say somebody he ees aimin' to lynch our *amigo,* Jack Perry?"

"That's what she said, Tortilla Joe."

Tortilla Joe shook his heavy head. "I wonder who the girl she was, and why they chase her? And why they want to lynch our friend, and for where is the lynchin' to take place?"

Buck shrugged.

The hoofs roared closer. Both of the partners turned. Now they could see the riders. They spilled over a hill, and they rode with hard and patent purpose. They were a colorful outfit.

Gaudy pintos—black and bay and gray—were in the group. One man rode a long-legged bay; another sat saddle on a deep sorrel. They saw the partners and came toward them, dust kicking under steel-shod hoofs. They swerved to evade catclaw and sagebrush, and they roared across the bottom of the dry wash toward the partners.

Buck and Tortilla Joe watched. Tortilla Joe's thick face held an almost stupid look, but Buck knew that back of that apparent docility was an alert awareness. This Mexican could show a very deceptive face. As for himself, Buck felt danger tug at his innards, building a cold wall around his belly. These men were not out looking for cattle or running wild horses.

They rode with stiff intent, and they were after the girl, Buck realized. Danger was in the wind.

Buck turned and looked toward the direction taken by the fleeing woman. She was out of sight. The wind, he realized, had died down somewhat; its wild fury had blown itself out, and now it was tapering off. But he had no thought for the wind. Jack Perry, according to the strange woman, was in danger of losing his life.

Buck put his thoughts into words. "Judging from past experiences, they lynch men because those men have killed somebody. This girl said they aimed to lynch Jack Perry. Therefore he must have killed somebody."

"And thees girl—she ees ride to Ceenchring Camp, wherever or whatever eet ees. Hola, that man in the lead—he ees a big fellow, Buckshots."

"Plenty of man there," Buck had to admit.

CHAPTER TWO

They came in fast, reining in their blowing broncs. And the big man was in the lead. He was big in body, and arrogance had marked him. He rode a tough black-and-gray pinto, sitting a hand-engraved Phoenix saddle. He wore a wide Stetson hat, and the chin straps, meeting under his craggy jaw, were held together by a shiny gold nugget that now glistened in the sun.

Buck saw that a buckskin jacket, gaudy with red and black beads, covered his wide shoulders and thick chest. He saw a flaming red shirt, and the man wore new California pants under wide-winged Cheyenne chaps.

Behind him were his riders. Buck gave them all a momentary glance. They packed Winchester rifles in saddle scabbards and each carried a shot gun, and one or two even toted two pistols. Guns were tied down, and Buck thought, This is a tough outfit, and he looked back at the big young leader.

The man's eyes, glistening and steely, ran over to the lamed sorrel. When he spoke his voice had a superior edge that somehow rubbed against Buck McKee's good nature.

"Where's the girl?" he demanded.

Buck grinned. "She done got away," he said slowly. "She done stole my bronc an' boom—afore I could hold her, she was gone!"

"She stole your horse, you say?"

Buck nodded. "You heard me rightly, Mister Man. She lights into my saddle, and here I am—with her crippled sorrel." He assumed a hang-dog appearance. "Ain't no justice in this here world—"

The young man stood on stirrups, looking in the direction taken by the young woman. The storm had blown itself out and the horizon was rapidly clearing.

His face took on a hard look. "Yonder she rides, men! Over there, and she's so far away a man could never catch her. Our broncs are winded and the chase is over. Thanks to these two strangers, she got away."

They turned hostile eyes on Buck and Tortilla Joe; probing eyes that held anger and rough emotion. The blame for letting this girl escape was laid on the shoulders of the partners.

The big leader said sternly, "Forget the heifer, men." Wind blew hard against him suddenly, then spent its fury. His pale blue eyes rested on Buckshot McKee and Tortilla Joe.

"Who are you two strange buckos?" His voice held authority. "And what for you riding this Salt River country over here in Arizona Territory?"

His voice was harsh and rough as desert sand. It was the voice of a man accustomed to giving orders, and having those orders quickly obeyed. It rubbed against Buckshot like sandpaper. And when the lanky cowpuncher spoke his own voice held naked authority.

"I could ask you the same questions, fellow!"

Behind the big leader a man stirred in leather, hand going toward his holstered gun. Buck flipped him a quick glance, and the man stared at him with dull eyes. Buck looked back at the leader.

A merciless grin, tough and narrow, touched the thin lips, giving the eyes a slanting, rough look. A big hand went up and played with the gold nugget that held the chin straps together under the big jaw. Big knuckles moved; long fingers shoved the nugget up and down the straps. Behind him a horse rolled the cricket in his bit, the sound suddenly shrill and potent with danger.

The big leader spoke slowly. "I take it you two buttons are newcomers to this Hammerhead range. Am I correct in this assumption?"

Buck nodded. Tortilla Joe's heavy head bobbed up and down. The Mexican said nothing; he was leaving all conversation to his partner, a habit of his in time of trouble and stress.

"You're on Hammerhead range."

Buck studied him. "Hammerhead range, eh? Well, it means nothing to me, fellow. Me an' my partner was ridin' along in the sandstorm when this woman rides plumb into my partner's bronc. Both horses go down. The wind muffled her coming. She's got nice knees, fellows."

A rider laughed.

The big man turned on his stirrups. He sent a hard glance toward the man who was laughing. The man closed his mouth and became glum. Then the big man returned his gaze to Tortilla Joe and Buckshot McKee.

Buck had a moment of raw anxiety. The girl had said they were going to lynch Jack Perry. And Jack was the son of an old, old friend of theirs, cowman Sam Perry.

"She'll never git to Cinchring camp in time to get help into Buckskin town," a man said slowly. "By the time them Perry construction hands git into Buckskin, Jack Perry will be hangin' high an' dead, Curt."

The big man nodded. He seemed suddenly to become agreeable and friendly. "My name is

Curt Lawrence," he told Buck and the Mexican. He emphasized the word *Lawrence*. Buck got the impression that the name was supposed to mean something on this desert range. "Now who are you two drifters?"

Buck gave the riders his name and introduced Tortilla Joe.

"This gal mentioned something about this gent named Jack Perry," he said. "Why for do they aim to lynch the fellow?"

"He killed my dad, old John Lawrence." Suddenly Curt Lawrence's brows drew down and gave him a predatory look. "Say, your names sound familiar, men."

Buck asked, "How come?"

"Do you two know Jack Perry?"

Buck played ignorant. He was learning nothing darned fast. "Never heard of Jack Perry until now," he assured Curt.

Curt Lawrence said slowly, "Seems to me I've done heard your handles mentioned before now. . . . Seems to me Jack Perry boasted about a couple of drifters coming into this area to side him. And unless my memory proves wrong—which it seldom does—them two gunmen were to tote the names you just mentioned to me, Mc-Kee. . . ."

A stiffness had gone through the riders. Buck could feel it and taste it and sense it. Hard eyes were on him and Tortilla Joe. Eyes that appraised and watched with wary steeliness.

Curt Lawrence toted a pearl-handled six-shooter. Now his right hand, big and thick-knuckled, rested on the gun's grip. The air was knife-sharp with suspicion and controlled violence.

Buck glanced at Tortilla Joe.

The Mexican's tongue, as wide as that of an ox, came out slowly and attempted to dampen thick lips. Dark, short fingers rested on the handle of the old .45 in its well-oiled holster.

And the Mexican's eyes, seemingly dark and childishly innocent, moved from one man to another, touching this man, that man. They took silent stock of the tough danger.

Buck saw that this situation called for caution and the correct words. The main thing was to get to Buckskin town and keep the citizens from hanging Jack Perry. The thought came that the lynching would not take place until the old wolf's son, Curt Lawrence, could officiate, for Jack Perry had killed Curt's father, and what would be more fitting than to have the son kick out the trap?

Buck and Tortilla Joe had never seen Jack Perry. But he was old Sam Perry's only off-spring and they were deeply in debt to old Sam, who ran a cow spread up in Colorado.

Again Curt Lawrence spoke. "How about it, you two? You two gunhands comin' in to side Sam Perry?"

Buck shook his head. "Never have heard of the name before," he lied.

Curt Lawrence nodded, eyes scheming. "Okay," he said, but Buck knew the matter was not ended.

Buck said, "We need grub. We need shaves and haircuts. We need some sleep on a good bed, not the ground. My partner's bronc is broke to tote double. Why not all of us head into Buckskin town, after we unsaddle the girl's bronc?" He looked at Curt Lawrence. "What handles does that prairie chicken travel under, Lawrence?"

"Her name is Clair McCullen. She'll· bring your horse back, McKee. Get on behind the Mexican and ride back with us, and move pronto."

Buck stood stock-still. He studied the big man with cold insolence. "Are you trying to order me around, Lawrence?"

Again came that stiffness, binding these men in a unit, freezing them tight in saddles. Evidently nobody ever spoke roughly to this son of the dead cattle king. But Lawrence smiled, although the smile was forced.

"You're a salty rooster, McKee. . . . Somebody

might pull your tailfeathers, fellow, if you stick around Salt River long enough. . . ."

"It won't be you," Buck warned.

Tortilla Joe said, "Forgets it, you two," and he swung into saddle. He left his left stirrup free, and Buck put his boot into it. Buck lifted his length across the horse and settled behind the cantle. Tortilla Joe restored his boot to the stirrup.

"Come on, men," Lawrence ordered.

The posse swung its horses and rode back in the direction from whence it had come. Buck bounced a little, arms around Tortilla Joe. They loped across the sandwash, horses kicking sand and gravel. They almost ran over a jackrabbit, which suddenly leaped out from under a sage-brush.

The darting rabbit, jumping out of the sage-brush, made Curt Lawrence's bronc shy, and the big man, anger grooving his face, hit his bronc solidly with his quirt, straightening him out. For a moment then Buck saw raw, terrible violence on the big face, and he knew that the man was driven by harsh passions. And because he knew this, he knew that Curt Lawrence, when aroused, was dangerous.

"Bone-headed bronc," the big man snarled. "Three gaits, the fool—walk, stumble, and fall down. Make good glue, he would!"

"Too tough for glue," a rider hollered. "The Hammerhead is a tough spread, and its broncs are too tough for the glue factory, Curt!"

Buck did some thinking. He added up a few facts and he got some answers. This thing was clear to him now, he figured. He and Tortilla Joe had been heading for Yuma, the town down on the Colorado River on the corner of Arizona Territory and the State of California. They were heading in that direction to get a job punching cows for Gallatin, who ran a spread right at the junction of the Gila and Colorado Rivers. Fall of the year had taken possession of the Colorado country, where they had spent the summer punching cows for old Sam Perry. Soon there would be snow, and both hated snow.

So they had asked old Sam Perry for their time. Faded blue eyes had studied them from under heavy eyebrows.

"So you two aim to drift out, eh?" the old cowman had asked.

Both of the partners thought the world of old Sam. Sam had bailed them out of jail that spring, for the partners had got into a little trouble. The trouble had consisted of starting a gang fight and breaking the windows and furniture in a local saloon to smithereens. Sam had got them out of jail by using his influence with the judge and sheriff. Had it not been for old Sam, the partners would still have been in jail, up there in Colorado.

Buck had nodded. "Drifting south, Sam. Thanks for the boost and the summer wages. Up here a man spends all his summer wages buying winter clothes. Know an old bird named Gallatin—down in southwest Arizona—and he's got a winter job for us. Don't need to buy no winter clothes down under that hot sun."

"Lucky dogs. Can drift when you want to. Not tied down to anything." Old Sam had counted out gold pieces. Arthritis had made his once supple fingers into talons. "Do me a favor, men?"

"Name it," Buck had said.

"When you cross the Continental Deevide, you come down into the Salt River desert. Swing south into a little town called Buckskin an' give my greetings to my only boy, Jack."

Buck had been startled. "Never knowed you had a boy, Sam. Never heard you mention him."

The old man's eyes had become dreamy. "I haven't seen Jack for eight long years, men. But he's a busy one, thet boy of mine. Right now he's developin' some desert land down there—irrigation, I figure. Yep, eight long years—whale of a long time for a man not to see his only offspring."

Buck had promised, "Be glad to give him your greetings, Sam."

"The cook is goin' write Jack a letter today—write it for me. With this rheumatiz, I cain't write good no longer. Never was no hand with a pen, either. I'll warn him you two is comin'. Stay out of barroom fights and jails, men. And don't forget your old friend, Sam Perry."

They had shaken hands. "We'll be back next summer," Buck had promised.

Tortilla Joe had said, "We punch cows again next summer for our old *amigo*. You can bet the life on that, Samuel."

Evidently the cook had written the letter. Evidently the letter had reached Buckskin ahead of them, which was natural. They had loafed along, angling down toward the Gallatin spread. No hurry. They took their time, riding along, enjoying God and Nature. Evidently the cook had mentioned to Jack Perry that two friends of the old gent, named Tortilla Joe and Buck McKee, would drop in. And somehow Curt Lawrence had gotten hold of this information. But the names had not registered with enough impact, and Lawrence was doubtful. The impact would come later, Buck thought with a wry smile.

Curt Lawrence saw that smile. "Something funny, McKee?" he murmured.

Buck said, "Smiled at your ugly face, Lawrence."

Evidently the cowman had a hidden sense of

humor, for apparently Buck's words did not rankle him, or maybe he did not get angry because of Buck's wide grin.

"You're a rough gent, McKee. You blundered into trouble right off the bat. I take it you two are getting this shave and haircut, fillin' your bellies full of restaurant chuck, and then you're drifting on, I figure."

"An order?" Buck asked.

Now the man was hard. The humor was gone, his face was bleak, his words were chopped.

"Judge for yourself, McKee."

Buck felt the push of impatience. They had to reach Buckskin and keep old Sam Perry's only son from being hanged.

"I'm a bettin' man," Buck told Lawrence.

Lawrence studied him. "You want to bet I cain't run you off Hammerhead range?"

Buck grinned and shook his head. "They's two of us astraddle this old nag. Only one man on your pinto. But a pinto hoss, I still say, ain't got no bottom." He sent a scornful glance over the other mounts. "Hammerhead outfits ride pore horseflesh, looks to me. I'm still a bettin' man, Lawrence."

"Which way do your bets run?"

"Even with a double load, this Mexican's bronc can outrun that mangy pinto—and leave the other Hammerhead hosses behind, too!"

A number of men laughed. Curt Lawrence showed a smug grin. "We run good horseflesh on Hammerhead, McKee. Your eyes has been affected by the wind and desert heat. By the way, have you got a few bucks under your felt that you'd feel like usin' to tempt fickle Fate?"

Buck nodded. "Twenty bucks, in gold. Coin of the realm, Curt Lawrence. Bite into it and it bites good. . . ."

Lawrence scoffed, "Chicken feed, fella. But a deal—if it's all you got. Okay, scissorbills, let's hit the gravel wide open. Try to keep from eatin' the big rocks, McKee!"

They roared toward Buckskin. Tortilla Joe rode like a jockey, gross body leaning forward, shoulders bent to deflect the wind. He knew how to get every ounce of energy out of his horse. Buck hung onto the Mexican, also bending forward, and occasionally he glanced back at Curt Lawrence, who whipped his horse with savage slashes of his shot-leaded quirt.

The sun was hot, slipping down behind high igneous peaks. Dust rose and the wind whistled around granite boulders. A catclaw branch hit Buck, catching his shirt sleeve, the spines reaching through the shirt and tearing his forearm. It hurt. But he had no time to nurse his wounds now.

Hammerhead broncs had been ridden hard in

pursuit of Clair McCullen. Buck and Tortilla Joe had loafed along. Therefore the Mexican's horse was fresh while Hammerhead horseflesh was winded. Buck had not expected that the horse, carrying two riders, could outrun the Hammerhead horses; such, though, was proving the case.

He had merely wanted to get more speed up to get into Buckskin sooner. As it was, despite its double load, Tortilla Joe's mount forged ahead. They raced across another sand wash, then hit a wagon road that angled through sagebrush.

"Take the road," Buck shouted in his partner's dark ear.

"We beat them, Buckshots!"

"Thet little signboard back there said it was still a mile into Buckskin," Buckshot McKee warned. "By that time this old hay-burner might be fagged out, totin' both of us."

"He good horse."

"Get your big carcass down so you don't stop so much wind."

Grinning widely, the Latin crouched down, lying along the mane of his horse. Buck also bent his body forward. Now the Hammerhead men were swinging their broncs onto the wagon road.

They were inching up when the partners rode into Buckskin. The town was a weather-beaten and sunburned little burg sitting on a small mesa, and surrounded by sandhills and sage-brush. Mesquite grew in clumps, and juniper trees and scrub oak dotted the hills, green clumps jumping out of the brown bareness. Saguaro cacti rose and held up their spiny arms. Some of the saguaros were very old and very big, reaching around forty feet in height.

But Buck had no eyes for the cacti.

From out of an alley came a cur, fangs snapping. Gaunt, shaggy, he snarled, leaping for the hamstrings of Tortilla Joe's bronc. But the horse was no newcomer and he leaped, almost throwing Buck who hung on, the saddlestrings cutting his hands.

Buck glanced back.

The dog, missing his lunge, had rolled over. Now Hammerhead broncs, roaring in, rode him down. One kicked him, and he rolled end over end. Buck saw him get to his feet, yelp, and dart back into the alley.

Up ahead was a crowd, Buck saw.

And a motley crowd it was—grown ups and children and dogs and even a burro. He saw the gay flash of a Mexican *serape,* the wide-brimmed sombrero of a Mexican *vaquero*. Most of the kids, a glance told him, were Mexican children, and lots of them were rather unwashed.

They were grouped in front of a long adobe building. Squat and rambling, it hugged the hot earth, occupying almost a block.

But it was not the crowd—or the building—that claimed Buck's attention.

Tortilla Joe had drawn rein, and the sides of his horse moved in and out, as the bronc grabbed for air.

Tortilla Joe's eyes were wide, the pupils distended. Automatically his brown, dirty hand rose.

He made the Sign of the Cross.

Now the Hammerhead broncs, also blowing hard, were around Buck and Tortilla Joe. Curt Lawrence's pinto sobbed for breath. The young cowman leaned forward, stirrups holding his weight.

"You win, McKee."

Buck nodded.

He felt sick.

Curt Lawrence dug in his pocket and came out with a twenty-buck gold piece. He held it out to Buck.

"Here you are, McKee."

Curt Lawrence watched Buck. Buck made no move to reach for the coin.

Anger colored Lawrence's face, for Buck paid him no attention. Buck's attention was riveted on the adobe building. Built in the proper Spanish style of architecture, it had jutting ceiling-joists.

Now, from one of these joists, hung the body

of a man. And the wind moved in and turned that body and showed his hands bound behind him. His shadow danced on dust; his body hung limply; the rope had broken his neck.

"They beat us to it," a man murmured.

"Perry'll never murder another man," a man said hoarsely.

Buck thought, in that instant, of Old Sam Perry, up in Colorado. Back in the alley a hound lifted his nose and howled toward the blue bowl of the Arizona sky.

Buck shivered.

Curt Lawrence seemingly had no interest in the hanged man. "Here's your money, McKee," he repeated.

Buck slapped the gold piece to the ground.

Rage colored Curt Lawrence's predatory face.

CHAPTER THREE

Two boots were hooked over the brass rail. One boot was made by Hyer. The other boot was a Justin. Both boots had run-over heels and were scarred and battered. The Hyer belonged to Tortilla Joe. The Justin boot belonged to Buck McKee.

Tortilla Joe sighed and said to the bartender, "I'll take tequila."

The bartender looked at Buck McKee, a question in his eyes. He was a fat man, and his big head was anchored to wide shoulders with a neck as thick as the trunk of a scrub-oak.

"What'll yours be, tall gink?"

"Whiskey," Buck supplied. "Straight, white aprons."

The barkeeper lumbered toward the back-bar. He moved with the agility of a sick Hereford bull whose legs were stiff with blackleg. A fat hand went out and wrapped itself around two bottles. These he spun down the polished top of the bar.

The tequila bottle stopped in front of Tortilla Joe.

The whiskey bottle stopped in front of Buck McKee.

Tortilla Joe said, "He ees the expert, no, Buckshots?"

"No," Buck said.

The bartender scowled.

Buck said, "An old trick. Now try it with two glasses."

The fat hand wrapped itself around a glass. This slid down the bar and stopped in front of Buck. The big face wore a happy grin. Another glass slid down the bar, and this stopped in front of Tortilla Joe.

Then the bartender looked at Buck. "Now what do you say, hairpin?"

Buck said grudgingly, "All right . . . fer a beginner."

The bartender put his wide back against the back-bar rim. He yawned like a sleepy cougar and slowly closed his eyes. He seemed very tired and very weary; yet, despite this cloak of negligence, Buck McKee seemed to sense an alert vigilance. Sometimes these local big shots had bartenders staked out as stooges to listen and report back.

Buck glanced at the man. The barkeeper's eyes were closed, his head drooped—but his ears didn't tote ear-plugs.

Buck poured and spoke out of the corner of his mouth. "Speak Mexican, Tortilla," he advised.

Tortilla Joe drank and studied the bartender over the rim of his glass. "Maybe he ees onder-stand the Mexican?" he said.

The bartender spoke without opening his eyes. "I'm not lissenin' to you fools yap," he snarled.

"Thanks, pal," Buck returned.

Tortilla Joe suddenly swore at Thick Neck in Mexican. He used some pretty tough words; they rolled off his tongue. Thick Neck studied him with amused indifference. Tortilla Joe added some choice fighting words. Thick Neck scowled and then went back to his nap, showing no offense at the Mexican's words. Plainly he did not understand the Spanish tongue.

Tortilla Joe said in Mexican, "He does not understand, Buckshots. Now let us have the long talk, *no es verdad?*"

Buck took another drink. The liquor was a combination of the devil's breath, liquid fire and carbolic acid. He blew on his tongue and grim-aced. Tortilla Joe took another snort. His eyes bugged out, his eyes rolled in moist sockets, and he blew and looked down at his breath.

"No see any fire, Buck?"

"Smoke," Buck said, grinning. "No fire, though." The whiskey was eating the varnish off his stomach. "This burg has a tough stiff setup, *amigo.*"

Tortilla Joe looked at the front window. A wide window marked by streaks of dust and the markings of houseflies. His face took on a long and pathetic look of suffering.

"The death of his son weel be a hard blow on ol' Sam Perry. Hees only son, Jack was— Eef we had got here only the seconds sooner. . . ."

"But we didn't," Buck said practically. He turned his glass slowly and admired the damp rings it made on the bar. "This Curt Lawrence don't cotton to us, *amigo.* First off, he figures we're gunmen who have come in to side the Perry construction outfit. Second off, he just don't like us 'cause we won't bend to his orders. He's a big shot, Tortilla Joe."

The Mexican nodded. Never one to keep his attention upon a single point or person for any length of time, his mind promptly leaped over the form of big Curt Lawrence and settled on the more pleasing image of a woman, a woman named Clair McCullen.

"That Mees McCullen, now . . ." He sighed with blowing lips. "She ees the beauty, no?"

Buck grunted, "A female hoss thief, nothin' more. Operatin' in a rotten town filled with two-bit lynch-mad people. . . . But I gotta wait here until she comes back to town with my horse."

"They theenk she breeng een men from Ceenchring Construction, Buckshots. The whole town he ees talk about that. They say there be a beeg fight with the Lawrence outfeet, and the Lawrence *hombre* he ees got gunmen staked out around the town, they tells me."

Buck nodded. "I cain't help but think of poor old Sam Perry, up there in Colorado. His heart will be busted, an' he'll walk on his chin in sorrow. And we gotta notify him, Tortilla."

"We have to send him a *carta,* a letter."

Buck said, "I'm no hand with a pen or pencil. Can hardly write my own name, 'cept to a check payable to me. You'll have to write to Sam, Tortilla Joe."

"But me—I cannot do the writing, even in the Mexican, Buck. So eet ees up to you, fella."

Thick Neck spoke without opening his eyes. "You two bums are plumb big fools, in my language."

Buck looked at the bartender. "Why them unkind words, fella?"

"You might suddenly find your carcasses weighted down with lead—hot lead, too. Well, if you stick round Buckskin, only one thing I got to say to you."

"And that?" Buck wanted to know.

Thick Neck had his eyes open now. They were wide sad eyes—they were very, very sad. They had the sad look that a man has when he says goodbye to his bosom friend directly before that beloved friend starts the climb upward to the hangman's noose.

"You poor, poor mans," Tortilla Joe murmured, mock sympathy dripping from his words.

"And that one thing?" Buck asked again.

"Goodbye."

Buck grinned. "Thanks."

Thick Neck closed his eyes. His thick chest rose and fell to his measured breathing. To all appearances he was a lizard dozing on a warm rock, at peace with his belly and the world.

Buck paid him no more attention.

Tortilla Joe also had no eyes for the bartender.

Their eyes—rapt and admiring—were on the woman who had sidled between them. Buck saw a small woman not over five feet tall. She was built right in the right places. She had glistening red hair that gleamed and shimmered. Her eyes were green and bright and sharp. Her buckskin blouse, hand-made and embroidered with brilliant beads, contrasted with her buckskin riding skirt.

Buck said in awe, "Holy smoke, and it isn't a doll, either. She's alive, Tortilla Joe." He touched her hand and she did not draw it back. "She's warm and soft, too."

Tortilla Joe stared in make-believe disbelief. "I feel of her other hand." His brown hand went over her tanned hand. His eyes widened. *"Hola,* alive she ees, sure as the shootin'!"

She did not draw back her hand from the Mexican, either. Her green eyes went from the tall Texan back to the squat Mexican. Each held a hand.

Finally she said, "Yes, I'm alive. You can pull back your hands now, men."

Buck grinned. "We ain't been formerly introduced, have we?"

"You mean *formally,* not *formerly.* I have some shocking news for you two bums. Bolster up your knees and prepare for a shock."

"I ready," Tortilla Joe said.

"Me, too," Buck chimed in.

The red lips pursed. The green eyes twinkled with mirth. "I am Mrs. Curt Lawrence, gentlemen."

Buck pulled his hand free.

Tortilla Joe pulled back his hand. He looked at Buck, and Buck, for the first time, looked away from Mrs. Lawrence.

"Some dogs," mourned Buck, "have all the luck."

She smiled. "Maybe the big wart isn't as lucky

as you think, men. The given name is Sybil. Call me by that handle. You're Buck McKee and you're Tortilla Joe something or other. . . . That right?"

"Keerect," Buck said.

She studied Buck coldly. "Where are your manners, Sonny Boy? A man should always tend to the wants of the women first, you know."

Buck came back to earth with a start. "Name yore poison, Mrs. Lawrence," he said grandly.

"Whiskey, bartender. Straight, as usual."

She drank the liquid fire with one gulp. She had a handful of diamonds, Buck saw. As she tossed the drink down Buck suddenly winced, remembering his own burning belly. He studied her ears. She caught his glance, and a look of surprise came across her little face.

"Why look at my ears, stupid?"

"Lookin' to see if any flame or smoke was comin' outa them," Buck said. "My left big toe is dislocated from that last snort I had from the same bottle."

"Hope it hurts bad," she said dryly.

Buck looked down at her. "You're a runt and Curt Lawrence is a big gent. Never the trains shall meet, or somethin' like that."

She shrugged pretty shoulders. "He's big in body, and sometimes too big across the levis. Somebody should take him down a size or two.

Sometimes his hat is too small." She looked at Thick Neck. "You got tears in your eyes. Hope they're not for me; I don't want them. This time pour me a double shot, bartender."

The bottle hit the rim of the glass. The glass went up, met her pretty lips, and the glass came down . . . empty. Buck's big toe on his right foot suddenly hurt. Tortilla Joe said, "I'll watch her ears thees time, Buck."

Sybil Lawrence looked at him. "You're not watching my ears, bucko. Your gaze is sort of covering the whole face."

Buck laughed.

Sybil laughed.

Tortilla Joe blushed like a schoolboy on his first date. He choked on his tequila. He sprayed tequila like a bull walrus coming up for air. Buck kept on laughing, but now there was conjecture in him. What the heck kind of wife did the curly wolf Curt Lawrence own, anyway? Drinking with two strangers who had run against Lawrence. . . .He remembered the terrible, hate-filled look on the big man's face when he had looked down at the twenty-buck gold piece Buck had knocked from his hand; looked at the gold piece, there in the liquid Arizona dust.

Buck spoke with slow solemnity. "If I had a wife, I'd be danged if I'd let her hang around saloons, gabbing with strange, tough men."

The green eyes swung to him. They touched him with cynical appraisal. There was more to this woman than mere bantering, Buck realized. He got this impression and held onto it, and later he found his first guess had been correct. A touch of mockery formed on the pretty lips.

"You aren't married, McKee?"

"Had a wife once, but she run off with a drummer," Buck lied. "She liked his new suitcase."

Her lids were down thoughtfully. "Wonder what kind of a beau you'd make?" she mused.

Buck grinned. "Try me out, honey?"

Suddenly she was serious. "Let's drop this distasteful talk, gentlemen. Marriage, so they say, is an institution. Another definition of an institution is a place where they put loco people. . . . I'll lay the facts before you two saddle-warped sinners—you are both up to your Stetsons in trouble!"

Buck glanced at Tortilla Joe. The Mexican's dark eyes were dark fathomless pools of conjecture. Buck thought, What is this leading up to, anyway? But he gave the thought no tongue, waiting for Sybil Lawrence to clarify her statement. Which she soon did.

"My husband is ornery. He's mad at you two, too. First, you kept him from catching that Clair McCullen heifer, when she headed for Cinch-

ring to get help to keep the citizens from hanging Jack Perry. Then you slapped good money
out of his hand, McKee."

"Blood money," Buck murmured.

"Maybe so, McKee. But the whole town
watched and saw, and he's got pride. That's one
thing the son of cattle king Lawrence—shot
down two days ago by Jack Perry—has, gentlemen. You smashed that pride, McKee. And
you'll pay through the nose, unless you jerk
stakes off this Hammerhead range."

"He doesn't own the air," Buck reminded her.

"Maybe he doesn't, but he thinks he's got a
deed to it. His old man ran this range the way he
saw fit—like a king—and his son has the same
idea. Which brings us around to a dead man,
one Jack Perry."

Buck realized there was quite a bit here he did
not understand. Cinchring Camp, he judged,
was the irrigation camp. Therefore it would be
composed of muleskinners and fresno men. He
glanced out the window. Lawrence gunhands
moved back and forth on Buckskin's main street.
This town was a dynamite cache . . . and a big
one. If a construction hand rode into town, the
match would be dropped. . . . Tortilla Joe's voice
cut into Buck's unhappy thoughts.

"We never had the honor of meeting Jack
Perry, when he was alive."

She frowned. "That's odd. Jack spread word around that two gunmen were being sent down by his father, who is up in Colorado. Those gunmen aimed to help him fight the Hammerhead spread, so he boasted."

Buck groaned.

Tortilla Joe groaned.

Buck said, "Look, Sybil, look. We're jes' dumb, common everyday citizens. We're taxpayers—that's always good for an argument, you know—and we're home lovers, too . . . if we had homes to love. . . . Last summer we punched cows for Jack Perry's good old father. A fine man, good to his help. Sam asked us to drop in and say hello to his son. He wrote the son and told him we were coming. He didn't write—the cook did—rheumatiz has the old man's hands crippled. We rode this way to meet the son and boom—smack into trouble. We wanted to talk to the son, but the son couldn't talk. That's the deal, so help me Hanner."

Green eyes touched him. They were girlish and young and yet, back in their depths, glistened something jade-colored and strong. Again, Buck glimpsed this; again, he did not like his thoughts.

"That's the gospel truth, huh?"

Tortilla Joe said, "Look, I cross myself."

Buck said, "The whole setup, honey."

Tortilla Joe asked, "What ees thees Ceench-reeng Camp, Meesus Lawrence?"

"Cinchring Creek is northeast of here. Jack Perry had a dirt-moving crew working there. He's building a dam on Hammerhead range. That gal you ran into—"

"She runs eento me," Tortilla Joe corrected. *"Hola,* weeth her horse, she knocks me an' my horse down, she does. She ees lovely, no?"

"I don't think she's pretty," Sybil Lawrence said sourly. "Kind of a comely wench if you ask me . . . which nobody has. Well, this McCullen woman is the local seamstress. She and Jack Perry were—well, engaged. When they dragged Jack out to lynch him, she headed out for his construction men."

Buck had dreamy eyes as he remembered the loveliness of Clair McCullen. "Too bad Jack got hung," he said thoughtfully. "With her he'd have had a interesting life, to say the least."

"So you might think." The green eyes went from one man to the other. "Which leads us up to a pressing question—what are you two sons of Satan doing in Buckskin? The road out of town, gentlemen, is clear."

Buck glanced at Tortilla Joe. "She's been sent by her big husband to warn us," he told his partner.

"She ees a female spy, no, Buckshots?"

"Yes."

Sybil Lawrence scowled at them and took another drink. "Both of you are simple darned fools." She spoke next to Thick Neck. "This hooch of yours is getting weak. You got the barrel too close to the town pump." Again she spoke to the partners. "My husband is out to nail your hides to his corral. And he'll do it if you persist in walking around town, being a red flag swung in his face—"

She never got to finish her sentence. From behind them came a harsh, danger-filled voice— the voice of an angry man.

"Sybil, get outa here, savvy! And move pronto, too!"

Buck paused, glass rising. Tortilla Joe's fingers stopped turning his tequila glass. The green eyes of Sybil Lawrence glistened with metallic anger.

All three turned.

Curt Lawrence stood behind them.

CHAPTER FOUR

Again, Buck got the impression of bigness. And with this was another element—anger. Curt Lawrence's craggy face was mean-looking. His lips were wry with anger. He looked at Buck. Cold eyes, mean eyes—the eyes of a ruthless man. Buck got the full measure of their wrath. They did not scare the tall Texan; rather, their insolence angered him slightly. No matter how big a man was in life—or imagined he was—the earth leveled him off. That was part of Buck's philosopy. He did not realize this was a philosophy. Time leveled all things—the earth, man, beast, plants. No man was a big man, Buck realized. He just thought he was big.

The eyes went to Tortilla Joe. By now shock had left the Mexican and his jowls were simple and full, hanging like the jowls of a hungry and peaceful St. Bernard dog. And the eyes of the Mexican were filled with liquid sadness.

"Get out, wife."

Still Sybil did not move. She still stood between the partners.

Buck said, "We don't aim to lead her astray, Lawrence." His voice dripped sarcasm. "We was kinda amused at her talk, figgerin' all the time you had sent her to warn us and to feel us out."

"I fight my own battles," Lawrence said. "I stomp my own snakes. I build my own trail. No woman fights for me, men."

Buck noticed that two men stood behind Curt Lawrence. Gun riders, both of them—the mark of the six-shooter was on them, and its Cain-like brand was for all to see, and thereby judge them. Two guns on each, tied low to bole-like hips. And they had dull and deadly gunman eyes. . . .

"Get out of here," Curt Lawrence said.

Still Sybil Lawrence did not move. Two huge strides brought the young cowman forward. His spur rowels made harsh sounds. His big right hand went out and found his wife's small shoulder. He twisted her, and she yelped. Then his left had pushed her.

She went staggering backward. Arms flailing, she cursed him, and her face was twisted with hate. She went into the arms of one of the bodyguards, who held her in a hammerlock hold.

Lawrence spoke to Buck. "I'm telling you to

leave her alone, savvy. And I'm telling you two to hightail out of my town. Right now, too."

Buck said, "Here's my answer!"

Already the lanky cowpoke's right fist was rising. It was coming up with solid and quick determination. His knuckles smashed into Curt Lawrence's jaw. His fist slammed back the big arrogant head. Lawrence snarled something, and Buck's left clipped short his words. The left dropped the Hammerhead *primero*. It dropped him neatly and with final dispatch. It all had happened so fast, and with such cold precision, that the big man was surprised, in addition to being stunned.

Lawrence fell in a sitting down position. He was groggy, and for the moment the fight had been knocked out of him. Twice in one day this lanky compuncher had shamed him and had bested him.

Hurriedly, Buck glanced at the two gun riders. But he had no danger there. The one who held Sybil Lawrence stared with his mouth open, surprise etched on his homely face. Buck glanced at the other. To see him he had to look down at the floor. For the man was sprawled on his face, and he was unconscious.

Buck glanced at Tortilla Joe. The Mexican had his .45 out, but he still stood with his back to the bar.

"I no slog heem, Buckshots. Thet man, he do eet weeth hees war club."

Buck stared at the newcomer. The newcomer had come in behind the gunman and had dropped him. He was a total stranger to Buckshot McKee. He was one of the oddest specimens of humanity Buck had ever seen in his travels . . . and he had traveled plenty far in his twenty-six years.

"Holy smoke," he grunted.

The man was short, very short. He was a skinny, desert-dried hunk of orneriness. Greasy buckskin trousers were skin tight on skinny legs. On his feet he had moccasins—beady and black with dirt. Above the waist he was naked. He had a scrawny brown chest.

His head, though, was huge.

Buck stared at the immense head. Stringy black hair lay against the huge head, and around the forehead was a wide buckskin thong. His right hand held a heavy Indian war club.

Buck thought, Is he a sideshow freak? He did not put this question into words though; instead he gasped, "Thanks for the boost, stranger."

The skinny man lifted his club in front of his face. His lips pursed and he blew on the hardwood. "Don't mention it, Mr. McKee. It was indeed a deep and lasting pleasure. I am, sir, the editor of the local newspaper, lovingly called the *Cactus.*"

"A editor?"

"Yes, the man with the blue pencil, sir." He looked down at the unconscious man. "For some time I have yearned to knock this son of the devil ice cold. The time finally came. His name, sir, is Will March. When he comes to, anger will be with him—he will undoubtedly reach for his gun, for he will want to kill me." The lips formed a soft sigh, and the pain of living was on the huge face. "This is indeed a cruel and bestial world, Mr. McKee."

Tortilla Joe could only gawk. The gunman released Mrs. Lawrence, who went to a chair and sat down. Thick Neck stared, eyes wide open now. The gunman stood undetermined, his courage gone as he looked at Tortilla Joe's big .45 pistol.

Lawrence groaned, head still down.

The editor said, "The name, sir, is Jones—Sitting Bull Jones. One of the Jones boys, no less. I scouted for General Nelson A. Miles when he tangled with the Sioux up in Montana; therefore my gallant nom de plume." The war club swung out and designated Curt Lawrence. "There sits, sirs, His Royal Nibs, the Crown Prince of Hammerhead Range. Evidently His Honor wants to say a few intelligent words.

From this angle, even to my untutored and ignorant eyes, this seems apparent. But for some reason, his huge jaw seems to be reluctant to move, or am I wrong?"

Tortilla Joe said sadly, "You have the good eyes, Seetin' Bull. Thees crown princess, she should not manhandle a woman, no?"

Buck studied Curt Lawrence. The man was gingerly getting to his feet. Buck's knuckles on both hands ached.

Buck said, "She's your wife, Lawrence. From what I'd say, right off-hand, you got a house full of dynamite in her. Still, she's a woman, even if she is married to a thing like you. And being a woman, she demands a woman's respect. Am I right about that angle, you high-ridin' son of Satan?"

Lawrence spat blood. He looked at Buck in silence. His quiet glance held a raw and livid anger. He looked at Tortilla Joe's naked .45. He turned and looked at the gunman Sitting Bull Jones had buffaloed. Then he walked over to the fallen man. Buck watched, wondering what plan the big cowman had in mind.

Lawrence looked at the man. Cynicism touched him, driving him to anger. His right boot swung back, then ahead. He kicked the unconscious man in the face. He kicked him four times. Two teeth skidded out and became lost in the sawdust. Then Lawrence stepped back, sanity coming to his eyes again.

Sitting Bull Jones chided him with, "Bad, bad little boy, Lawrence. Isn't cricket to kick your little playmate when he is down cold, you know...."

Boom....

Sybil Lawrence had got her right hand free. She had just slapped the gunman on the jaw. The sound sounded like a pistol report. Her open hand left a vivid mark across the gunman's face. Anger flared in his eyes.

"Let her go," Lawrence ordered.

"With pleasure," the gunman said hurriedly.

Hurriedly the gunman released Sybil. Then he rubbed his stubby nose. He got blood on his hand and he looked at it. Her fingernails had ripped the hide off the bridge of his nose.

Lawrence spoke angry words to the gunman. "When Will March comes to, tell him to get out of Buckskin and off Hammerhead range, and for good—or I'll kill him personally, savvy?"

"I'll tell him, boss."

Lawrence looked at Tortilla Joe, then at Buck McKee. His angry eyes rested on Sitting Bull Jones who returned his glare. Buck noticed that the editor's knuckles were white as he gripped his war club. Then Curt Lawrence stabbed a glance at his wife.

"You've had your little play day in town, woman. By now you're ready to leave for the ranch! Get out of here and do it right pronto, savvy?"

"You can't run me off, you big baboon."

Lawrence's smile was thin. "You get tough with me, you little runt, and across my knee you go. I've paddled your purty behind before this ... and I ain't too old to repeat the process!"

Sybil Lawrence looked at Buck McKee. "Thanks for slugging the little fellow," she said. "First time any man has knocked him off his feet!"

Then, without warning, the woman turned quickly on a boot heel. Buckskin riding skirt swishing, she went out the door, and they heard her boots move down the plank walk.

Sitting Bull Jones watched Curt Lawrence with a steady glare. Lawrence said, "You an' me ain't done yet, Sittin' Bull."

"You use terrible English," the editor pointed out. "You should have said, You and I, not you an' me."

Lawrence grinned, but it was not a mirthful grin. He spoke now to his gunman. "Let's get out of here." The gunman nodded and moved ahead of the Hammerhead owner. Lawrence was in the doorway when Buck spoke.

"What—no threats?" Buck asked.

Lawrence turned and his eyes probed Buck's. They stood there and appraised each other, and tension was an elastic band between them. Thick Neck stood to one side, and he seemed bolted to the floor. Sitting Bull Jones had narrowed old eyes, and he still hung onto his war club. Tortilla Joe, seemingly sleepy and dopey, still held his big .45. He held it in a lazy, stupid manner, the barrel pointing down at the floor. Lawrence looked at the naked gun. One movement, and up would come that barrel; a flick of the dark thumb, the hammer would rise and fall. The gun didn't fool Curt Lawrence. This was written plainly on his face. Then he swung his gaze back to Buck McKee.

"Only a fool makes threats, McKee."

"That's right," Buck admitted. "Only a fool. . . ."

Lawrence said, "You aim to stick around Buckskin, I take it?"

"We might stay," Buck answered. "We might not stay."

Lawrence nodded, seemingly busy with his thoughts. "We'll meet again," he warned. He said no more. He went outside. Buck heard his boots pound on the worn and dried out plank walk. Soon the cowman moved past the window. He walked with determination, and he was big and powerful and tough. Then he moved out of sight and the sound of his boot heels faded away, too.

"Only a fool," Thick Neck repeated. And his voice held sarcasm. Buck looked at him with a smile.

"You're sandpaperin' my patience," Buck told him. "Now don't get me so I don't like you, Thick Neck."

Thick Neck had no reply. He swallowed once, then moved out of reach. He was remembering the rapidity with which Buck had knocked down Curt Lawrence. Thick Neck therefore was prudent.

Buck looked down at Will March, who was still sound asleep. "You don't figure you done caved in his skull for keeps, do you, Sittin' Bull?"

The old printer went to one bony knee. Ink-stained fingers found Will March's wrist. He cocked his huge head and there was a silence; then the editor got to his fet. He brushed sawdust off his knee.

"Heart as solid and strong as a grandfather clock, Buck."

Tortilla Joe said, "A rider, he ees come."

They listened and the hoofs came closer. The rider was loping down the main street. Tortilla Joe listened again.

"Only one rider," he said.

Buck said, "Thought mebbe the Cinchring bunch was coming into town. Thought mebbe the fireworks would break loose."

They kept watching the window. Soon the rider would move into view. The hoofs came closer. Tortilla Joe watched, Buck watched, and Sitting Bull Jones watched. Thick Neck dozed. Will March slept peacefully.

Then the rider came into view. The horse was rimmed with sweat, and plainly the bronc was dog-tired from a long ride. Buck said, "My bronc," and then he looked at the rider.

"Clair McCullen," Buck said.

CHAPTER FIVE

They went outside, Buck in the lead, Tortilla Joe second, and Sitting Bull Jones taking up the rear, war club and all. By this time Clair McCullen had dismounted. She had tears in her eyes and her lips trembled in anger.

"You two still around?"

Buck shrugged, spread his hands. "Had to wait for my horse," he supplied. "I could swear out a warrant and jail you for stealin' my bronc, you know. We're friends of a man we've never seen, now lynched. Worked up in Colorado last summer for Jack's dad, old Sam Perry."

"You did! I'm sorry about taking your horse— I had to get out to Cinchring camp—"

Buck asked, "What happened out there?"

She leaned against the hitch-rack, sobbing. The whole town of Buckskin watched. They stood on the street and watched and hid behind windows and watched. A Lawrence gunman moved in to listen.

Buck said, "Get outa here, gundog!"

The man stood there, studying Buck with a cynical grin. His hand was on his .45. Buck moved toward him. Tortilla Joe twirled his gun on his forefinger. Sunlight flashed off the barrel.

"Okay," the gunman said, "okay. Don't get hot under the collar, people."

He walked away. Buck grinned. He turned his attention to the weeping girl. He got the impression that this girl had really loved Jack Perry. This was a bitter, terrible day for her. His heart went out to her in her grief. And when he spoke his voice was low with emotion.

"Tell us, Miss Clair."

"Those constructions hands—they wouldn't believe me. They said Jack was safe in jail, that the Hammerhead would never dare lynch him. They wouldn't head back with me, the cowards. . . ."

Buck waited. Tortilla Joe waited. Sitting Bull Jones rubbed his eyes. Sitting Bull Jones said, "Wind. . . . Always makes my eyes water." Sitting Bull Jones was lying. He knew it. Tortilla Joe knew it. And Buck McKee knew it.

"I begged them to ride into Buckskin and save Jack. Then a man rode out to camp. He told them Jack was already lynched. I should kill that Curt Lawrence, just like Jack killed his old man!"

Buck said, "They showed wisdom."

She glared at him. "Wisdom? What do you mean, you fool? Their boss—the man who foots their payroll—he got lynched! They aren't even men enough to fight for their outfit!"

Buck nodded patiently. "Curt Lawrence has this town spiked with guns, Clair. Him and his Hammerhead hands are just hoping those dirt men will ride in. Then they can wipe out the whole dirt camp and the fight will be over, with Lawrence and his Hammerhead the winner."

"I'll kill him."

Her voice was savage. She was either really sorrowing, or either a competent actress. Buck suddenly grabbed her by the right wrist.

"Come with me, woman!"

She stared at him, tears glistening in her eyes. Surprise had instantly taken the place of rage and sorrow.

"What do you want, Mister?"

"You stole my bronc. They hang people for stealin' horses, you know. The best place for you is in the county jail!"

"Jail!" Her voice showed she doubted his sanity. "I brought yore horse back, didn't I?"

"Come along with me."

Buck pulled her after him. She did not resist very long. She trotted along, with Tortilla Joe behind her, and Sitting Bull Jones behind

the Mexican. And the town of Buckskin watched
and wondered.

"Where are we going?" she panted.

"To talk to the sheriff," Buck replied.

"Why the sheriff?"

Buck did not answer. She did not see the wink
he sent Tortilla Joe. The thought had come to
the tall Texan that the longer this girl stayed
in circulation the sooner she would get into
trouble. She might even try to kill Curt Lawrence. She would be better off behind bars, he
reasoned. But he did not tell her this. It was a
rough deal all the way around.

The sheriff had a small log office. He sat behind a table that held various items: old Western
story magazines, two worn-down law books, a
rifle and an old scattergun. When they came in
his boots were on the desk, too. Spur rowels
were digging into the battered top. New boots
they were, highly polished and glistening. Buck
thought of his old battered boots. Maybe a man
should settle down, get a soft county job, and get
new boots every two months.

He was a short man, the sheriff, and he had
an enormous belly. He had a bald head that
glistened like a billiard ball smeared with lard.
Long handlebar mustaches hung down on each
side of his thick-lipped mouth and his eyes were
big and watery. He looked as if he had about as

much backbone as a jellyfish.

"What's the commotion about?" the lawman wanted to know.

"This gal," said Buck, "stole my bronc."

Clair McCullen tried to jerk away unsuccessfully. She still didn't know whether Buck was drunk or crazy or a combination of both.

"Let go of me," she stormed.

Buck said, "You sure got a nice arm, honey."

The sheriff let his boots hit the floor with a thud. His watery eyes studied Buck, went to the girl, flicked to Tortilla Joe, then landed on Sitting Bull Jones. They studied the big-headed editor and his war club. Evidently these two did not have too much mutual affection.

Then the lawman said, "She brought your horse back, McKee."

Buck nodded. "That she did. But remember, lawman, she had to steal it first, or she couldn't have brought it back."

Clair McCullen had stopped struggling. Buck let his hand slide down her wrist and he squeezed her little hand. She glared at him with cold indifference.

"You dirty rat! All you want to do is hold my hand. That's why you're creating this scene!"

"My, my," Buck chortled. "What a lively imagination."

Tortilla Joe's dark eyes were roving around

the room. Finally they settled sadly on the pot-bellied sheriff.

"What she ees your name, starman?"

"Potter. Henry Potter. You two, they tell me, is Buck McKee and Tortilla Joe." He looked at Buck again. "I can't hold this woman."

Buck tried another angle. "She threatened to try to kill Curt Lawrence," he told Potter.

Potter came instantly awake. "She did! Well, that's different—a threat to kill is far more serious than a charge of stealing a horse." His watery eyes narrowed in sudden thought. "How come you're so careful of the well-being of Curt Lawrence, McKee?"

"File the complaint, and shut up."

The lawman's eyes glistened, despite their moistness. He plainly did not like the tall Texan's authoritative tone of voice. But he said, "All right, after I take her to a cell. Come along, woman."

Clair McCullen planted both little feet solidly against the worn pine floor. The lawman got her by both arms and dragged her out the door and they heard him pull her down the cell aisle. Buck glanced back into the cell department. Potter was just slamming the door shut on Clair McCullen.

"Why you jail her?" Tortilla Joe asked.

Buck grinned. "A night in the clink will sober her up. She'll be mad when she comes out but she won't act on impulse. By then the edge of her grief will be worn off. Come tomorrow, I aim to drop the charges."

"Good idea," Sitting Bull Jones chimed in.

Sheriff Potter ambled back and almost pushed his chair through the floor, he sat down so suddenly and so hard. He took out an old blue bandana and tried to rub the sweat off his greasy forehead, but the sweat popped out right behind the dirty handkerchief.

"I've had a tough, rough day," the lawman lamented.

Buck studied him. "I don't see how you did have, if you want the blunt truth. They lynched a man in this town today. A lynching is against the law—direct violation of the law books."

Potter's thick lips trembled in anger. "McKee, watch your big mouth! This peaceful town don't like trouble makers. My prisoner was delivered out of jail by a mob—all masked—"

"Why didn't you stop them?" Buck asked.

Potter bent down to show his bald head. "I was slugged, knocked cold, wrapped over the head with a club. No wonder my head has a splittin' headache! I never identified a one of the lynchers. All masked. If Curt Lawrence hadn't been out chasing that female, I'd have jugged him as one of them. But he was out in the desert—"

"Maybe that's why he was out there," Buck said.

Potter studied him. "Explain that statement, bucko."

Buck spread his hands. "Maybe Lawrence didn't want to catch the girl. Maybe he used chasin' her as an alibi to get out of town while his other men, masked and ugly, pulled a man out of a cell and lynched him. By chasing her he was in the clear."

"Them is harsh words, McKee."

Buck shrugged. "Could be true."

Potter studied him with unblinking eyes. Buck sensed a hardness permeate this thick man, and he realized Potter was getting madder by the moment. Buck decided to quit deviling him.

"You two fellas have caused a lot of trouble today. Twice you insulted Curt Lawrence."

"Only once," Buck corrected. "The first time I insulted him. That was when I knocked that gold piece outa his hand. The second time I didn't insult him— I just knocked him on his rump."

"Then you knocked out one of his gun—er, his men, they tell me."

Sitting Bull Jones said, "He didn't do that—

I did. With my little club." He kissed the war club, his lips making a smacking sound. "My little war club and I."

Buck tried something. "Did Curt Lawrence come in here and want a complaint filed against us?"

"No. . . . The Hammerhead fights its own battles, McKee."

Buck nodded. "Yes, and the Hammerhead apparently lynches its enemies, too. Even takes them out of the county jail to string them up, too. . . ."

"They slugged me cold!"

"I forgot that," Buck said.

Potter leaned his bulk forward. The spring on his swivel chair howled in oilless protest. He did not seem angry. He seemed fatherly and benevolent suddenly. His fat forefinger jabbed a hole in the air.

"McKee, you two are in trouble. You don't hit a man like Lawrence and live. That goes for you too, editor. You slugged a Lawrence man. You three got two things to do. One is stay here . . . and stop breathing; the other, to drift out and forget this whole nasty affair. That clear?"

"Sure is," Buck said.

"Like the mud," Tortilla Joe said.

Sitting Bull Jones had a long lonesome look.

"I got too much invested to pull out and leave," he mourned.

Sheriff Potter leaned back. Again the spring protested. "That's the size of the deal," the lawman said.

"Thanks," Buck said.

"Gracias," Tortilla Joe said.

Sitting Bull Jones bowed in a grandiose manner. "My friend, many thanks for the fatherly warning." He straightened, his face deadpan. "It shall be heeded, also. Again, thanks."

They trooped out then, Sitting Bull in the lead, Tortilla Joe in the middle, and gangling Buck McKee taking up the rear. Behind them Sheriff Henry Potter chewed the end of one handlebar mustache and watched and wondered just who had made a fool out of whom.

They stopped and gave attention to the sunset. The sinking sun had lost its heat, but heat danced out of the sand. Somewhere a sagebrush bloomed, its aroma sweet. Buck thought, Only nice thing in this town, and let it go at that. Then the thought came that he had met something nicer than the desert aroma. Clair McCullen. She'd be a nice one to hold and hug, he decided. Yes, and Sybil Lawrence—she was an attractive woman, too.

Tortilla Joe said, "That sheriff, he no ees get the slogged. He bend over an' hees head—she has no marks. No bruises. He ees the beeg liar, Buckshots."

"Lawrence man," Buck grunted.

Tortilla Joe yawned. "We get the bunks for thees night, an' when the sun he comes up we dreeft for Yuma, no? Nobody she testify against Clair—she be free—"

Buck said, "Bet you twenty bucks I kiss her before we leave."

"I take that."

Sitting Bull said, "I'm gonna go to my shop. Get out my sheet. Drop in when you walk by. Right down the street, men."

He hurried away. Buck watched him go and smiled. The world was full of odd characters. Then the thought came that maybe he was one himself, and his smile died.

Sitting Bull Jones disappeared in a door.

"We leave come the daylights, Buckshots?"

Buck looked at the squat Mexican. "What about Jack Perry?"

"He ees the dead, lynched. What about heem?"

"He's the only son of old Sam Perry, remember?"

"I know that."

Buck spoke softly. "We punched cows for old Sam. He treated us like we was his own flesh and blood."

"I theenk of that, *tambien.*"

Buck grinned. "Hades, partner, you're way behind time—the train left a hour ago."

"What you means by that, Buckshots?"

Buck spread his long fingers. "Simple. . . . Curt Lawrence couldn't afford to let us ride out of this country scot-free. . . . Talk is going around about the two drifters that knocked Lawrence down and showed him up in front of all these people. They've lived in fear of the Hammerhead for years. Lawrence has to keep up his rep as a tough gent. We couldn't ride out if we wanted to. Do you want to pull out?"

Tortilla Joe shook his head. "No *senor,*" he said.

"Then close your big mouth."

They went down the street. They came to an adobe building. A door sagged on its hinges in dejection. From the unlit interior came the booming voice of Sitting Bull Jones.

"Come in, *compadres,* come in. *Entrez-vous,* hombres."

They went inside. The interior was gloomy. No candle or lamp was lighted. The place smelled of mice, paper, ink, and oil. A hand press made a metallic sound. Sitting Bull Jones stood in front of a type case picking out type. He wore a long leather apron—so long he al-

most stepped on it when he came to meet Buck
and Tortilla Joe.

"You so poor you can't afford to buy coal
oil?" Buck asked. "Dark as a tomb in here and
stinks twice as much."

"You ever been in a tomb?" the old man en-
countered. He did not wait for an answer. "We
have to keep it dark. Somebody shot at us
through the window the other night. Lawrence
bunch, we're sure. So . . . no lights. When it gets
too dark, we quit working. Ain't that right,
helper?"

The helper grinned toothlessly and nodded.
He was working a hand press and Buck doubted
if he had heard a word his boss had said. All
his skinny weight would go forward against the
lever. The old press was as noisy as an approaching earthquake. The heavy stamp lifted, hesitated, then fell with a clanging noise. A skinny
Mexican boy, naked except for torn pants, fed
paper into the press.

Sitting Bull Jones shook hands with the partners. Evidently he was of the handshaking
fraternity. He acted as though he had not seen
Buck and Tortilla Joe for years. He fairly
pulled Buck over to the press. He got one of
the sheets of paper and held it under the cowpuncher's nose.

His voice held triumph. "Read that headline, McKee."

Buck read aloud.

> McKee Beats Tar
> Out of Lawrence;
> Knocks him down!

Sitting Bull Jones chuckled. He sounded as happy as a squirrel who had just discovered a shiny new walnut under some leaves. His eyes were the sharp eyes of a gopher as he studied Buck's weather-beaten face.

"What do you think of it, McKee?"

Buck put the paper on the bench. "Curt Lawrence will hang your hide onto his bunkhouse wall when thet extra hits the streets, Sittin' Bull. You're rubbin' his fur the wrong way an' you're using a hard curry-comb to do it."

"We print the truth," the old man said, beaming. "The whole truth an' nothin' but the truth."

Tortilla Joe got philosophical. "Sometimes they keel mens for tellin' the truth."

The press had stopped. The toothless printer gawked at them. The Mexican boy watched them. Buck got the impression that he and Tortilla Joe were as odd in this town as a white man is on Mars. They had gone against the Crown Prince and were still alive.

Buck said, "It will get Lawrence even madder at us, too."

Sitting Bull Jones let words tumble from his lips. "Are you two men cowards?" Again, he waited for no answer. "Let me tell you two buckos a bit of delicate information. This might shock your sweet little constitutions, so brace yourself. Curt Lawrence has issued orders, men—orders, get me?"

"To what effect?" Buck wanted to know.

The old man watched; the Mexican kid gawked. Tortilla Joe said nothing. Outside, the dusk thickened. Somewhere a dog barked and somewhere children played. They called in Mexican to each other.

"His men are to pen you in on Hammerhead range, McKee. You can't ride out of this area. When you knocked him down in the saloon, you did more than hammer him on the jaw—you hit him in his pride."

Buck nodded. "Figgered that." He started for the door. Again, the words of the old publisher halted him.

"McKee, a moment."

"Yeah?"

"Will March, the gent I knocked cold. There's talk around, McKee. Curt Lawrence dressed him down with his tongue, and laid it to him, so they tell me."

Buck said, "March should be mad at you, not me. You was the one what chilled him with your club."

"Watch him, Buck."

Tortilla Joe asked, "Who keel ol' John Lawrence, Seetin' Bull? Jack Perry, he keel Curt's father?"

Sitting Bull eagerly went into action. Nobody knew for sure who had shot down the old cattle king. He had been found dead, shot through and through, out on the desert, just south of the Cinchring construction camp.

"Sheriff Potter, he found some empty cartridge cases. The firing-pin had landed on them in a peculiar manner."

"Yeah?" Buck said.

The sheriff had taken Jack Perry's Winchester .30-30. He had fired it about a hundred times. Each time the firing-pin landed on the cartridge case just as had the firing-pin that had exploded the cartridges that had killed John Lawrence.

Buck grunted, "All circumstantial evidence, eh?"

"What Jack Perry he say in hees deefense?" Tortilla Joe asked.

"He claimed he didn't kill the old cowman. He said he had two Winchester rifles, both .30-30 caliber. I talked a long time with him. He said one of them was stole from him. Taken from the construction camp. Gone for a few days and then suddenly was on the rack again. This was the rifle that shot old John. Of course, suspicion immediately pointed toward Jack, because he and John Lawrence had had a couple of arguments."

Buck rubbed his long jaw thoughtfully. "If Jack Perry didn't kill the cowman, who did kill him?"

"Nobody knows, Buck," the editor returned.

Tortilla Joe shrugged. Buck McKee shrugged. They went outside. The last light of day rimmed the far scarp mountains. Suddenly Buck stopped. He stared between two buildings into the alley.

"You see somebody—sometheengs?" Tortilla Joe demanded.

Buck said quietly, "A woman just sneaked into that door we see back there. The door to thet brick building, Tortilla. She went in fast, too—she didn't want anybody to see her. By accident I glimpsed her."

"Who was she?"

"Sybil Lawrence."

CHAPTER SIX

Tortilla Joe stared at the door. He spoke in a quiet voice. "That door she ees the back door of the bank, eet looks to thees son of Sonora, Buck. What ees wrong with her going into the bank, even eef by the back door?"

"She sneaked in there. She didn't want anybody to see her. And why would she sneak in?"

The Mexican lifted his heavy shoulders. "I no know." He let his shoulders fall. "We go back eento the alley, no?"

"Yes."

They traveled between the two buildings, heading for the alley. Tortilla Joe could hardly squeeze through the space but Buck walked along easily in the narrow confines. They came to the alley with its tin cans and garbage and its dust. They were at the rear of the brick bank, and Buck sidled close to a barred window. A lamp was lit inside the bank and the blind was pulled low. Buck squatted and squinted under the blind. He whistled softly as he watched. Tortilla Joe got on his knees and looked under the blind, too.

"Well, I'll be the dog that was goned," the Mexican murmured.

A man and a woman were in the room. Evidently it was the banker's office. They stood in the middle of the room. Sybil Lawrence stood on tiptoe, arms around the man's neck. She was kissing him fervently and long. Shamelessly the partners watched.

"She kees heem long time," Tortilla Joe muttered.

Buck asked, "You jealous?"

"She can kees me any time she wants, Buck."

Buck grinned. "That ain't Curt Lawrence she's swappin' kisses with, either. Good-lookin' gent, whoever he is. Well, we know one thing, for what it's worth—if it's worth anything."

"Si?"

"She's not faithful to the Curly Wolf. Hey, get down—pronto—"

With a sweep of his arm, he sent Tortilla Joe to the dust. Up ahead in the alley Buck had caught the last rays of the sun flashing on a rifle barrel. The rifleman was crouching behind a wooden garbage barrel. Sunlight had drifted through between two buildings to flash from his rifle barrel.

Tortilla Joe grunted, "What een the heck—?"

Buck was on one knee, short-gun out. The rifle spouted lead. The man missed because of Buck's sudden slip to one knee. Buck's .45 talked, flame spouting out of the barrel. All the time, above the roar of rifle and short-gun, he remembered old Sitting Bull Jones' prophecy.

Buck shot through the edge of the wooden barrel. Above the pounding of his .45 he heard a man's high-pitched scream. The man staggered out from behind his protection. His rifle hit the dust, slid to one side, stopped.

The man's knees sprang out. He fell on his belly, head buried in the dust. Buck got to his boots, knees shaky. Tortilla Joe got up and brushed dust from him. The Mexican's jowls were chalk white.

"Ambush," he murmured. "Dirty range, ambush range. . . ."

They walked ahead, with Buck shoving new cartridges into his cylinder. The town had jerked itself awake. People hollered, kids screamed, dogs barked. Even a burro took up the noise by braying in a doleful manner. Buck toed the man over and stared down at his dead and ugly face.

Will March would never kill another man.

Buck said, "Lawrence sent him against me,

Tortilla Joe. We don't leave this range, friend, until this is settled."

"I say okay to that, Buckshots."

People were converging down on them. They were gawking at the dead man. Buck had hit him three times in the chest. They were admiring the bullet holes, for they covered a small area. Sheriff Potter came on the run. His run was a slow dog-trot. His bald head glistened. He stared at the dead man, then at Buck, then at Tortilla Joe.

"What happened, men?"

Buck told him.

The lawman stabbed a glance at Tortilla Joe. "Will you verify that version, Mexican?"

Tortilla Joe knew what *verify* meant, but he played ignorant. He shrugged and spread his hands, and a look of great stupidity colored his jowls. "I know not what you mean, lawmans."

"Is that true?"

"Oh, sure, that ees the truth. Like Buckshots says, lawmans—that ees the right truth."

Buck grinned. "Ask March how it happened, Sheriff?" he taunted.

"Don't rub me the wrong way," growled Sheriff Henry Potter. "Anybody else see the gunfight?"

"Not me," a man said. "I want no part of this."

Nobody volunteered. Potter had two men tote the corpse into the morgue. Buck noticed that Sybil Lawrence was in the crowd. About ten feet from her stood the man whom she had been kissing in the bank office.

She looked at Buck, her green eyes sharp. "You're a handy man with that gun, McKee. Curt won't like this one bit."

Buck said, "That's okay with me, honey. Tell the big lug to come himself the next time. A man who orders an ambush is as low and filthy as the man who carries out the ambush. That makes your loving spouse a low and filthy man."

"He'll rise up in wrath," she said.

Buck looked at the man who had kissed her. He was about thirty, he figured—well built and well dressed and neat. Evidently he shied away from all physical labor. He was a good-looking man, roughly handsome, and one who would appeal to women, Buck guessed.

Buck noticed that the man, despite his well dressed appearance, toted a six-shooter.

"Here comes Curt," a man said.

The gathering split. The Crown Prince of Hammerhead range pushed through. Behind him trailed a gunman. He was the fellow who had jerked Sybil around, when Curt Lawrence had thrown her into his arms. He scowled. Lawrence scowled. There was a deep, deadly silence.

"You killed March, McKee?"

"I did."

"Why?"

"He tried to kill me."

Buck noticed that Sitting Bull Jones was standing beside Tortilla Joe. The old editor was busy taking down notes on a piece of paper tacked to a wide board.

Lawrence merely nodded. His eyes, though, held a scheming look. "Why would March tie into you, McKee?"

"Your orders, I reckon."

Curt Lawrence watched him. The gunman studied Tortilla Joe. The gnarled and dark hands of Sitting Bull Jones kept on writing. He was making some funny-looking characters on the paper. Buck found out later it was short-hand.

Lawrence seemed to be talking to himself. "This ain't logical. March didn't cross you when we had the ruckus in the saloon He got knocked cold by old Sitting Bull. I kicked out two of his front teeth myself. Yet he ties into you. Did you and him ever have trouble before, on some other range?"

"Don't talk like a fool," Buck said stiffly.

The big man's wide, hard face showed nothing. "Explain yourself, McKee?" he asked quietly.

"You made a deal with March. Paid him to move against my gun. The whole town knows about it."

"Can you prove that?"

"No. . . ."

"Then keep your big mouth shut, McKee."

Buck moved toward Lawrence. The cowman stood his ground. His hand was not toying with the gold chin strap nugget now. His hands were down with his thumbs hooked in his gunbelt and with his fingers splayed over the handles of his guns. But still his face was deadpan, without expression, without thought. He was schooled and tough, this man.

Sitting Bull Jones said, "I heard about the talking you handed March, Lawrence. The swamper at the saloon heard it. He blabbed all over town like a lovesick old woman."

"Shut up, you printer's devil!"

Buck said, "Make your play—"

But before either could draw, a man had forced his way between them. He was the well-dressed man whom Sybil Lawrence had kissed in the bank office. He did not talk to Buck.

He addressed his words to Curt Lawrence.

"Lawrence, don't pull your gun here, please.

Some innocent people might get killed. I want to talk to you in my office. Your wife should come along, too. Let this ride for now, Curt."

Potter pushed in. "That's right," he said. His sweaty forehead glistened in the twilight. "For Gawd's sake, will this trouble never stop?"

"Your job is to stop it," a man said.

Potter whirled his enormous bulk turning. He scanned the crowd with bitter eyes. "Who said that?"

Nobody answered. A kid hooted, a woman laughed. Potter again spoke to Lawrence. "Halloway is right. Go with him, Curt."

Lawrence looked at Buck, then at Tortilla Joe, then at Sitting Bull. Suddenly he showed a twisted smile.

"There's always another day," he said.

He and Sybil went toward the back door of the bank. The man named Halloway spoke to Buck.

"I'm the local banker. Name of Halloway— Martin Halloway. You boys have been in Buckskin only a few hours. Already you have killed a man, you've knocked down Curt Lawrence, and Sitting Bull here knocked out Will March."

Buck said, "What is it to you?"

"I'm a member of this town. An influential member, I might add. Until you came in these people knew peace—"

Buck kept anger out of his voice. But he clipped his words. "They sure did know peace," he said scornfully. "They're so peaceful they even lynch a man in broad daylight because Lawrence so ordered. Were you one of the killers who was hiding behind a mask, banker?"

The handsome face paled. The lips trembled in anger. Buck saw that this man, despite his well-groomed appearance, was hard and tough underneath. For a moment, he thought the banker would draw his gun.

Then he saw caution come in and veil the harsher emotions. And the lips of the banker moved slowly.

"We'll find out who slugged the sheriff, McKee. When we do, the guilty party—or parties—will pay. We'll find out who was behind the lynching of Jack Perry. Those people will pay, too."

Buck smiled tightly.

Sitting Bull Jones broke into the conversation with, "You'll find them! You'll make them pay! Hogwash of the foulest quality, Halloway. If you arrested them lynchers, maybe you'd have to throw yourself into jail, eh?"

"I wasn't in on it."

"All men look alike with masks on," the old editor said savagely.

The banker looked at him with narrowed eyes.

Buck got the idea there was no love lost between these two. Evidently Sitting Bull Jones, because of his sense of fairness and justice, because of his sharp tongue and sharp pen and press, was not too popular in this town of Buckskin.

Halloway said, "Ever since you came to town, Sitting Bull, this town has been in a turmoil. Why the blazes don't you move out of here if you don't like the burg?"

"I aim to make it so I can like it, banker. These farmers spell one word, *progress*. They're coming in legally and using legal homestead rights. The Lawrence outfit has tried to run them out since the day they started building their dam. You can't stop progress you know. Not even greed stops progress."

"I oughta twist your neck around so you can look down your spine!"

Sitting Bull Jones retreated not an inch. He raised his war club and looked at it solemnly. He talked to the club, not to Halloway.

"If this club hits a man alongside the head, it'll knock his head off. That knot in you can scrape the hide off a man's skull. Wonder how this Shylock would look if you accidentally got bounced off his thick skull? This town is full of accidents, you know, War Club. Maybe an accident could happen to this banker."

Halloway turned and spoke to Sheriff Potter. "That's a threat against my well-being," he snapped. "Arrest this printer bum, Sheriff."

"I'm not talking to him," the editor told the lawman. "I was merely talking to my friend, my war club. He had no reason to eavesdrop."

"Right he is," Buck chimed in, grinning.

Potter was caught between the deep freeze and the steam house. Sweat popped out on his face. The crowd was laughing.

"Halloway, go, please," the sheriff said.

Halloway grinned. Buck sensed that the banker realized public opinion was running against him, and the longer he stayed in the public eye the more unfavorable that opinion would become.

"Hope you two heed me and my advice," he told Buck and Tortilla Joe.

Buck said, "We might . . . and we might not. . . ."

"If you have any sense, you will."

Buck shrugged. "Both of us is plumb senseless. Down in Sonora state one time we went to *siesta* in the shade of a mesquite. Mexican goat came nibbling along and et our brains."

"Chewed up all our brains," Tortilla Joe lamented, his face long and dour.

"A couple of trigger-happy idiots," the banker spat.

He walked away, heavy with self-importance. Somebody started laughing. The banker turned and looked at the man with hard eyes. The man stopped laughing.

"Sorry, Halloway."

Buck noticed that the speaker was an old man, and he seemed crippled in his right leg. He and the banker glared at each other. Potter watched, Buck watched, and Tortilla Joe watched. Sitting Bull Jones sported a wide grin.

"You shouldn't have laughed at Money Bags," Buck told the crippled oldster. "He might foreclose on your mor'gage and turn you out into the cold, cold world. Age means nothing to a banker, you know."

"He ain't got no mor'gage on me," the old man said.

The cripple spat. Brown tobacco juice spurted out. Whether he meant to spit on Halloway, or only land close to him—Buck did not know. But he did know one thing.

The brown stream jetted out to hit Halloway on the left hand. Anger flushed the banker's face and he came rushing toward the cripple, fists doubled. The old man, hurrying to get away, fell down. Halloway grinned savagely and his right boot went back to kick the oldster in the ribs.

The kick never landed.

That was because Buck McKee stepped into

the trouble. He used the same twin blows that had dropped Curt Lawrence. A solid rising left, flush on the button, followed by an overhand right. The next thing Halloway knew, the ground came up and hit him.

Eyes blurred, blood on his lips, he stared upward at Buck McKee, who still had his fists doubled.

"A man don't hit women, kids or cripples," Buck gritted.

Halloway spat blood. His face still held a dazed, stunned look. Slowly, gingerly, he got to his knees. For a moment he stood like an animal, on all fours. During this interval Tortilla Joe stepped forward and got the banker's gun.

He handed it to Sheriff Potter.

"Keep it safe for the leetle banker boy," the Mexican said scornfully.

Potter held the gun by the barrel. It must have been red-hot. He held it awkwardly. He watched the banker get unsteadily to his feet. The banker swung around and looked at the sheriff.

"I demand you arrest this man."

"On what charge?" Potter asked.

"Assault and battery, of course. You saw him hit me, you stupid fat pelican!"

Buck saw a hardness enter the sheriff's hanging jowls. "Don't get rough with me, Halloway. You hold no mor'gage over this boy. You went to kick an old helpless man. I darned near slugged you myself. McKee just beat me to it."

Buck said, "You stumbled over a rock, and fell on it."

Halloway studied the tall cowpuncher. "You gone plumb loco, McKee?"

Buck kicked at a good-sized rock. "You fell over that. You clipped your jaw on it."

The old man said, "He sure did, McKee. I seen it."

Banker Halloway had had enough. He pivoted and went into his office. He slammed the door so hard the hinges bounced.

Buck looked at Sheriff Potter.

The sheriff winked.

CHAPTER SEVEN

Buck looked at the pretty, dark-haired young waitress. This range, he decided, had some lovely women. Beside him sat Tortilla Joe, dumbly studying a menu. He couldn't read a word of English and darned little Spanish, either.

"What we eat, Buck?"

Buck sighed. He and Sheriff Potter had had a talk. There would be a coroner's inquest over the body of Will March. Two days from now, the sheriff said. The body would keep. A fellow in town would shoot the veins full of alcohol.

"Not the kind a man drinks," the sheriff had informed him. "That other kind what kills him if he gets it in his belly."

"I'm going to my office," Sitting Bull Jones had said.

So now Buck McKee and Tortilla Joe sat in the Greasy Plate Café. At long last they were going to get something to eat. But neither had much of an appetite. It had been a rough, tough day, and maybe it wasn't over yet. . . .

Buck remembered Potter's wink. Evidently Banker Halloway and Potter were not such firm friends. He got the idea that they could push the fat sheriff so far, and then hell would pop. Or was he wrong? Potter had seemingly worked in cahoots with the lynchers.

"Darn those kids," the waitress said.

The boys had their noses pressed to the front window. They were hero-worshipping Buck McKee and Tortilla Joe.

The waitress shooed them away.

"I just washed that window today," she informed Buck. "Now they're going to get it all dirty with their dirty noses." She put their plates in front of them. "You two are sort of town heroes, if you don't know it."

"Heroes they sometimes get keeled," Tortilla Joe said. "Now you make me two more of these *tortillas*, no?"

"You must like them."

"That ees what ees geeve me my maiden name."

"Not maiden name," Buck corrected him. "Given name, you mean."

"What she ees make the deeference? As long as they no call me too late for meals, I am happy."

Buck watchced the waitress walk back to the kitchen. She had a nice back and a nice carriage and nice legs. She was built just right, he realized. Well, so was Clair McCullen. He grinned. She was still in jail. Do her good, he figured. Knock her off her high horse a little. Too bad he couldn't get Sybil Lawrence in the same cell with Clair. A jail term would do Sybil good, too. He pondered on this intriguing possibility. Finally Tortilla Joe's words, coming around a mouthful of beans, took him back to the present.

"Some theengs they ees rotten here een Arizona Territories, Buckshots."

"Like what?"

"Sybeel, she ees kees thees banker. She ees another man's wife."

Buck grinned. "That ain't nothin' new," he said.

"Notheeng, he ees sacred no longer?"

Buck glanced at his partner. For a moment he had taken the Mexican seriously. Then he saw the long and dour look on his partner's face. He jabbed his elbow deep into the fat ribs.

"You ol' Romeo. You've kissed many another man's wife in your time. And don't try to lie out of it, either!"

"That ees the wrong attitude."

More kids pushed their noses against the clean window. Already dirty streaks were beginning to form on the glass.

The waitress came in with the *tortillas*. She was hot and angry and irritable. She kept brushing her hair back. She chased the kids away.

Matrimony, Buck thought sourly, was a devil of a mess. Good for married men and women, but not for single drifters. No wonder the human race was distintegrating so quickly—fools got married, and only fools. Suddenly he had a vision of Clair McCullen. Blonde and small and lovely—ever prettier when those pretty eyes flashed in anger.

She was plenty angry in that cell.

The waitress came back from chasing away another bunch of young fry. She was angrier than ever.

"Will you two men do me a favor?" she asked.

Buck looked up. "That's not a fair question, miss. What if I say yes, then you tell me to blow out my brains? First, what do you want?"

"How long you two aim to stay in town?"

Buck looked at Tortilla Joe, who was studying her over a forkful of *tortilla*. Then he looked back at the girl.

"We don't know for sure," he replied in all honesty. "Lawrence says he won't let us ride out of town. If he kills us I reckon we'll be here a long time. Why do you ask, miss?"

She brushed back more hair. Buck discreetly

held his hand over his soup.

"If you stay here," she said, "please eat at some other café."

Tortilla Joe's wide dark forehead showed a wide dark scowl.

Buck also frowned. "Why?"

"Those kids. I'll have to wash that front window again soon. I'll lose money on you two, counting the time required to wash the window. Not to mention the cost of the soap."

"Oh," Buck said.

Tortilla Joe had long jowls. "Nobody, not even thees girl, do they want us een thees town of Buckskeen."

The waitress said nothing. She had a frozen, stony face. Buck decided his first impression had been wrong. She was not lovely. She was not even pretty. She was, in fact, almost ugly. She looked better walking away than she did walking toward a man.

The door opened. Sheriff Henry Potter waddled in. He said hello to the girl. He nodded at Tortilla Joe, who nodded back. He slid his big bottom onto a stool and the stool was absorbed. He looked at Buck.

Buck looked back at him.

"What about that girl?" the sheriff asked.

Buck knew he meant Clair McCullen. But he decided to act stupid. He scowled and sucked his soup as a carp sucks mud along a Montana creek bank.

"What girl you mean, Sheriff?"

"You know who I mean. Clair McCullen."

Buck got to his boots and reached for a toothpick. "What about her?" he wanted to know.

"Why don't you drop charges against her?"

Buck got the toothpick working. "I will," he assured Potter. "But on one condition, Sheriff."

The waitress listened. Tortilla Joe reached for a toothpick. The sheriff watched Buck through his red-socketed eyes.

"What's the condition?" Potter asked.

Buck put the toothpick at an angle. "It's this way, Mr. Potter. She thinks she's too wide for her—well, her dress. I'll drop the charge against her if she does one thing—"

"And that?" the sheriff asked.

Buck grinned. "If she kisses me of her own free will, and of her own accord. Otherwise, I press hoss-stealin' charges."

Potter's eyes widened. His wide face got a dazed and pained expression. His voice shook as he asked, "Have you gone loco, McKee? Surely you're joshin' with me?"

Buck kept his face straight. "That's the deal," he said. "And the only deal. You tell her that, Sheriff?"

"Sure will."

Buck picked his teeth. Tortilla Joe noisily stuck his toothpick between two teeth and sucked on it.

Sheriff Henry Potter said, "You can't make that horse-stealing charge hold, McKee. You got to remember she took the horse back. No jury in the country would convict her on such evidence."

"Are you a lawyer?" Buck asked pointedly.

"No, but . . ."

Just then a man came into the restaurant. He stopped right inside the door. He spoke in a harsh, sonorous voice.

"Stranger, are you Buck McKee?"

Buck went automatically into a crouch. Tortilla Joe moved to one side, hand on his gun. Buck's first impression, coming out of nowhere, was that this man—this human moose—was a Hammerhead gunman Lawrence had hired to match guns with him. He had his hand over his gun.

He glanced at Tortilla Joe. His partner was ready. The Mexican was a hard ball of humanity, crouched and tense. Only Henry Potter seemed unconcerned as he pushed his fork down through a hunk of apple pie.

"Yes, I'm Buck McKee."

The big man wet his lips. He had a tongue the size of a cow's. He stood about six-six, Buck figured. His torso was as thick as the bole of a solid old oak. His long arms dangled down to end around his knees.

Buck noticed then that he was not ready to draw. Therefore the tension left him, and Tortilla Joe also straightened.

Buck saw a huge face covered with black whiskers. The giant had eyes as big as those of a horse, and they were the color of a bronc's eyes, too. They were brown and moist.

"What do you want?" Buck repeated. "I'm Buck McKee."

The man boomed out again. His voice sounded as if it came from the bottom of an empty wooden barrel. It rolled across the café and smashed against the wall.

"Friends of Jack Perry, you two?"

Tortilla Joe answered. "We know Jack's papa. Up een Colorado. Now who are you, beeg hombre?"

"Name is Fiddlefoot Garner."

Buck did some hurried remembering. He could not manage to place the name. He glanced at Tortilla Joe.

"I know heem not, Buckshots."

Buck said, "What about it, Garner?"

Again that booming voice. "I'm boss of the Cinchring Construction Company. Jack Perry owned it, you know. I rode into town to scout things. Also to claim the body of my boss, who was my friend. Some of my skinners are hot under the collar pads about these hellions lynching the boss."

Buck resumed work with his toothpick. "You scared me breathless," he panted. "I figgered you were another Lawrence gunman comin' to notch me off. Set down an' tie into a V of pie while we talk, Garner."

They shook hands. He had a grip like a bear's paw, although Buck had never shaken hands with a bear. Then Fiddlefoot Garner sat on a stool. Buck glanced at the floor, half expecting the man's tremendous weight to push the base of the stool through the flooring. But the flooring held.

"What kind?" the waitress asked.

She pushed back more hair.

"Apple, miss."

"Don't blow me down," the woman said angrily. "I can hear without you hollering, Fiddlefoot."

"Sorry." The giant grinned. Even his ears seemed to move. She slid out a fork. His enormous grizzly paw swallowed it, leaving only the tines sticking out. These went down to smash a hunk out of the pie.

"Jack Perry boasted about you two comin' in, Buck. His dad wrote down that two hell-roarin' gunslingers were on the way down from Colorady."

The fork rose, the piece of pie balanced. The pie hesitated, the big mouth opened, the pie was lost forever.

Juice ran down Garner's jaw. He wiped it away with the back of a hairy hand. "Nice to have two men fast with their guns to side us," he said.

Buck groaned. "We're not gunslingers, fella."

"You shot down Will March. March was the fastest man on this range, so they said. Thet makes you a gunfighter in my book, McKee."

Buck shook his head.

Tortilla Joe looked very sad. The ease with which Fiddlefoot Garner got outside half a pie —in three bites—seemed to fascinate the Mexican.

Buck said, "Jack had the deal all wrong. We merely were droppin' in on him to give him ol' Sam's greetings. I don't know where the mistake occurred. Either Sam was joshing with his boy, or else Jack was reading something into the letter that wasn't there. We're jes' two poor little drifters, with no kin or even a roof over our heads...."

Sheriff Henry Potter, for once, was smiling. Tortilla Joe also sported a wide grin. Buck was smiling at his own wit. Then he looked at the waitress. She had a glum and gloomy face. No sense of humor, Buck thought. Worst class of woman a man can tie onto.

"Another pie," Garner told the girl.

Buck said nothing. More kids watched. By now the girl did not bother to chase them away.

Fiddlefoot Garner spoke around more pie, blueberry this time. "Well, anyway, Buck, we got a deal for you."

"Yeah?" Buck's tone dripped skepticism.

"Our men want you to lead us," the construction boss said.

"Lead you where?" Buck asked, playing ignorant.

"Against them Hammerhead devils, of course. We ain't gonna set back an' let Lawrence lynch our boss." Blueberry juice streaked down both sides of his mouth. He reminded Buck of one of those Cocopah squaws who tattoo a line from their mouth's corners each time they get married. "Jack was a darned swell fellow, Buck. Hard worker and a man of vision. He had eyes that saw the day when this desert, with water on it, would bloom like the proverbial rose. Now he sleeps in a restless death, and his soul cries for vengeance."

"You talk een beeg words," Tortilla Joe said. "You should be writin' the books, no?"

"What was that?"

"I forget what I say, maybe. . . ."

Outside a boyish voice was raised in wild roughness. "Read all about it, people. Buck McKee comes to sling a gun for the Cinchring outfit. Tortilla Joe is with him. McKee beats the tar out of Curt Lawrence. Jack Perry's neck is stretched by lynchin'."

The waitress stuck her head out the door. "We want two papers, Pancho."

She gave one to Buck. The tall Texan read the headlines and winced openly. Darn that Sitting Bull Jones! The old editor sure wasn't out to make him, Buck McKee, a bosom friend of Curt Lawrence! Sitting Bull Jones evidently had more courage than he had good sense. Plainly he stood on the side of the Cinchring outfit.

Fiddlefoot Garner boomed, "Sittin' Bull is a brave, brave man, gents."

Sheriff Henry Potter grunted, "A bullet don't care whether it kills a brave man or a coward." This bit of wisdom dispensed, he stood up and paid his bill. He speared a toothpick. "Miss McCullen will see you, McKee."

"When?"

"Any time."

The obese lawman waddled outside. Fiddlefoot Garner crammed half a pie into his volcanic mouth. He did some talking, and Buck and

Tortilla Joe listened. They found out that the Cinchring crew consisted of farmers who had taken up desert homesteads. They had hired a few dirt stiffs—men who knew fresno and slip work. They were going to build a dam and then build some ditches. Irrigation water would flow over the desert. Water that came from Salt River, which had its headwaters high in the mountains.

"Got the dam built yet?" Buck asked.

"Buildin' it now." Fiddlefoot ran a tongue around his plate and looked hungrily at the waitress. "Reckon they ain't no use of me askin' for more pie, is they? Or is my credit good for another half a pie?"

"Ain't no good," the waitress said.

The big man assumed a hurt look. "I figured you was money mad, but I never thought you'd allow a man to starve to death on a stool in your restaurant. Ain't a good advertisement for your café—a man dying of starvation settin' on one of your stools!"

"You won't die of hunger."

The giant eyed the six pies in the case across the counter. "Jes' as you say, woman."

The door barged open. In came Sitting Bull Jones. He chuckled and smiled as if he had just inherited a million bucks cash. Buck noticed he had a new ribbon tied around his forehead. This one was blue. There was an acrid odor about the man, not all of it caused by printer's ink. Sitting

Bull Jones could have stood a soaking in Salt River.

He held up his newspaper. "Look at that headline, McKee!"

"My death warrant," Buck said gloomily.

"We got them Hammerhead scissorbills on the run, McKee. When you two come in to side us—you two professional gunslingers—"

Buck winced openly.

Tortilla Joe shuddered visibly.

Sitting Bull laid his war club on the counter. "Done drove a spike into it," he said, admiring the club. "Left the head out about a inch. Hey, McKee, where you all headin' for at this time of the evening?"

"Cinchring," Buck said.

The publisher's tan face became pale. His ink-stained fingers grabbed Buck by the shirt sleeve. His fingers were talons twisting the sleeve.

"What about me, McKee?"

"What do you mean?" Buck said.

"What if the Crown Prince ties into me, when you are gone? I'll be an old, sick man, bucking his gun. Consider me, please, Buck!"

Buck had to grin. "What did you do before I arrived?"

"What do you mean?"

"You bucked Hammerhead then, didn't you? I wasn't around to pertect you then."

"But, Buck—things have come to a head since

then. Since you an' Tortilla Joe came into Buckskin I've shot off my mouth more than ever—I knowed you two gunmen would help me if Lawrence pushed me."

Buck stared down at the wide eyes. He looked at the hairband holding in the greasy hair. A sort of pity came over him.

"What if Lawrence kills me?"

Buck grinned. "I'll preach your funeral sermon. Never preached one in my life, but there's a first time for everything, so they tell me."

He disengaged the talons. Fiddlefoot Garner swung his gaze back to the pies. The waitress wiped a plate and listened. Tortilla Joe wore a wide, good-natured grin.

"Eef he shoots you bang bang dead, we put the white leely in your hands, Seetin' Bull."

"A great consolation you two buttons are," the old man mourned. "Girl, black coffee—gallons of it, and pronto."

Buck and Tortilla Joe went outside, Fiddlefoot Garner waddling along behind them, his mind still on the pie. He had driven a buggy into town. At the hitchrack in front of the general store he had tied the team of black geldings to the tie-rack. He said he would go out in his buggy. The partners would get their horses from the town livery barn and ride along with him.

"All right," Buck agreed.

CHAPTER EIGHT

Unknown to the partners, Curt Lawrence watched them from the bank. He peered out from the corner of the low-drawn blind. Behind him, seated at his desk, was Martin Halloway. Halloway looked at the cowman's wide back and thought, A bullet through the spine would end him for once and for all. He liked that thought.

But this was not the time or the place.

Banker Halloway looked at Sybil Lawrence. She sat on the corner of his desk. She had her legs crossed. Halloway looked at her pretty knees. Suddenly he wanted to put his hand on her knee. The urge was almost irresistible. But he choked it down.

He looked up at her.

She looked down at him.

Curt Lawrence had his back to them.

He gave her a long slow look, the look of a lover. She smiled and winked at him. The smile had a brassy and forced edge to it. But Martin Halloway did not notice this. He was too deeply in love.

And love, so some sage once said, wears blinders.

Curt Lawrence spoke without looking at them. "Fiddlefoot has come in for them, I'll bet. They're heading for the town livery barn. That means they aim to get their broncs. He's turnin' his team and the buggy. They'll head out to Cinchring with him.

"Sittin' Bull Jones is going into his office. Blast him and his *Cactus*. We have to get him outa our way, people."

Again Halloway watched the woman's pretty knees. "A bullet—just one little bullet—in the right part of his anatomy, in the correct place," he said slowly.

Lawrence added, "And with no witnesses, either."

The banker repeated, "And with no witnesses."

Lawrence straightened. Although it was semi-dark in the office, Halloway could see the rugged set to the man's bony face. Curt Lawrence stood there and thought wrapped him, making him gloomy. His wife watched and swung a pretty leg and said nothing.

Halloway watched, too.

Outside, Pancho called out, selling his newspapers. The words *Lawrence* and *McKee* and *Cinchring* seeped through the brick walls of the bank.

Lawrence said suddenly, "See you later."

Long strides carried him across the room. He went out the back door. Halloway listened to his boots grind down the alley, ringing on gravel. Back there in that alley a man had died under Buck McKee's hard lead. Halloway, for some reason, did not like this thought.

He got to his feet. He walked around the desk. He stood in front of Curt Lawrence's wife. They looked at each other. Neither spoke. His hands came up and rested on her shoulders.

"I love you," he said.

She said, "And I love you."

His eyes searched her face. She slid off the desk and got to her feet. She went into his arms.

They kissed.

The kiss, to the banker, seemed ardent.

"We've got to get rid of him, Sybil," the banker said suddenly.

"We will, Martin."

"When?"

"Now is a good time."

"Why now?"

She said, "McKee and the Mexican are in town. Already they've had run-ins with him.

Don't you see, Martin?"

He stepped back. He rubbed his jaw and studied her. "Smart little gal," he praised. "Somehow we'll put the blame of his death on McKee and the Mexican. Smart girl, Sybil."

"I have to own the Hammerhead."

Halloway kept rubbing his chin. His eyes got a crafty and scheming gleam. She had said, *I* have to own the Hammerhead, and she should have said, *We* have to own the Hammerhead. Or was it just a slip of her pretty tongue?

He kissed her again.

Her lips clung to his. He stepped back, again deep in his thoughts.

Sometimes she seemed too metallic and too brassy and too scheming. Sometimes it seemed that her mouth pulled down into hard and ugly lines. Sometimes it seemed that her eyes became a little bit too stony and, at these times, he wondered about her.

But he never wondered long.

He was sure she loved him.

She asked, "Where did Curt go?"

"I don't know," he said.

She said, "I hate the big blowhard devil, Martin. I could kill him myself. He thinks for sure that Jack Perry killed Old John. He thinks for sure that Perry killed his father—"

"Hush, for heaven's sake!"

Her smile was touched by cynicism. She cocked her pretty head and regarded him with a long glance.

"The walls don't hear," she pointed out. "Man, are you getting jittery?"

He studied her. "No," he said. He added, "But why take chances?" He walked back and forth, hands behind his back. She watched him but he did not look at her. She was the schemer now, and this showed on her face. But when he looked up the face was smiling and innocent.

Halloway stood there with his head cocked. He was thinking of Hammerhead—the biggest ranch in this section of Arizona Territory. The immense ranch house spread out along the mesa, big and long and made of adobe—the house built by John Lawrence almost half a century before. And he was thinking of Hammerhead cattle. Cattle, moving ahead of riders during roundup —thousands of cattle, coming out of the mesquite and underbrush, running with wide eyes, smashing through the chamiso and red-shank. They were running across his brain . . . and he wanted them. And he was working out his plan, too. Some men went out with a gun or a club, and they got what they wanted—John Lawrence had been that type, and his son was that type, also. They were the kind who tore what they wanted from the earth, from their fellow men. They were tough and domineering, and they walked across the earth with huge strides, the chime of their spur rowels echoing across the rangelands. They took their land and their women and they broke their broncs and they ran out their wild cattle . . . and they fought not with brains, but with brawn.

He was not this type. He knew how to wait, and those men did not know the meaning of the word *wait*. He was patient, as the spider is patient. He had spun his web; now let the boisterous blowfly get ensnared. . . . He would wait and he would scheme, and he would have what he wanted; if things rushed too fast, and waiting became futile, only then would he move to meet his adversaries, and his gun would be in his hand.

"A dime for your thoughts, Martin?"

His smile was quiet. "Are you worth a dime, pretty lady?"

"What do you mean?"

"I was thinking of you. . . ."

"Oh, quit the joking." She was on the desk again, swinging one pretty leg. She watched him for some time, and he studied her face to find out her thoughts. But her face showed nothing. He saw her scowl suddenly.

"What's the trouble?" he asked.

"I'm thinking of two men."

"Yes. Could I guess?"

"Go ahead," she said.

He said, "A fat, waddling Mexican, and a string-bean cowpuncher. Tortilla Joe and one Buck McKee. . . ."

"That's right."

He started his pacing again. The thought of the two partners had shoved the pleasing thought of Hammerhead out of his mind. His boots made their sounds—five paces over, five back. He put his hands behind his back.

"We're lucky they came into town," he said suddenly.

"I think so. If we can get one of them to kill Curt."

"I got it figured out," he said.

She nodded. "How will it work out?"

"Fiddlefoot Garner has come into town for them. They'll go out to Cinchring. They'll look the deal over out there. Neither of them are farmers, nor do they know a thing about irrigation. But one glance at the fresno men and they'll be sure of one thing, Sybil."

"And that?"

"That there are no fighters on the outfit. Farmers, yes—and a few drifting dirt men—but no tough fighters. The farmers are from the east and the midwest; they have been raised in peace. The dirt men are drifters, working only for wages.

Am I right?"

"Then what will they do?"

He scowled. He rubbed his gaunt jaw. His eyes showed doubt. "I don't know," he had to admit. "They might move against Hammerhead in open warfare. They might play their cards close. They look stupid and dumb, but McKee killed Will March, and March was no cowpuncher on the Hammerhead payroll. Will March was a professional gunman. . . ."

"Maybe McKee was lucky."

Halloway grinned. "Well, he must have had lots of luck since coming to Buckskin, for he's won most of the time." He touched his jaw gingerly. "He knocked me down, for one thing; he laid Curt down, too." Suddenly anger flushed his face and it reddened. "He'll pay for dropping me, woman."

"How?"

He looked at her sharply. "Are you teasing me?"

"No."

Her face was deadpan.

He pulled air into his lungs. "I'll find a way," he assured her. "Maybe I can lay the killing on the shoulders of your beloved husband."

"Hope so." Again that pretty leg swung. Again he watched it. She said, "How about Clair McCullen?"

"What about her?" His voice was sharp.

Sybil Lawrence moved her shoulders lazily. "She's in the calaboose, remember? Horse stealing, the charge—and McKee filed the complaint. Why is he keeping her in jail?"

"He can't hold her."

"She stole his bronc."

He said, "She borrowed it, not stole it. She took it back. How that dumb Potter could have allowed McKee to file a complaint is beyond my understanding. But Potter hasn't got too much between the ears except space."

"You can only push him so far," the woman said. "Then he plants both hoofs and is as bull-headed as a lovesick burro."

"He's small fry. So is Sitting Bull Jones. Two necessary nuisances, one might say. Curt is a fool to take Sitting Bull so seriously. Wonder where your loving husband went?"

"I wonder. . . ."

CHAPTER NINE

Buck pulled in his bronc. Tortilla Joe, riding behind him, also stopped his horse.

"What ees the matter, Buckshots? Why you stop your *caballo* at thees place, here een the darkness of thees building?"

"Curt Lawrence," Buck murmured. "Just went in the back door of the saloon. Why don't he use the front?"

"Maybe he come down the alley from the bank, no?"

Buck dismounted, ground-tying his horse. He was the type of man who always played his hunches, and right now he had a hunch something was wrong. He kept remembering the pinched, frightened face of old Sitting Bull Jones. The old publisher had reason for being afraid; that extra about Curt Lawrence would not make the Hammerhead owner a bit happy.

Tortilla Joe also came down out of saddle. He

breathed with hoarse sounds, a fat animal on foot. They were hidden in the darkness of the building. Heat still came up from the desert. It hit them in the face, and it was very hot. But neither had any thought for the heat.

"Wonder what he do een saloon?" Tortilla Joe conjectured.

"Come along," Buck said.

They left their mounts and went along the alley. They came to the back window of Thick Neck's saloon. Again they looked through a window. Curt Lawrence was talking to a man who was playing cards with three other men at a table . The man's back was to them and therefore identification was impossible. Still there was something familiar about the man, Buck decided.

"Who's he talkin' to, Tortilla?"

The Mexican looked at the man. "I no know, Buckshots. Steel, there ees sometheeng about him— Now he stand up, no?"

The man had laid down his card and had cashed in his chips and had got to his boots. Lamplight showed his face clearly. He was the gunman who had held Sybil Lawrence, the one whom she had scratched across the nose. He and Curt Lawrence moved to one side and talked. Lawrence did most of the talking. The gunman merely nodded occasionally. He rubbed his nose gingerly. Then he pulled his gun around and went out on the main street.

Lawrence went to the bar. He put his boot on the rail and Thick Neck poured him a drink.

"He ees ask that gonman to do sometheengs for heem," Tortilla Joe said. "I wonder what the task she ees for heem to do, Buckshots?"

Buck frowned. "Let's find out."

Again they went between two buildings and came out on the main street. Already Buckskin was retiring. Lamplights were going out in various adobe cabins. The Mexicans got up early, loafed all day, and retired early. No wonder so many dark-skinned Mexican kids ran around, Buck thought wryly. A dog trotted across the street—he was long and lean and wolfish. The store was dark and the only lights in town, on the main street, were those in the saloon, the Greasy Plate Café, and in the *Cactus* office.

Buck pulled at Tortilla Joe's sleeve. "Duck back in this doorway."

The gunman came sauntering along. He did not see them because of the darkness that hid them. He walked by about ten feet away. He was mean and evil and dark, and Buck watched him closely. The gunman sauntered by the *Cactus* office. The press was quiet, the edition had been printed, and the gunman glanced inside. Then, satisfied by what he saw, he walked on. He anchored himself between two buildings. He was a dark, ugly outline against a dark background. Had Buck not seen him enter the slot, he would not have known a man hid there.

Buck said, "I got a hunch Sittin' Bull was right, Tortilla."

"You mean thees gunmans—he ees out after Seetin' Bulls?"

"He looked in the print shop. Sitting Bull wasn't there, of course—he's in the Greasy Plate. The gunman will wait. Nobody on the street. He could grab ol' Sittin' Bull by the hair, drag him into the alley, and club him to death with his gun. And who could prove what?"

"I go een the alley, Buckshots."

Buck nodded. He heard his partner move away. Despite his bulk the Mexican moved on silent boots when he wanted to move in silence. Buck stood also in silence and watched. A few minutes ran by. The thought came to the tall Texan that perhaps his assumptions, his hunch, were all wrong. Could be. . . .

Sitting Bull Jones, complete with war club, came out of the Greasy Plate Café. He turned toward his printing shop. The moment was ripe, and Buck stepped out of hiding. He moved down the street toward the old man. He could well imagine the gunman's surprise upon seeing him on the street. Buck knew that eyes were constantly watching him; the gunman probably figured he, Buck McKee, had gone out to Cinchring Construction. But here he walked the main street, coming toward Sitting Bull Jones.

Sitting Bull Jones, unaware of the killer in the shadows, stopped and stared at Buck McKee.

"Thought you headed for Cinchring, Buck?"

"Gonna get some terbaccer," Buck said. "Found my Durham supply had run out. So postponed it a spell."

"The saloon has Durham."

Buck shook his head. "Don't cotton to the saloon too much. Curt Lawrence is in there and I've had enough trouble with him for one day. The girl in the café has tobaccer, hasn't she?"

"Sure."

"S'long, Sittin' Bull."

"So long, McKee."

The old man continued on down the street toward his newspaper office. Buck went toward the café. He was sure the hidden Lawrence gunman had heard every word he and Sitting Bull had said. That was all right. They had told him nothing. Buck didn't need another sack of Bull Durham any more than he needed another head. He had three full sacks in his saddle-bag.

He got opposite the hiding place of the gunman. A cold feeling came in and touched the Texan. He got a queasy feeling in his belly. The

gunman could blast out, and he, Buck McKee, would get the works. He realized he was going into danger for an old man who, by all rights, should have meant nothing to him. Fate had pulled queer strings. A few hours ago, when he and Tortilla Joe had ridden into Buckskin, neither had even known that a queer old galoot like Sitting Bull Jones walked the earth.

Now he was moving against a gunman—a Lawrence gunman—because of the old printer.

Suddenly, without warning, Buck pivoted, gun out. He point it toward the gunman who imagined he was hidden.

"Come on out, you two-bit killer."

His words were low and were heard only by the gunman. Sitting Bull Jones, going down the street, did not hear them. Buck could well imagine the gunman's surprise.

Buck cocked his .45. "Come on out, Lawrence man," he said quietly. "I seen you hide yourself back there waitin' for ol' Sittin' Bull. I can see you clear. Take your hand off your gun or I'll send lead howlin' through your brisket."

"Don't shoot, McKee!"

The gunman walked out of hiding. He had both hands discreetly away from his gunbelt. He came close to Buck, staring at his gun.

"You're a hard man to get the best of, Mc-Kee."

Buck looked at him. He was no coward. He would fight if he got a chance. Buck egged him on.

"Somebody went through my saddlebags down at the barn." This was a deliberate lie. Buck had glimpsed Tortilla Joe behind the man. The Mexican was working toward the killer. By the deliberate falsehood Buck hoped to rivet the gunman's attention on him.

"They did?"

"You were snoopin' around my rig. Somebody told me that. You searched them saddlebags." Buck stiffened his gun, pointing it at the man's belly. "I should shoot you through the guts and let you die a slow, lingerin' death. . . ."

"You can't kill a man without givin' him a chance, McKee!"

"You aimed to kill that old printer. Lawrence went into the saloon and ordered you out here to bump off Sittin' Bull. I saw the whole thing. Did you search my saddlebags?"

The man's lips trembled, then tightened.

"McKee, you jes' want trouble, that's all."

They were two wolves circling, fangs bared, manes raised; ready to fight, to snarl, to bite.

By this time the Mexican was directly behind the gunman. How he moved so quietly Buck could not understand. The gunman had no idea a third man had entered this. He was aware only of Buck.

Buck deliberately holstered his .45. The barrel swished as it went against the oiled holster leather.

"You givin' me a chance, McKee?"

The gunman spoke in a hoarse, rattling tone of voice. His gross body became compact, a human ball of hard flesh, and his hands were down, fingers out over handles of two big .45s.

"I sure am," Buck said.

The gunman watched, eyes glistening even in the dark. He was evil and mean, and he licked his lips. His tongue was out when Tortilla Joe's club came down. The blow almost made the gunman cut his tongue in two with his teeth. He never knew what had hit him. One minute he had his full senses, his faculties were in coordination; he was a fighting, tough machine of flesh and blood. The next he was on the sidewalk, lying on his face—an inert, broken piece of meat and blood, senseless and unaware of the world.

Buck grinned, wiped sweat from his forehead. "I timed it just right at that," he said, and his voice sounded limp. "I thought for a while I had holstered my six-shooter too soon and you wouldn't slug him afore he got to draw. You walk on silent boots, friend."

"I leave my spurs een the alley, Buckshots."

Buck stepped across the unconscious gunman. Not a soul on the street, and nobody to tell the gunman—when he regained consciousness—what had happened. Nobody to report back to Curt Lawrence, either. Buck pulled his partner into the pitch darkness between the buildings.

"Come along, Tortilla."

"We leave heem back there?"

"Sure."

"He not know what heet heem. He weel come to and then he weel stagger around—*hola,* like a drunk mans, no?"

"Lawrence will look for him, I reckon. Where did you get that club, and what is it made of?"

The club was made of manzanita, that tough and flexible red wood of the desert. Tortilla Joe had cut it from a tree back in the alley. He was very cheery and proud of himself, and he chuckled continuously. The Mexican kissed the thin club as loudly as Sitting Bull Jones had smacked his war club.

They came to the alley.

Buck said, "I got another call to make."

"*Si.* Where ees she to be made, Buckshots?"

"The jail."

"Ah, the muchachita—the little girl, no? Maybe she kees you now and get out from behin' them col', col' bars, no?"

"Maybe," Buck grunted.

They went in through the front door. From the outside the place had looked as if it had no lamplight, but that was because the blinds completely killed all chance of light showing in the windows. They went in without knocking.

A lamp burned on a wall bracket. It was turned down very low. Sheriff Henry Potter slept in his chair, head on his desk. Lamplight glistened from his greasy bald pate. He was sound asleep. He snored like a jackass braying. His thick lips moved, his big nose quivered; he was deep in the arms of the dark god Sleep. He did not awaken, either, when Buck and Tortilla Joe entered.

"Dead mans," Tortilla Joe joked.

They crossed the office and opened the door leading to the jail. A lantern hung from the ceiling supplied dim and inadequate illumination. The jail consisted of six cells, three on each side. A cell corridor ran between them. The partners went down this.

Clair McCullen had been lying on her bunk. When she heard them she sat up and looked around and then she came to the bars.

Buck said, "Even in this dim light, you're sure purty, sweetheart."

"Lovely," Tortilla Joe chimed in.

Her voice was husky. "You come to turn me loose?"

Tortilla Joe shook his dour head. Buck also shook his head. Hope left her face and turned it hard, and anger was on her mouth, twisting down her lips.

"McKee, why the devil have you got me in jail?"

"A purty girl—a perfect woman—never nags," Buck chided devilishly. "After all, you have prestige here—you're the town millinery shop—"

"Not shop, you idiot! I'm the seamstress. Oh, Lord, you talk stupid. You talk like I was a store, and I'm only a woman—" She stopped when she saw his smile. "You're getting me mad on purpose."

"And you're fallin' for it," Buck said. He admired her trim and womanly figure, and his grin was friendly. "You stole my hoss. Hoss thieves, so they say, have to pay. And you have to pay me, honey."

She tried to slap him through the bars. He grabbed her arm and held it. She tried to pull her arm back but he kept his grip on it. She stopped struggling. Lamplight showed her eyes clearly.

"What is this deal, McKee?"

"You can get out of here on one promise."

She watched him. "If that promise is what I think you mean, then you're out of luck, you long-geared galoot!"

Buck grinned.

Tortilla Joe watched, his smile wide.

The silence grew. Buck still held her arm. He stroked her little hand. He kept on smiling. Finally impatience possessed her.

"What is that promise, McKee?"

"You kiss me, of your own accord—and like you meant it."

She jerked her arm back, the movement savage. "You go to and stay put," she snarled. "Why, you—you—"

"Goodby, Honey."

"Don't honey me— you good— you good-for-nothin'—"

Buck cut in with, "You're stuttering. Doesn't look good for a purty girl to get so mad she stutters. Well, when you change your mind, get Potter to come after me. I'm a fool around the women, sister."

"You're a fool all the time."

Suddenly Sheriff Henry Potter loomed into sight in the doorway leading to the office. He had a pistol in his hand and his eyes were wild.

"What the blazes—? You scared me silly, McKee. Figgered mebbe it was another jail delivery, I did." He holstered the .45 clumsily, the barrel of the gun first missing the mouth of the holster. "You two walked right past me, eh?"

"You sleep hard," Tortilla Joe said.

Buck said, "She won't come across. For one little kiss, she could go. But she's like a mule with the ringbone. Won't move a step, Sheriff."

They went into the office. The air was cool, but still the sheriff mopped his bald head. Sweat popped out behind his dirty bandana. His huge eyes rolled in their damp sockets. He rubbed his wide nose.

"McKee, do me a favor, please?"

Buck looked at Tortilla Joe. "This deal is kinda got the cart ahead of the hoss, Tortilla. Usually I have to ask the sheriffs for favors. This sheriff is askin' me for one." He spoke now to Potter. "What's troublin' your purty little head, lawman?"

"My wife."

"Never knew you had a wife. What about her?"

Again, the bandana plowed through sweat. Again, the sweat popped out behind its passage.

"My wife is suspicious of me an' Clair. Claims I'm holdin' the girl to have her close to me. Imagine a man my age—and a woman that suspicious— McKee, drop the charges against her, for me?"

"No."

"My oldest daughter—Aggie— Why, she won't even talk to me! McKee, she thinks I'm holdin' her because I—"

"You said that before."

They went outside. Down the street Lawrence was kneeling beside his gunman. Buck said, "Let's have some fun."

"This won't be fun," Tortilla Joe said.

"Might be."

The gunman was still out cold. When they approached Lawrence got to his feet. Buck said, "Somethin' wrong, Curt."

"To you, McKee, the name is Lawrence— not Curt!"

"Okay, Curt."

Tortilla Joe looked down at the gunman. "Maybe he have his gon go off, an' he keel heemself, no?"

"Somebody's slugged him," Curt Lawrence snarled.

The owner of Hammerhead looked at Buck. His gaze moved over to Tortilla Joe. Buck said, "Too bad, fella."

They went to their horses and rode toward Cinchring.

CHAPTER TEN

Everywhere there was dust.

Dust was in the still air, in the coffee, in the hotcakes. It hung across the desert, and it coated saguaros and manzanita and sagebrush and greasewood with its gray and gritty coat. It was the tough desert dust of Arizona Territory. Gray dust, fine as silt, tough as sandpaper. Dust rose behind fresnos. It came from under the pounding plodding hoofs of working mules and horses. It rose from under the boots of plodding men. It coated the men's clothing and put a gray blanket across their faces, leaving only their eyes visible. It filled their mouths and the cracks on their lips, and they cursed it and they ate it and they slept in it and it filled the pores of their sweating, stinking bodies.

Men were fighting the desert. Water was on their side, a patient and dumb ally. Men were going to whip the desert. Water would whip it.

But first there had to be dust, and they were fighting the dust so water could be brought in—clear and dashing mountain water—to kill the dust once and forever.

"Darn this dust," Buck said.

"Darn thees dust," Tortilla Joe said.

Buck looked at the Mexican. "Are you a parrot, too?"

Thick shoulders lifted, fell. "I am accommodatin', *señor*. You cuss at the dust, I cuss too. You not sleep too well last night, no?"

"Bunk hard as a granite boulder," Buck grumbled. "Pillow filled with lead hunks. Dead men running across my head all night. These hotcakes are a combination of copper filings and sand. You bite into them and the vibrations of your teeth on the grit make your ears wobble and jump."

"Makes my toes ache," the Mexican said.

Buck, said, "A man wastes his breath when he talks to you. So keep on chewin' sand, chum, and let this long boy nurse his own bitter thoughts. I wonder how dumb two humans can get?"

"You ees tell me not to talk, remember?"

"Then why are you talkin' now?"

Again the Mexican shrugged. Buck would soon get over his angry mood, the fat man knew. Anger never stayed long with his partner. It passed, and soon Buck would be joking again. But the dust was thick. Tortilla Joe suspended part of a hotcake in front of his cavernous mouth and sent a glance around the cook-tent. Already the skinners were out moving dirt. The cook was at the far end, peeling spuds for the noon meal. Buck and Tortilla Joe were alone at the long plank table without a tablecloth or oilcloth. Tortilla Joe shoved the hotcake into his mouth. He chewed on sand.

Buck's teeth grated on sand, too.

But the lanky Texan kept on chewing. A man had to eat to live, was his philosophy. But he didn't give a hoot about this Cinchring dirt-camp. He was a saddle-man—a gent wedded to a horse. And here he was eating a combination sand-and-flour hotcake in a stifling old tent that had once been white but now was dark with dust.

"We was born for trouble, Tortilla Joe. Here we are, stuck with a bunch of sodbusters and fresno men building a irrigation system, just because we punched cows for a sick old man up in Colorady. Over on the Gila River awaits the Gallatin spread, and the sun is warm and there's no dust and cattle are grazin' in the foothills, waitin' for us."

"Me, I no talk, remember?"

"Jes' cause we mentioned to Sam Perry we

was ridin' acrost Arizona Territory, he writes to his son—and the cook or somebody makes gunhands out of us. And here we are up to our little dirty necks in gunsmoke."

"I no *habla,* remember."

Buck looked at him. "Say somethin', you fat son of a saddle."

"That Clair, she ees got a purty smile, no?"

"Ain't all she's got that's purty," Buck said.

"Ah, lovely womens, no?"

The Latin sighed gustily. Buck swung his attention over to his partner. He looked at the wide dark face and the thick nose. Tortilla Joe stared blankly back at him.

"Why you look at me, Buckshots?"

Buck grimaced. "That mug of yours would drive a hungry dog off a garbage wagon." He climbed to his tall height and stepped back over the bench. Then he put his knife and fork and spoon on the plate, put his coffee cup around a little finger, and carried the mess over to where the cook's flunky was washing dishes in a copper tub.

"Fine saddleblankets, cookie."

The fat cook glared at him. "Not saddleblankets, fella. Hotcakes," he corrected in a tight voice.

"I still stick by the word saddleblankets," Buck said.

"You're makin' yourself unpopular, McKee."

Buck shrugged. "Makes no never-mind."

Tortilla Joe dumped his hardware and plate in the water. "Come on, Buckshots; we go outside, no? The sand ees fresher and tastes better out there, so they is told me a while back."

They walked out, Buck tall as a toothpick; Tortilla Joe waddling like a bear. The cook, arms akimbo, glared at them.

"Sure ain't grateful," the *cocinero* grumbled.

The flunky, not saying a word, continued washing wishes. Sand continued to sift through the tent.

"Wonder if the wind will come up again today," the cook conjectured. "Sure hope it don't blow in more sand."

"Don't know," the flunky said shortly.

While it had been stifling hot under the tent, outside it was blistering hot. Sunlight hit the sand, reflected, bounced, and gained in heat with each bounce, or so it seemed to Buck. The distant mountains danced in the heat, looking like mirages. Out of the dust and the heat came the huge form of Fiddlefoot Garner.

"Hot," he said.

Buck said, "Hot."

Tortilla Joe said, *"Muy calor."*

These words said, Fiddlefoot Garner wiped his forehead with his hairy hand. He looked at

the mountains.

"Nice and cool up there in them pines," he said. "That's where the Salt River comes from. Nice and cool up there."

"Nice and cool," Buck said.

"Muy cool," Tortilla Joe said.

Fiddlefoot Garner asked, "Good meal?"

"Sure," Buck said. "Fine grade of sand."

Garner smiled. "You'll get used to it." He ran his forefinger around the inside of his mouth. "Even got it between my teeth. Poor Jack Perry —loved this sand. Hey, wanna see the dam, eh?"

His ox-like eyes went from man to man. Plainly the most important thing in this sand-filled earth to him was the dam.

"Why not?" Buck said.

"Si, sure," Tortilla Joe agreed.

"We'll ride out there," the big man said. "In my buckboard. Come along; I got my team tied over here in the shade."

"Didn't know this country had any shade," Buck said sourly. To himself he said, I don't give a hoot about the dam.

Garner had a team of sorrels tied behind the tent. They were dusty sorrels now, and the buckboard to which they were hitched was also dust-rimmed. Tortilla Joe got in, the buckboard sagging to one side. Garner climbed in on the other side, almost tipping the rig over. With Garner on one side, and Tortilla Joe on the other, the buckboard settled back on an even keel. They filled the seat completely.

Buck said, "I'll ride behind the seat, standin' up."

Garner had already untied the team. He cramped the front wheels around, almost tipping the rig over.

"Quite a dam," he said.

Buck nodded.

Garner got the team to a plodding walk. Sand hung to the steel rims of the wheels. Garner said, "Hot day."

Neither partner spoke.

Garner bit off a chew. "You may not know this, McKee, but this mornin' afore you was awake the farmers voted."

"Yeah. . . . Voted on what?"

"They voted you in as their leader. They want to avenge Jack's untimely passing. They nominated you and voted you in as gun-boss."

"I ain't got a thing to say about it, eh?"

Garner cocked his head and studied him. "Why, you're an ol' pal of Sam Perry, and Jack is Sam's only son. Think of the honor, McKee."

Buck grinned. "Great honor. What kind of a plan have they hatched up, Garner?"

"Kind of a watchful waitin' plan, I reckon."

"Good," Buck said.

The team slowed to a stupid plodding. Wind whipped in, dust and sand rose, and Tortilla Joe blew his nose.

"Sandman, that's what I am," he said.

Nobody answered.

Here the desert ran into the brush-covered hills. They went along a trail that led now through cottonwood trees, for the river was close by. They followed a road ground into the hot earth by wheels and hoofs and boots. The dust rolled out of the coulee. It came in billowing, stifling clouds. Plainly they were nearing the dam site, for fresnos raised the dust. Fiddlefoot Garner put the team to the west, and the rig climbed a low hill. Below them were the workers.

Fiddlefoot Garner said, "Down in thet dust is the dam. As you kin see, the river is low at this time of the year; about December it almost disappears. Then the rains fill it again and it runs with more water. Our plan is to get our dam finished afore the winter rains start."

Buck studied the project. He was amazed at the amount of work the workers had done. They were not disturbing the normal flow of the river. But on each side they had reared their earthen wall. They had the spillway built—a solid sheet of concrete, situated at the west end of the dam.

They were lining the face with boulders hauled down from the hills.

Buck said, "When the spillway is completed and the rest of the dam is solid, you aim to run a coffer-dam acrost the river, eh, an' divert the water through the spillway until you get the old bed of the river covered?"

"That's the deal. And we got to get it built before the rains start, or we lose the hull thing."

Tortilla Joe grunted, "You do lots of work— good work—"

"Jack Perry had his heart and soul—and all his money—in it," the big foreman said. "All of us got our lives' savin's in it, McKee. These farmers has homesteads below here. Most of them are married. Wives stayed back East." He looked toward the south where the desert stretched, saguaros raising ghostly hands against the heat. "This country will all be bloomin' like the Garden of Eden, come a few years. Yes sir, fruit, crops, gardens. Nice homes. . . ."

Buck glanced at Tortilla Joe. The big man had a dreamy, faraway look in his horse-like eyes. Up to this point Buck had openly doubted the possibility of turning the desert into farms. Now, seeing the immense work these men had done since spring, that doubt left him. These men would get their goal, come hell or high water . . . or even Curt Lawrence.

Tortilla Joe said, "Good deal, Gardner." He nodded his head vigorously. "You make this land good land, I theenk."

"I know it," the foreman said emphatically.

Garner's huge index finger pointed out points —there the main canal would go, angling along the hills, and side-canals would come off this, running down to homesteads. There would have to be land leveled, a drainage system installed, but they would come with time. The main thing was to get the dam built before the winter rains.

Buck agreed with this.

"You got guards out?" he asked.

"Night and day—twenty-four hours a day— they patrol, Buck. No violence as yet, but we fear Lawrence, when the dam is almost through. It would do him little good to dynamite now, or attempt to destroy the dam."

Tortilla Joe again nodded. "He smart, the son. He wait unteel she ees almost the feen-eeshed; then he would make hees play."

Buck said, "Don't for one minute underestimate him."

"We ain't."

They spent some more time talking about the dam. Buck began to catch the homestead fever.

Garner asked boomingly, "You boys ever use your homestead rights?"

"No," Buck said.

"No," Tortilla Joe echoed.

"We can get you some choice homestead sites." Fiddlefoot Garner was as happy as a boy with a new horned toad. "For you two, anything—"

Buck said, "Not for me."

"Why not?"

"Work," Buck said. "With your hands, too. Not for this boy. I'm so lazy I ride a horse from the corral to the bunkhouse. I wouldn't walk more than a block, unless forced to."

"I only walk half the block," the Mexican said.

Garner's face showed disappointment. "The boys has some nice sites picked out for you two," he reminded them. "Think it over. Well, you've seen the dam—now let's drive around the homestead sites, out on the desert."

Buck glanced at Tortilla Joe. The Mexican shook his head. He also didn't relish the idea of bouncing over sand hummocks in a buggy when the thermometer out of the sun stood around one twenty.

"Can't do it," Buck grunted.

"Why?" Fiddlefoot Garner asked.

"Got to get back to town. Your men are all right out here. We got to get a letter off to old Sam Perry telling him about his son's fate."

"It'll be a hard one to write," Garner said mournfully.

Tortilla Joe nodded. "But we has to do it."

They drove back to the dirt camp. The only shade was that made by the few cottonwood trees along the river bottom. It was so hot that a jackrabbit refused to run. He squatted under a sagebrush, ears back. Garner shot him with his .45, while Tortilla Joe held the lines. But there was no danger of the team trying to run away. Too hot for such gymnastics.

Garner creaked out of the buggy and held up the jackrabbit by the ears. "Chuck for the table," he said. "Figured there wasn't another rabbit around here."

"Why?" Buck asked.

The man creaked back into the buggy, settled his wide bottom on the seat. "We has to live close to our pocketbooks, men. So rabbits make meals. One boy says he's et so many jacks he's hoppin' around."

Nobody smiled or laughed.

Too hot.

CHAPTER ELEVEN

Despite the heat, she was still lovely. She leaned forward, arms on the fork of her expensive hand-carved saddle. The wind ruffled her silk blouse, and the buckskin riding skirt clung to her slim figure. The polished silver on her hand-made spurs glistened in the Arizona sunlight.

"Well," she said, in that throaty voice of hers, "fancy meeting you two here. Tortilla Joe and Buck McKee. . . ."

Buck grinned. "I'd take off my hat, Missus Lawrence, but I'm afraid the sun might knock me out of my saddle."

"The same she ees apply to me," Tortilla Joe said, grinning. "I am a polite man, but not when the sun ees not polite."

Sybil Lawrence's green eyes moved over them. For a moment there was a brief silence. Buck wondered why the wife of Curt Lawrence rode

desert range on such a hot day. He watched her face. There was a lot of woman here, and she would respond to the right man. . . . He wondered if Curt Lawrence were the right man. From what he had heard, they had been married only a few years. She had come with a show troupe, and she had stayed. Outside of that, he knew about her little, if anything, else. She was, he understood, a sort of a mystery. She made no friends, and she plainly wanted none. She liked to drink and she could swear like a trooper, if and when the occasion demanded. . . .

A few head of Hammerhead steers grazed around a hummock of mesquite. To a person not knowing the desert the steers apparently were doomed to starvation. But, strangely, they were fat. They found a little grass around the roots of the mesquite, and they also ate mesquite beans.

"Don't addle your poor little brains," she said scornfully. "I take it you two sons of Satan have been out visiting the dirt camp?"

Buck was the spokesman. "That's right, Green Eyes."

"Anything new?"

Buck loafed in leather, heat seeping into him. "I had them double the night guard. They're gettin' along fine, they told me."

"And now," she said sweetly, "I suppose you boys are running out of this country, afraid of

Curt Lawrence?"

"We got two inquests to go to," Buck pointed out. "One over Jack Perry; the other over Will March's carcass. We jes' can't leave, woman."

"No can go," Tortilla Joe said, and shrugged.

She leaned forward even further. Buck saw a ghost of a smile touch her pretty lips. She was all woman and charm. Sunlight reflected from a roll of copper-colored hair that peeped out from under her cream-colored Tom Watson Stetson.

"Going to take up homesteads?" she asked.

Buck said grandiosely, "You're darned tootin', Sybil. Both of us is takin' up a hundred an' sixty, with desert claims to side in, hill claims, mining claims, and the whole works."

"When it get done, we have over a section of land," the Mexican said, falling into line.

She pouted. "Tell that to some fool who believes you, McKee."

"You don't believe us?" Buck said, grinning.

Tortilla Joe assumed a beaten, hangdog look. "All the time nobody she believes us, partner. . . ."

Buck said, "We're farmers now, Sybil. Died in the wool sod men, we are. We're forsaking our hard old saddles for a life of ease. I suppose you are out riding range looking at cattle?"

"If you two classify yourself as cattle, I'm

looking at two bovines, I suppose."

Tortilla Joe mourned, "All the time the eensults, Buckshots."

Buck said, "Stay away from that dirt camp. Those men will figure you're out spyin' for your beloved blowhard husband. They'll jerk your arms out by the roots, and beat you to death with them."

"Oh, gosh."

Buck stretched and swallowed sand. "Well, we got to be on our way to Buckskin, honey. There's a woman in there behind bars, and it's drawin' close to the time she'll want to smack me."

"With a board?" she asked.

"Not with a board," Buck said.

She smiled. "Everybody on this range has heard about your crazy proposition, McKee. Do you only play that game with the one girl?"

Buck studied her. "You got a husband," he pointed out.

"He's not in the way," she told him.

Buck put both hands on his saddle-horn and leaned back and looked at Tortilla Joe, who had a face about as active as a dead lizard in the sun. Tortilla Joe dug a tortilla out of his saddle-bag and unwrapped the corn-husk wrapper with slow determination. His face, Buck saw, was about a thousand years old. Suddenly he winced as his teeth ground on sand.

"Even through the tortilla husk the sand she comes, Buckshots."

Buck said, "One husband should be enough." It was just bantering, conversation. It meant nothing.

"He is," she said.

"We got to get to town," Buck said.

Tortilla Joe howled suddenly. Both jerked their attention to the Mexican. He had his thumb and forefinger in his mouth.

"I theenk maybe I breaks the tooth, Buck."

Buck grinned.

Sybil scowled.

Tortilla Joe said, "And the Big Fella, he keeck two tooths out of pore Weel March. . . . Waste of tooths, that ees." He stared at his thumb as though he expected to find a tooth impaled on it. "I could use them two tooths."

"Who couldn't?" Buck asked.

Tortilla Joe looked at Sybil Lawrence. "There ees the dentist, ees there not, een Buckskin?"

"Blacksmith pulls teeth."

"No," Tortilla Joe said suddenly. "I no see heem. . . . Already my tooth she ees better."

Buck looked at Sybil. "Ever do any rasslin'?" he asked innocently.

She studied him as though doubting his sanity. "Wrestling? What do you mean, McKee?"

"With the boys," Buck said. "Don't you like

to have their tender arms around your little waist—"

"You two," she said convincingly, "are loco."

This opinion dispensed, she turned her horse sharply, used her spurs and, despite the heat, loped away. Buck watched her and grinned. Tortilla Joe watched and said, "My tooth she ees no break. That was the what you call eet— the act, no?"

"She got mad," Buck said.

Soon mesquite and manzanita hid the wife of Curt Lawrence. The partners jogged along, suffering under the sun.

"Why for she ride range een thees hot weather, Buckshots?"

"I dunno," Buck had to admit. "Maybe out spyin' for her ol' man, eh? But still, she cain't love the big stiff."

"Not when she ees kees that good-lookin' banker."

They rode at a walk. Neither was in a hurry. Buck gave Curt Lawrence some thought. When irrigation came in, free range went out. Hammerhead ran cattle over free range, government grass. With irrigation water flowing through canals, more farmers would come, and Hammerhead would go broke. For the success of Hammerhead ranch, in this range of marginal land, depended upon free grass. They rode about a mile, and then Tortilla Joe said, "Rider she ees come."

The rider turned out to be Curt Lawrence astraddle a bay stallion. A heavy, tough animal, this stallion, and his hard ride had brought sweat out on him. Buck wondered if the big man were out to kill the bronc by riding him so hard in this terrible heat.

The partners drew rein and waited.

Lawrence curbed the stud around. The magnificent bay reared against the cruel indignities of the spade-bit. Lawrence hit him with his quirt and forced down his head and hoofs.

"You two gents seen anything of my wife?" he demanded.

Buck shook his head, his face very stupid. Lawrence looked at Tortilla Joe, who looked as if he had just lost his entire family.

"We no see her, beeg man."

Buck said, "Only human we've seen since leavin' Cinchring has been you, Lawrence. And man alive, are we glad to see you!"

The heavy face scowled. "Don't get sarcastic, McKee. I don't cotton to your tone of voice, fella."

"Send another gunman against me, then," Buck taunted. "Get another boy along the cut of Will March, and send him against me, eh?"

"There's plenty of time, McKee."

"That's good," Buck said. "So long, Lawrence."

"Maybe I ain't leavin'."

Buck shrugged. "We don't want you," he said evenly.

They looked at each other. Lawrence ran his fingers slowly over the gold piece in his chin strap. His hand left the nugget and settled on the fork of his saddle ahead of his .45.

Lawrence remembered things. The body of a man, hanging on a rope, turning slowly in the slow wind. . . . Buck slapping the twenty-dollar gold piece from his hand to the ground. . . . Yes, and the hard knuckles of Buck McKee knocking him, Curt Lawrence, to the floor. . . .

Hate filled him.

Buck saw this hate ebb into the man's face, tighten the cords in his thick neck. For a moment he figured the owner of Hammerhead might make his draw. Buck stiffened, fingers moving slightly as he flexed them. His eyes were riveted on Lawrence.

Then Lawrence remembered Tortilla Joe.

He sent a hard quick glance toward the silent Mexican. Tortilla Joe was tight in leather, his dark eyes bright and sharp.

"Two against one, odds no smart man would take," Lawrence grumbled.

"Maybe you're not smart," Buck ventured.

Lawrence turned the stallion, cake-walking him around on his hind legs. His grip was savage and hard on the reins. His spurs hit the stud, straightened him, and he loped into the brush. He rode south.

Tortilla Joe said, "He go south. Hees *esposa* she go north."

"His back ain't as purty as hers," Buck said.

Tortilla Joe spared enough moisture to spit on a lizard on a rock. "She ees een the love with the banker."

"How do you know it isn't a pose—a fake? Maybe the banker has something she wants."

"No fake. Her eyes, they light up—kerosene lamps, they behind her eyes. Love, they say, ees the great theeng."

Buck did not dispute that. Each man, he figured, had a right to his own opinion, as long as he did not try to force his opinion on others. . . . For some reason he kept thinking of Banker Martin Halloway. He was a slick customer. Buck sighed and mopped his forehead and restored his stetson to position. Where did the banker tie into this, and what was his game, if any?

"Maybe we should rob a bank, Tortilla Joe."

Tortilla Joe sighed. "Eef they catches us, eento the jail we goes. We no need *dinero,* Buckshots. We steel got some of our sommer wages. We got the jobs waitin' for us in Yuma weeth Gallatin . . . eef ever we gets to the Gila. I no want to go to the jail."

"They'd have to catch us," Buck said.

"*Si,* but lately the luck we have ees all bad." The Latin sighed again, gusty and loud. "What bank does we rob?"

"Halloway's bank."

"We theenk eet over, no? Thees Seebil, now. Maybe she be married before she marry Lawrence, no?"

"Why ask?"

"Jes' wonder, Buckshots."

Buck gave this consideration. "Sybil is the type what can't live alone," he finally said. "So you can reckon she was married afore she met Lawrence. Wonder how long this banker has been on this range?"

"I no know."

They jogged along, nursing the silence and their thoughts. A road-runner, weary from traveling ahead of their horses, stopped and rested, wings out to let air get to his wiry body. He stood with his beak open and watched them ride by, secure in the shade of a mesquite clump.

Tortilla Joe looked at the ungainly bird. "Weeth hees beak he can cut the rattlesnakes een two. Hees beak she ees sharp as the knife, no?"

Buck nodded. He glanced at six head of Hammerhead cattle out in the brush. They were crosses between herefords and *cimmarones,* the native Arizona cattle. They were working toward a spring in a draw. Their habit, Buck knew, was to drink in the morning, spend that day working away from the water-hole or spring, then to work back the next day, spending a night around a water hole.

"They no graze much off the soil," Tortilla Joe said. "They brouse like the deer—*hola,* there ees one streepin' mesquite beans off the trees, no?"

"Yes," Buck said wearily.

Suddenly Tortilla Joe pulled in his mouth. His stubby brown forefinger pointed to a rimrock ledge ahead on the butte.

"There ees a rider on thet butte. I see the sun reflect from something shiny, Buck."

Buck reached back and unbuckled his field glasses. He put them on the rider, who was about four miles away. He could not identify the man. He handed the glasses to his partner.

Tortilla Joe focused the adjusting screw.

"That ees the banker, Buckshots."

"You sure?"

"Sure, Halloways eet ees."

Buck put the glasses back in the case. When it came to eyes and ears, Tortilla Joe was human wolf. He always attributed his good eyesight to the fact he had never learned to read and write.

"Why for he ride up there on thet heel?"

Buck said, "He's ridin' so he should meet Sybil, ain't he?"

"They both ride straight, they meet."

"Oh," Buck said.

"Love," Tortilla Joe chortled.

About a mile out of Buckskin, another rider came toward them. He rode with such mad haste that Buck said, "The devil must be chasin' him with a red-hot iron, eh."

"Maybe he try to keel his horse."

The rider came closer and turned out to be none other than Sitting Bull Jones. He crouched on the horse like a miniature ape. When he saw the partners he reined in with sand shooting upward. He still toted his war club, Buck noticed.

His face, streaked with sweat, was wild and unruly.

"Clair McCullen—she busted jail, men—"

Buck had to smile. "What's so bad about that, Sittin' Bull? What I'm interested in is this; how did she do it?"

"The sheriff—Potter—he ran off with Clair!"

This news made Buck stare. Tortilla Joe's eyes showed surprise. Buck shut his mouth and studied the man. Was he crazy?

"That the truth, Sitting Bull?"

"They run off together, McKee."

Buck had to laugh. He had a sudden mental picture of Sheriff Henry Potter, big as a moose, slow-moving as a glacier, and as ugly as a skinned skunk. He thought of Clair McCullen and her cool blonde beauty. When it came to making perfect pairs somebody had sure mismatched these two.

"Well, I'll be damned," Buck said.

"That purty girl," Sitting Bull said. "And that homely, ugly man. . . . Buck, be careful, when you ride into town."

"Why?"

"Mrs. Potter's got a shotgun and says she'll shoot you on sight!"

Buck scowled. "I never have even met the woman. Why does she crave to shoot a hole through me?"

"She blames it all on you. You had Clair tossed into jail, remember?"

Buck looked mournfully at Tortilla Joe. "First thing you know, Tortilla, they'll blame this heat on me. . . ."

"Always the trouble," the Mexican said mournfully.

CHAPTER TWELVE

Hands behind his head, Buck McKee lay on his back and admired the ceiling, which had apparently recently been painted an egg-shell blue. The bed he lay on was soft, the mattress good, and the blue silk spread had not been rolled off. But Buck was considerate; he had taken off his boots.

Beside him lay Tortilla Joe, who already was dozing off. Buck studied the egg-shell blue ceiling and gave vent to some deep philosophy.

"Now why would a woman who is unmarried want a big double bed like this one we are flopped on, Tortilla Joe?"

"Maybe she gets married once in a while." Tortilla Joe spoke with a large yawn. "First time I've been on a clean bed since the time we stayed in the hotel in Great Falls, up in Montana. *Hola,* we were the beeg ones that time, no—moneys in all pockets, an' ready to head south for the weenter."

"That was five years ago," Buck said.

"That long already?"

Buck said, "That's gone, past. This sure is a nice mattress. A woman sure can keep a room clean, compared to the way a bachelor keeps his quarters. Sometimes I think marriage is worth puttin' up with a woman. . . ."

"What eef you marry one who keeps the dirty house?"

Buck grinned. "I'm jes' talkin' to hear my big mouth say words, I reckon. If you—even you—was a woman, I'd never marry you."

"Thanks for the compleement."

Tortilla Joe started softly snoring. He could go to sleep instantly anywhere at any time. Buck looked at the walls. They too had recently been painted, and their color was light green. When he had been in grammar school years before, one of the teachers had told him the world was green because green was easy on the eyes.

A heavy, thick rug covered the floor. The edges of the floor, showing around the outside of the rug, were slick and clean. Against the one wall stood a mahogany dressing table with a big mirror. There were two matching chairs, a big cedar chest, and a wardrobe trunk. The door to the clothes closet was open. Dresses hung from the rod—blue, yellow, all colors.

The air had a slight trace of perfume. Buck

wrinkled his nose and sniffed. He liked that perfume.

"Evening in Buckskin," he said.

Tortilla Joe slept sounder, and his snores increased in volume. Buck poked him in the ribs with his elbow and the snoring stopped momentarily. Outside, feet approached, and Buck heard them scuffle the sand. He listened closely.

"Sitting Bull Jones," he said. "I can tell the sound of moccasins."

Tortilla Joe came awake. "What was that?"

"Close your mouth," Buck said.

The moccasins scraped sand, came to the closed door, then stopped. There was a short pause, and the partners listened and were silent. Then there came a knock on the door.

Buck said sweetly, "Come in, honey."

He made his voice sound feminine.

The door opened. Sitting Bull Jones, complete even to war club, slipped inside. He closed the door behind him. Then he stood there, back to the door, blinking his eyes. His homely face showed anger and surprise.

He stared at them.

"Buck an' Tortilla Joe layin' on thet bed! Where is the woman?"

"What woman?" Buck asked.

"The one what invited me in jes' a minute ago."

Tortilla Joe smiled widely. Again Buck made his voice sound like that of a woman. He said, "Hello, Sitting Bull."

The publisher's ugly face turned very red. He swung his war club in a circle, narrowly missing a chair.

"Darned female impersonator," he roared. "I wondered why Clair would call me such sweet names. . . . I never was very friendly with her. Not my fault, though. Did my best to get chummy with her, I did."

"So did I," Buck admitted.

The eyes probed them. "What you two sheepherds doin' in her room, floppin' on her bunk?"

"Waitin'," Buck said.

"Fer what?"

Buck spoke to Tortilla Joe. "What are we waitin' for, *amigo?*"

"We wait for reduction in the taxes, no?"

"No," Buck said. He looked at Sitting Bull. "How come you come up to Clair's home?"

"Jes' wanted to look around. Don't seem possible a purty girl like her would run off with a walkin' garbage pail like Potter. Older than her by years, an' ugly as sin with its paint washed off."

"You're no beauty contest winner," Tortilla Joe said.

"I know that." Without being offered an invitation, the editor sat down on a chair. He looked at his war club. "Done polished the head of that spike. Now when I swing it, sunshine reflects off it. Tells me instantly whether the spike is on the upper end or bottom, so I can hit right with it. Wonder what happened to thet Lawrence gunman last night?"

"Which one?" Buck asked.

"The one thet they found cold on the sidewalk. You fellas talked to Lawrence about him. Found him right after I said goodnight to you, remember."

"Wonder what happened to him?" Buck asked.

"Maybe he get seeck and fall down," Tortilla Joe said.

"Hawkins don't know what happened to him either," the publisher said. "He says the first thing he knew he was out cold. Somebody said he'd got a big welt acrost his skull."

"Prob'ly fainted," Buck said. "Hit somethin' with his head as he fell."

Tortilla Joe closed his eyes. Buck looked at the egg-shell blue ceiling. Sitting Bull spat on the head of the spike driven in his war club. He got some fine sandpaper from his pocket and started polishing the head of the spike.

Buck asked, "How come you're here, Sittin' Bull?"

"Thought maybe Clair McCullen would

sneak back for her clothes. Don't seem natural she'd leave with the sheriff, to start with, and it looks like she done left all her clothes behind, too. Thought mebbe I could waylay her and get an interview for the *Cactus* from her."

"An exclusive interview," Buck said.

"Yeah, exclusive. . . . I still don't believe she fell in love with Potter. His bald head is too shiny and his belly too big. A fat man—especially one what's bald—he ain't a romantic figure."

Neither partner answered.

Sitting Bull adjusted the ribbon around his head. This time he had a wide green ribbon holding down his hair. He then resumed polishing the head of the spike.

Finally Buck asked, "How long you bin in Buckskin, Sittin' Bull?"

"About four years." Sitting Bull polished the spike some more. "Never selected the town. It chose me."

"How come?" Buck asked.

"I run out of funds. The stagedriver done booted me off the stage. Ol' boy here was runnin' a lousy-lookin' sheet. I went to work for him. He wanted to go to Californy. He done gave me the whole caboodle. I couldn't let him do that, so I borrowed a few bucks from the bank and gave it to him as a partin' gift. I still remember them tears in his eyes and how his old Adam's apple bobbed up and down in gratitude."

"Borrowed the money from Martin Halloway, eh?" Buck asked.

"Not from Halloway, 'cause he wasn't the banker at that time. Old Man Jessups owned the bank then. He sold out to Halloway about two years ago . . . yep, two years gone this very month, men."

"Where did Halloway come from?" Buck wanted to know.

"He read ol' Jessups' ad in the Tucson paper."

Buck again devoted his attention to the ceiling. His mind was full of ideas. They were groping around and now they were beginning to arrange themselves into a somewhat orderly fashion. The information given him by Sitting Bull Jones was being woven into this sheme.

Deliberately he changed the subject. "Thet Mrs. Lawrence shore's got a hour-glass figure. Sure would like to get my long arms around her pretty little waist, Sitting Bull."

Sitting Bull Jones' eyes had glistening lights darting across them. He grinned lopsidedly and rubbed his nose.

"I've done been pestered by the same idea many a time, Buck. The big shot sure got dumped off his bronc when he saw her. First thing a man knew, they was man an' wife."

"That quick, eh?"

"That quick," the publisher reported. He squinted at the nail in his club. "Looks darned good to me."

Again, ideas started moving across Buck's brain. He wasn't the smartest man in the world, and he would have been the first to admit this fact—still, as he often said, he was smart enough to feel hungry, be cold, and feel heat. His mind went to work.

He added up all the things he had learned while in Buckskin. Into this mess he threw the memory of the events that he and Tortilla Joe had witnessed in the last few days. It was quite a mess of porridge. He threw one fact against the other, and he got exactly where previous thinking bouts had taken him—up against a blank wall of ignorance.

"So long, Sittin' Bull," he said.

"I ain't leavin' yet."

"Oh, yes, you are." Buck spoke with emphasis. "My partner and I crave some sleep. Goo'bye."

Sitting Bull Jones got to his moccasins. He made a sweeping swing with the war club. The nailhead whistled slightly. He juggled the club and smiled. He was as happy as a porcupine who had just discovered a field of tender young corn stalks.

"Sure got the right heft and feel now," he

said happily. "I'd sure like to hit Lawrence acrost the rump with it, nail out."

Buck said, "When you hit him, hit him acrost the head—not the rump. For the last time, so long."

Sitting Bull shouldered his war club. "You're an o'nery ol' woman," he said sarcastically. "So long."

He left.

Buck listened to the crunch of the old man's retreating moccasins. He tried to swing his thoughts into line again but they were stubborn. Tortilla Joe lay on his back with his mouth wide open and his nose vibrating with snores. Buck fell asleep before he knew it. When he awakened he came awake hurriedly. His first impression was that he had slept for some time, for the shadows of sundown were in the room. He glanced at the door.

It was slowly opening.

He had hold of his .45, and as he identified the figure, he slid the gun back under the pillow. He realized that Tortilla Joe had quit snoring. Evidently the Mexican had awakened even before he, Buck McKee, had come awake. The person who had entered had not as yet seen them lying on the bed because the shadows were thicker on this side of the room.

Buck said, "Why, hello there, honey!"

The figure stopped, became frozen. Buck thought, A lovely little bit of frozen girl, that woman. The woman had her back to them, for she had been going toward the clothes closet. She stood like that—stiff, awkward, unyielding. Then she turned around and peered at them.

"Who in tarnation are you?"

Buck said, "Shadows almost hide us, eh? This is Tortilla Joe an' Buck McKee, Clair."

Tortilla Joe said, "You come back to veeseet us, no?"

"No," she said stiffly. The shock seemed to have left her now. Buck saw her pretty outline and he wished it were lighter, for he could not clearly see her face. He sat on the edge of the bed.

"Sit down, Clair," he said.

Stiffly, she sat on the chair that Sitting Bull Jones had sat on while polishing the spike in his war club.

Her voice was strained and a little high-pitched. "What the blazes are you two devils doing in my home . . . and on my bed?"

Buck grinned. "We come in to take a nap."

"You elopes weeth the lawmans," Tortilla Joe explained. "Your beeg bed, shee ees the empty. We come een an' take the shuteyes, no. . . ."

"I'll holler."

Buck's smile widened. "Open your purty

mouth to scream, kid, and back into the clink you go pronto. This town is as fidgity as a bull what has been high-lifed and turpentined for the ring. One beller outa you an' citizens will descend like hailstones on a wheat field."

She bit her lip.

"Well," she asked, "What do you want?"

Buck watched her. "Where is Sheriff Henry Potter?"

"I don't know."

Buck shook his head. "I've never called no woman a liar afore, Miss Clair. You never busted jail, sister. Potter let you out, and he had a reason for turnin' you loose."

"Smart gink, eh?"

Buck was modest. "I'm not too darn' wool-blinded to see my long nose," he assured her. "Potter wanted you out of jail for a reason. And that reason wasn't to ride out alone and entertain you in the badlands."

"You're wrong there, McKee."

"Talk," Buck said.

Tortilla Joe sat on the bed, a human ape in the dusk. Buck watchced the girl closely. The thought came that he should frisk her for possible weapons. She did not look too calm. She looked jittery and tired and raw-nerved.

"He got me out in the hills, Buck. Then he tried to force himself on me. Get that, Buck!

That big stupid fat oaf—he tried to get the best of me."

Buck had a mental picture of that.

"What happened?" he asked.

"I busted him with a left hook. My knuckles still ache. I hit him right in that fat mug of his. And you know what?"

"What?" Tortilla Joe asked.

"I knocked him down. Believe it or not, a little thing like me—and him as big as a steer— and I knocked him flat."

Buck said, "Hard hitter, eh? Where is Potter now, Clair?"

"Said he was going to leave the country for good. He's had lots of pressure on him lately. His wife and kids jaw at him night and day, night and day. Then he lost Jack Perry to the mob—"

Buck shock his head. "He never *lost* Perry," he corrected. "He *gave* him to Lawrence's mob."

"You're plumb wrong there, McKee."

"In what way?" Buck asked.

She shook her head slowly. "Potter was knocked cold; it was a genuine jail delivery. Somebody slugged him cold, hitting him at the base of the skull. The blow landed low—that's why you two never saw it. Potter is honest, men."

Buck grimaced. "There goes a pet theory of

mine all up in smoke," he told Tortilla Joe.

"Maybe thees girl—she not honest?"

"Don't call me a liar, you Mexican!" Clair was ready to fight again. Evidently her fistic victory over Potter, out in the badlands, had only whetted her appetite for further fisticuffs.

"I takes eet back," Tortilla Joe said hurriedly.

Buck had another set of questions. "All right, Clair, look at it this way. We'll admit then that Potter may be honest. Then why doesn't he head back for town? Why is he out in the hills?"

"You got me stumped, Buck."

Buck eyed her steadily. "Potter has told you secrets, sister. You're anything but a nice quiet little seamstress, believe you me. Might Potter be out ridin' range an' layin' low for a spell while he scouts Hammerhead cattle?"

"I don't know."

Buck glanced at Tortilla Joe. The Mexican watched Clair McCullen. Buck sensed that the time had come, that the clock showed the right hour.

"Potter might be wise to something," Buck added, speaking in a slow voice. "Did he ever mention to you that the Hammerhead outfit was losin' cattle, Clair? He ever say that?"

"Yes," she admitted, "he did."

Buck was adamant. "What else did he tell you, honey?"

She was silent for a while. Another cur barked across town, and children hollered as they played tag. These sounds seeped into the room.

Buck said, "You and Potter have been good friends. Don't ask me how I know . . . I just know." He was shooting a lot of ammunition into the dark. He hoped an occasional bullet would hit close to the mark, if not on it. He was playing every angle he knew. "Why did he take you out of jail?"

"To get me out in the hills. He admitted that himself. When he saw he couldn't get to first base, he changed his mind."

"Why is he staying in the hills?" Buck's tone had risen a little.

She moved in the chair, her eyes on him. "All right, McKee, I'll tell you what I know. He's afraid they might kill him."

Buck wet his lips. "Who might kill him?" he asked.

"Curt Lawrence . . . or some Hammerhead killer. This has come to a showdown, Buck. You and Tortilla Joe have brought it to a head. According to Potter, Lawrence has to make a move, and do it fast. And he's afraid Lawrence might kill him."

Buck shook his head.

"You don't believe me?" she asked.

"Not Lawrence. Lawrence won't kill him."

Buck shot another question at her. "Sister, where do you fit into this dirty deal?"

Her eyes were on him. He thought, Wish the room was lighter, so I could see her face more clearly. The bed springs moved behind him as Tortilla Joe shifted positions. But Buck had no eyes for his fat partner. His gaze was on the woman who apparently was silently considering his question.

"Talk," Buck said.

She said nothing.

Buck said, "This is goin' to end soon. It might end in court and it might end in gunsmoke. I got a answer to this deal figured out. You claim you loved Jack Perry. Lawrence had him lynched. Therefore you must hate Lawrence. We can get Lawrence, but first you have to tell us all your troubles."

She said, "Yes, I loved Jack. Loved him with all my heart—I wanted to marry him—we had planned our home. I'll do everything in my power to get even with Curt Lawrence, Buck."

She started to weep. Almost silently she wept. Buck felt his throat tighten, and he looked at Tortilla Joe, who had a mute sympathetic look across his wide jowls. Suddenly Tortilla Joe stiffened. Buck had also heard the noise.

From out in the alley came the sounds of a violent scuffle. Men grunted, and gravel moved

under boots. Buck leaped to the door with his
.45 drawn. Tortilla Joe was behind him, pistol
also palmed.

Clair McCullen watched, sniffling a trifle.

She did not go to the door. She saw surprise
run across Tortilla Joe's face. She saw a smile
twist Buck McKee's lips.

"Come on in, Sittin' Bull," Buck said.

"That I'll do, Buckshot."

Sitting Bull Jones entered. He dragged a man
behind him. He had the man by the legs, and
the man was out cold. Buck grinned when he
recognized the unconscious man. Tortilla Joe
said nothing.

Clair McCullen said, "That's the Lawrence
gunman, Hawkins!"

CHAPTER THIRTEEN

Blood dripped down the man's face from his scalp. He needed a shave and his face was skinned, for Sitting Bull Jones had dragged him face down through the sand and gravel.

Buck looked at Tortilla Joe. "That's the button you knocked out last night with that manzanita club, Tortilla?"

"Thet ees the same mans, Buckshots."

Sitting Bull Jones cackled like a hen who had laid a striped egg. "Figgered you gents had laid him low last night. . . . And here you lied to me with such straight faces, too. You two are clever gents, believe you me. . . ."

Buck asked, "How come you slugged him?"

"Glimpse him snoopin' around, Buck. Gave him the war club, spike and all. Gotta drive that spike in a mite further, though. Cut into his scalp too deep, an' I only deliver the coup-de-grace with a glancing blow along the top of his dumb skull. Wonder if I kilt him?"

He felt of the man's dirty wrist.

"He's alive," he said.

Buck asked, "How come you was snoopin' aroun', Sittin' Bull?"

"Come down to check to see if Clair had snuck in." He looked at the seamstress. "Glad to see you back, girlie."

"I'm not glad to see you."

"That should hold you, Sittin' Bull." Buck grinned and spoke to Tortilla Joe. "This guy stinks. He belongs in the nearest garbage barrel, Tortilla."

"You grab hees boots, Buckshots. I take heem by the arms, no. We totes heem down the alley until we find a barrel, *hola!*"

Buck got the unconscious man by the boots. Tortilla Joe got hold of the man's arms. They toted the gunman outside. Buck had to smile. This was the second time within hours that Hawkins had been knocked unconscious. They found a barrel, and they doubled the man and sat him in it. His head hung on one side of the rim and his boots stuck out on the other side.

Hawkins kept on sleeping.

Tortilla Joe rubbed his hands together, studied the unconscious gunman, and then smiled widely.

"Weesh Lawrence could see heem now," he chortled.

Buck said, "We should be riding out of this jerkwater burg soon. I got a hunch this thing will all be over inside a few hours, Tortilla Joe."

"Young Jack—he then sleep in pieces. The cart I always get before the horse," Tortilla Joe lamented. "Bet thet Seetin' Bull, he get his interview now, no?"

They returned to the room. Sitting Bull had not got his interview yet. But he had got slapped across the mouth. He was rubbing his jaw when the partners entered.

"Try to kiss her?" Buck asked.

"My youthful ardor overcame my mature logic," the printer said. "She hits as hard as a young burro kicks."

"One jackass hittin' the other," Buck said. He spoke to Clair. "Give the ol' boy a private interview, honey."

"That's all I will give him," the woman said.

Buck and Tortilla Joe resumed their seats on the bed. Clair and Sitting Bull talked, with Sitting Bull taking notes in shorthand. Buck noticed the girl told the publisher an entirely different story from the one she had told him and Tortilla Joe. She was lying to Sitting Bull. Or had she been lying to them, and telling the truth to Sitting Bull Jones?

Buck decided she was an accomplished liar.

She had had much practice, he realized, in the deceptive science of fabrication. Sitting Bull concluded his interview, rubbed his jaw and looked at Buck.

"Gotta git this into print right pronto."

"When will it come out?"

"An extra, as soon as we can grind it out."

Buck said, "Make tracks."

Sitting Bull scurried outside. They heard his moccasins scamper down the gravel and go beyond the range of sound. Tortilla Joe stretched and yawned lavishly.

"I am the sleepy boy," he told Buck.

Buck yawned, too. "Well, let's hit the hay, Tortilla. Got this clean, wide bed What's the matter with you, woman?"

"You two get out of my bed! I'm sleepy myself—had no sleep last night—"

Buck said, "This bed is wide enough for three."

"I won't sleep with you two drifters!"

Buck lay down and smiled at the egg-shell blue ceiling. "There's always safety in numbers, honey."

Fully dressed except for their boots, he and Tortilla Joe dozed off. Clair still sat in the chair. Right before sleep took him, Buck heard her move over and bolt the door.

She went to bed between them. She shivered.

She whispered, "Buck, are you awake?"

"Yes. . . ."

"I'm cold. Put your arm around me."

Buck pulled her close to him. He liked the perfume of her hair and the feel of her curvaceous body against him.

"You're not cold," he said.

"I am too." She shivered again.

Buck pulled her closer. Suddenly she began to weep silently. Buck felt her shoulders shake.

"I miss Jack so much."

"Go to sleep, honey."

She was still weeping quietly when he dozed off. He kept his arm around her. Tortilla Joe slept like a dead man. Buck awakened at dawn and they were both still asleep. Tortilla Joe also had an arm around Clair. She slept soundly, mouth opened slightly. Buck looked at her pretty face with the dawn coloring it. She was a beauty. Her hair was tumbled across his shoulder, and her breathing was deep and secure.

He looked at Tortilla Joe.

The Mexican slept with his mouth opened. He breathed out a violent mixture of odors redolent of onions and garlic and beans.

Buck said, My God, he's homely.

Clair moved and opened her eyes. She looked at him and smiled. Buck had been groping for a decision, and now he apparently reached it.

"Tonight we got a job to do, Clair."

"All of us?" she asked quietly.

Buck nodded.

"What is it, Buck?"

"Tonight we rob a bank," Buck said.

CHAPTER FOURTEEN

Sheriff Henry Potter ate like a wolf who hadn't seen a jackrabbit for two weeks. He crammed sandwiches into his wide mouth. He spoke around half a sandwich, and his words were muffled. He kept on chewing and talking.

"I had to get out of town, McKee. They had the pressure on me plumb hard. Why, I was afraid they might shoot me down!"

Buck sat crosslegged in the shade of a granite boulder. "Then thet jail delivery was the real thing, eh?"

Potter bit deep into a ham sandwich. "Good chuck, fellas." His head bobbed affirmatively. Sun glistened on his bald dome as if it were made of polished silver. "Thet was the real thing," he said.

Buck looked at Tortilla Joe, who sat opposite him. He sat crosslegged, and he was humped over like a bullfrog sitting on a log.

"What strikes me as odd," Buck said slowly, "was that you never recognized a one of the lynchers. . . ."

"They all wore masks and raincoats and old overcoats—anything to hide their identities. . . . Two of them come into my office with them Jesse James disguises and *blotto*—this lawman is out cold."

Buck nodded.

"Talk more maybe?" Tortilla Joe asked.

Clair McCullen, leaning against the boulder, also in the shade, watched and listened carefully, but kept out of the conversation. The whole thing was tying itself into a compact unit now, Buck realized, and he was getting rid of the loose ends, doubling them back and making them take on meaning.

"Lawrence has to get Cinchring out of this country," the lawman said. "I know he got the lynch bunch to kill Jack Perry . . . but what can I prove?" He answered that himself. "Not a darn' thing, Buck."

"Go ahead," Buck encouraged.

"Jack had to get lynched. He was throwing the dignity of the Hammerhead in the mud. Them Lawrences has been a proud clan. Jack is of the same bolt of cloth as was his father, John. Jack murdered John Lawrence."

Buck asked, "Are you sure of that?"

Potter kept on eating. "All the signs pointed toward Jack," he said.

Buck got to his boots and brushed off his levis. Tortilla Joe, with a heave, also got upright.

Clair watched.

Buck said, "Has Hammerhead lost cattle, Potter?"

The lawman nodded. "Curt Lawrence claims it has. He claims that the homesteaders are selling his cattle south in Sonora, acrost the Border. He says they're eatin' Hammerhead beef out at the dirt camp. I trailed cow sign, lost it. Never was no good with my nose to the ground."

"You're not sure then?" Buck was persistent.

"Not sure. I might head into Phoenix town."

Buck asked, "Why?"

"Git the United States marshal's office to side me. Jail delivery is a serious offense, and if cattle are goin' acrost the line—thet makes it a federal offense. Might head out for Phoenix."

Buck spoke slowly. "You say you left Buckskin because you was afraid somebody might kill you. Who was that *somebody,* Potter?"

The ox-like eyes rolled in moist sockets. "Do I have to say some names, McKee?"

"You'd sure help us clear this up," Buck answered.

The sheriff looked at Clair. He swung his moist gaze over to Tortilla Joe. The Mexican studied him with wicked intent. Potter did not like the look in the dark eyes. He looked back at Buckshot McKee.

"I won't say, McKee."

Buck nodded, seemingly satisfied. "All right, Potter." Suddenly, without warning, the flat of his hand went against the big chest, knocking Potter back. Potter grunted, the push turning him just enough so that Tortilla Joe's right fist, arching out of nowhere, socked the lawman hard under the jawbone.

Potter sank down like a pole-axed bull.

Tortilla Joe pushed the man flat with his boot. He jumped on the big belly with both boots, and his smile was wicked. Potter's breath whooshed out of him. He screamed, "You'll bust my big belly open!" and Tortilla Joe put a boot on the man's windpipe. Potter struggled, kicked, swatted, and then his face grew blue. It got as blue as a blue-roan horse. Then it went red. At this point, Tortilla Joe took his boot back. Potter sucked in air, and then sat up, and fear was wild across his bulging eyes.

"Don't kill me!"

Potter stared up at Tortilla Joe. This time, for some reason, the Mexican did not have a long and stupid face. His face was rock-hard and rock-stern. Potter glanced at Clair, who watched fascinated; he swung his big eyes

around to Buckshot McKee, who was grinning tightly.

"You gonna talk?" Buck asked.

"Well, now—" Potter shook his head. "Maybe no—"

Tortilla Joe said gleefully, "We streep all his clothes off, no. We let hees beeg belly get sunburned as he lay on the ant pile. Them red ants, they bite like a roadrunner—they have knives for beaks. They make that belly crack open. Then the sun on thet belly—*Hola*, he die slow, eh, Buckshots?"

Buck grinned. "Ant hill around back of this boulder. Seen it when we rode in. Black ants, though—some of them a half-inch long, it looked like. Will black ants be as good as red, Tortilla?"

"Better."

"Get him by the legs and drag him over to the pile. Hey, he don't want to play with us, eh?"

"I ain't got much to say," the sheriff said hurriedly. "So I'll shoot off my mouth. I'm sure Halloway engineered that lynching, seeing Curt Lawrence was out chasin' this gal here. I was afraid either Lawrence or Halloway would try to kill me."

"Heck, Halloway is harmless, ain't he?" Buck asked. "Just a town banker, not a gunman."

"Him and Lawrence are good friends, remember that."

Buck smiled. Yeah, he thought, they're good friends—they're sharing the same wife. He asked, "Who owns the Hammerhead, sheriff?"

Potter had trouble with his voice. He had to clear his throat three times before he could answer.

"Lawrence owns it, of course. Inherited it from Old John."

"Any mor'gages on it?" Buck asked.

"I'm county recorder, Buck," the sheriff returned. "I'd know if there was a mor'gage, 'cause it would come for recording through my office. And there ain't none on record."

Buck mused on that bit of information. "Just had a wild idea that didn't work out, I reckon." He looked at Tortilla Joe. "Hades, Joe, this man is as dumb as we are."

"Dumber. Eet was a shame I had to jomp on his eentestines."

Potter glared at him. "I aim to jug you two sometime for beatin' me up. After I come back with the marshal, I'll throw you two in my clink —an' toss the key in Salt River."

"You got any witnesses?" Buck asked.

"Witnesses to what?" the sheriff asked.

Buck shrugged. "You say we beat you up, Potter. Have you got anybody who seen us manhandle you?"

"Clair saw it."

Buck spoke to Clair.

"You wouldn't want to help these two hellions, would you, Clair?"

"I wouldn't help either of you."

The sheriff grinned. "Are you goin' to Phoenix with me, girl?"

"No!"

Potter rubbed his throat slowly. "My wife might tangle with you if you head back for Buckskin. The ol' lady is hell on high heels, Clair."

"I'm not afraid of the fat slob."

"Heck of a way to refer to a man's lovin' spouse," Potter grumbled. "The ol' lady won't go as far as to use a pistol or shotgun on you, Clair. But she sure can hit from the ground, thet ol' gal can. An' them long fingernails of hers—why, you'll look like you matched class with a wildcat, woman."

Clair spoke abruptly. "I'll chance that, Sheriff."

Potter said, "Wish you'd stay with me, honey. We ran out of Buckskin together—you was congenial then. Why, you even kissed me of your own free will then. What changed your mind about me?"

"I got thinking of Buck," the girl joked, winking at one Buckshot McKee.

They mounted, leaving the sorrowful sheriff

there in the rimrock. They rode down on the desert sand. Heat hit the sand, bounced, hit them, then rebounded to the sand. Buck said nothing. Tortilla Joe sang an old Mexican song softly, and his key was wild. Clair rode and said nothing.

They went to Cinchring camp.

Clair and Tortilla Joe went to the cook-tent. Buck got Fiddlefoot Garner off to one side. They squatted in the shade of a giant saguaro cactus and talked. Buck did most of the talking.

The huge head of Fiddlefoot Garner mostly nodded affirmation. His head bobbed like a floater on a fish-line when a carp is nibbling on the bait.

"This crew, Buck, has never et one bit of Hammerhead steak, unless it was bought from the butcher, down in town," Fiddlefoot Garner asserted. "We never stole a single Hammerhead cow."

"I'm not asking about a single cow," Buck pointed out, smiling. "I'm asking about more than one, Fiddlefoot."

"Quit your joshin', Buck. This is serious."

Buck climbed up to his rawboned height. "Your word is tops with me, Garner."

Fiddlefoot Garner hammered one doubled fist into the palm of his hand. "If Lawrence is losin' cattle, they're not goin' to this camp. If he

keeps on pesterin' us farmers we'll stretch his hide out on a sandy spot in a dry wash, and the hide will be full of bullet holes, believe you me."

"Not so loud," Buck cautioned. "It's only five miles into Buckskin town. You'll knock over a house there with that loud voice."

Fiddlefoot calmed down. "Where the devil did that stupid sheriff go?"

"I don't know," Buck said.

The trio left the camp, after Buck had eaten something. Fiddlefoot Garner watched them leave. He stood there in the blistering sun, coated with grimy sand, and he shook his head mournfully. He looked like a dehorned bull shaking his head to keep the blowflies away.

Buck glanced back.

"Big man," he said. "Got some brains, too."

"What did you have that was so important to talk about?" Clair asked.

Buck said, "Women."

"Oh, joking all the time."

Buck said, "Would you like me more if I was the serious, studious type? You know—well dressed, good-looking."

She looked at him. "You couldn't be that if you tried, McKee. All you are is a saddle-bum. . . ."

Buck smiled. "Keerect, honey. And that's what I aim to be the day I close my eyes for the last time. Sandpaper collars for roughnecks, you know."

"Your neck is too rough even for rough sandpaper," she said, but she was smiling.

Buck spoke to Tortilla Joe. "You swing north, Tortilla, and scout the Hammerhead range there. Scout for signs of cattle on the move. Take Clair with you. She's safer with you than with me."

"Why?" Clair asked.

Buck looked at her. "I get you alone and I get bad ideas."

"I want to go with you."

Buck shook his head. "You're too much woman . . . I don't trust you or me, either. I ain't got my hammerlock hold down right yet; need more practice. I might get the worse of the tussle. Be ashamed as a man could be if a woman—a little woman like you—throwed me. . . ."

She stuck out her tongue at him.

"Right purty tongue," Buck complimented her.

"Come on, Clair," Tortilla Joe said.

She and the Mexican headed north. Buck knew the general direction of the Hammerhead ranch, and he rode in that direction. Within thirty minutes he was on a sand ridge overlooking the ranch house and buildings.

A big spread, he saw. Ironwood trees grew in

the immense yard. He saw huge manzanita trees with red trunks shiny in the sun. He also saw the guard . . . before the guard had seen him.

He hollered, "Peaceful man coming in, guard!"

The man was squatting under the shade of an overthrusting granite boulder. Buck's words jerked him to his feet. His rifle was half-raised when Buck rode in. Buck had his right hand high, palm out.

The guard watched him and didn't trust him. Buck saw a bowlegged man of about forty. The hammer on the Winchester .30-30 was at full cock. Buck had a cold spot in his belly.

"No trouble wanted," he said.

"You're McKee, ain't you?"

"I am."

"What do you want here on Hammerhead?"

Buck said, "I want to talk to Curt Lawrence."

"He's in the house."

Buck asked, "His wife there, too?"

"Both in the house, I reckon."

Buck said, "Take me to them, friend."

The eyes narrowed. "Lawrence don't cotton to you, McKee. Get off on this side of your bronc. Watch your hands. Then walk ahead of me . . . an' remember this Winchester is ticklin' your long spine, *amigo!*"

Buck did as directed. They walked across the hoof- and boot-packed yard toward the rambling *hacienda*. Hammerhead men squatted in the shade of buildings and watched. Buck looked at them and marked them for what they were: gunmen. They said nothing, but they watched him.

Gun wolves.

The long porch was covered with native flagstone. Their boot heels made sounds across the porch. The guard knocked on a huge oaken door.

"The guard, Missus Lawrence."

"Come in," a woman's voice said.

The guard said, "Open the door and enter, McKee." The big door swung in silently, and Buck was in a huge room. Flagstone was on the floor, and over these slabs were gaudy Navajo and Chimayo blankets. A big fireplace made of native copper ore was at the far end. The furniture was made by hand and was made of manzanita. Hand-carved beams stretched across the open ceiling.

But Buck McKee was not interested in the house. His eyes were on the woman who sat in the big chair, her legs curled under her. Sybil Lawrence was crocheting; she looked demure and domestic. This rather surprised Buck. Always, up to this time, she had appeared brassy hard and sophisticated.

"Take a chair, Mr. McKee," she said.

CHAPTER FIFTEEN

Buck was a little surprised. He said, "I'll squat here," and he settled on his heels, back to the wall. He looked at the gunman. "You can go now, Junior. Your little day's work is through, child."

The gunman scowled, then looked at Sybil Lawrence.

Mrs. Lawrence said, "Thanks, John," and the gunman left. Buck heard his boots pound across the flagstone-covered porch and then hit the gravel walk. Buck rolled a cigaret and asked, "Where is your old man?"

"In the library."

Buck had another surprise. It seemed odd to associate books with a person like Curt Lawrence. The interior of the room was cool. Sybil Lawrence kept on crocheting, her needle swift and sure. Buck watched her fingers. Sunlight came through a window and reflected facets of dancing light from her red hair.

Buck said, "Did you expect me?"

She didn't look up. "I thought maybe you'd come for a talk . . . sooner or later. Do you want to talk to Curt, too?"

"Will you call him?"

She called, and Curt Lawrence answered. Buck heard him come down the hallway, his boots making sounds. When he entered he scowled at Buck, who by this time had his smoke working.

"Okay, McKee. Talk fast and then get the blazes out of here, savvy? What's on your mind, fella?"

Buck sucked his cigaret. "Don't jump into the collar too fast, big man. You're in trouble up to your bull neck . . . and that neck of yours might get stretched for all you know. . . ."

Curt Lawrence studied him. Sybil Lawrence had stopped crocheting; her needlework was lying in her lap.

"Did you ride out here to threaten me on my own property?" Curt Lawrence clipped his words.

Buck grinned. "Jes' stay cool, an' we'll settle somethin', Lawrence. Sheriff Henry Potter is headin' into Phoenix."

"What for?" Lawrence asked.

Buck got to his feet and crossed the room and

threw his cigaret butt into the fireplace. Then he returned to his original position, back to the wall.

"He aims to get the United States marshal into this," Buck said.

Curt Lawrence asked, "Where do I fit in, McKee?" His tone held derision.

"Jail delivery and a lynchin'," Buck said. "Two awful serious charges, Lawrence. Maybe charges so big that even the Lawrence name won't save your neck, eh?"

"Maybe I wasn't behind the lynchin'," Lawrence said.

Buck nodded. "Maybe you weren't," he agreed. "But this ranch has lost cattle, lots of cattle, hasn't it?"

Curt Lawrence looked at his wife. Sybil Lawrence's gaze met that of her husband. Then the woman looked at Buck McKee.

Sybil Lawrence said quietly, "Go on, Buck. I think you're barking up the right tree, Texan."

Buck said, "Yesterday me an' Tortilla Joe met you, Missus Lawrence, ridin' open range. Behin' you trailed your husban'. Evidently you were out scoutin' for your cattle. Maybe you don't know that, all the time, somebody was trailin' you."

"Who trailed us?" Lawrence's voice was husky.

Buck climbed to his boots. "I think you know,

Lawrence." He put on his stetson. "Tortilla Joe an' me is ready to close this whole mess, once and for always. We've got all the loose ends picked up now. . . ."

"I doubt that," Lawrence stated.

Buck had his hand on the doorknob. "Frankly, as far as I'm concerned, you can doubt and be damned, Lawrence. I came here to warn you, for the last time, to stay out of my way, savvy?"

"And if I don't stay out of your way?"

Buck said, "I'll kill you, Lawrence."

They looked at each other. Rage was in the eyes of the young cattle king; Buck had no anger. He was merely stating a positive fact.

Lawrence said huskily, "Why, you two-bit drifter, I'll—"

But his wife cut in quickly. "Curt, watch your temper, please. Buck is speaking the truth, so please keep out of his way."

Curt Lawrence looked at his wife. Slowly the anger left him. "Sybil, I've stood about all I can hold, honey. I've been double-crossed from here to Sunday. You're the only one, honey, who has stood by me."

"Buck's going to work this out, Curt. I know he is. Leave it to him." She spoke to Buck. "Thanks for calling, McKee."

"The pleasure," said Buck McKee, "is all mine, Missus Lawrence."

He left them then, left them in the coolness of the immense ranch house built by Old John Lawrence. His boots beat across the flagstone porch, and then found the gravel walk. As he crossed the compound the human wolves watched him. They had ugly canine eyes. The guard had led his bronc into the shade of the huge rock barn.

Buck mounted and left the Hammerhead Ranch.

He kept remembering Sybil Lawrence. She was fighting for her life, and being a woman, she had only a woman's body, a woman's guile, to fight with. But still she was strong; her husband had obeyed her.

But what if it came to a showdown?

The shaggy wolf in Curt Lawrence, the fighting blood handed down from his fighting sire, would come through, Buck knew. Buck realized also that this range was sitting on top of a hill filled with dynamite. Gunsmoke and gunflame might be the match needed to ignite the fuse. . . .

He remembered the gunmen. Cold-eyed men of the saddle, hired for their gun-slinging ability —not their riding prowess. This was costing Hammerhead a lot in the way of dollars. Stolen steers and cows, and a bunch of gunmen on the payroll. That ran into lots of dollars, no matter from what angle the setup was viewed.

Buck left the creek and climbed a long alluvial cone, heading for the higher ridges. His plan was to gain altitude and pick out Tortilla Joe and Clair McCullen through his field glasses. Catsclaw snapped back, caught his shirt sleeve, and tore his sleeve, slightly touching his skin. "Wait-a-minute," some called this brush that, with its catsclaw branches, grabbed a man and tried to hold him. But Buck was not interested in the terrain. Nor was he interested in the brush that covered this wilderness here on the Salt River.

He was thinking of the Gallatin ranch, down where the Gila River and the Colorado joined forces, right outside of Yuma. He wanted to head southwest, and he wanted Tortilla Joe to ride with him. Down there they'd spend the winter punching cows, with maybe a few drinks occasionally in San Luis, the little town that hugged the International Border.

Old Man Gallatin would be glad to see them. Ma Gallatin would beam and welcome them in for chuck, and young Sonny, their grandson, would ride range with them—even if he had to sneak out of school to do it. Heck, Sonny would be thirteen now—or was it fourteen?

Buck searched the brush with his glasses. He saw cattle, and he swept the glasses across the rangelands, endeavoring to pick out his partner and Clair McCullen.

This was an endless, tumbling range of desolation. Here lived the prairie wolf, the coyote, and occasionally one could hear the far, high scream of the traveling cougar. Mountains arose on the north, but the snow had left even their highest tips, the sun running across them and melting the snow. To the west stretched the desert—long and wide and gray with sand, its breast marked by green verde trees, by the green of mesquite.

To the east, the desert stretched also, but in the far distance it hit the mountains, and Buck could make out the blue lines of high peaks. He turned his mount toward the south. The desert moved on and on, stretching toward Old Mexico; occasionally rimrock ledges rose to break the floor of sand. These ridges were dark and black, miles away. Buck saw some cattle moving in a coulee. They ran as though they were afraid of something, and Buck moved his gaze up the gully.

He saw two riders.

Clair and Tortilla Joe.

He turned his bronc and loped toward them. When he neared them he saw the rifle in Tortilla Joe's hands. Clair McCullen sat a still saddle, and then Tortilla Joe, recognition coming with certainty as Buck rode closer, shifted and lifted the Winchester, jamming it down securely into his saddle holster.

"Buck, what you find out?"

Buck told them.

Clair McCullen said, "These cattle . . . they're sure wild."

Tortilla Joe spat on a lizard. "Somebody he has been ronnin' these cattles, Buck. They are afraid of the mans on the horsebacks. What we do now?"

Buck watched Clair McCullen.

"Tonight," he said, "the three of us rob a bank. . . ."

Buck saw color leave the woman's face. For a moment, her bottom lip trembled violently. Then she controlled her emotions and became calm again. When she looked at Buck, he had discreetly turned his gaze on Tortilla Joe.

"We rob a bank," he repeated.

CHAPTER SIXTEEN

They stood in the Mercantile, Buckskin's biggest store, which was not, after all, very big. Clair McCullen kept anxiously watching the front street through the big fly-specked window.

Buck joked, "Lookin' for a boy friend of yours, Clair?"

She shook her head. She was stone-serious. "I'm watching out for Sheriff Potter's wife, Buck. She might hear I'm in town and tie into me. She must be nuts, to think I couldn't get anything better than that fat sap of a husband of hers to run off with."

Buck said, "I'll fight your battles from here on out, honey."

The skinny little storekeeper chimed in with, "Don't make no rash promises, Mr. McKee. You wouldn't talk so big if you ever met Mrs. Potter on the field of battle."

"You've tangled horns with her, eh?" Buck asked.

Tortilla Joe speared three crackers from the barrel. The storekeeper saw him, scowled, but said nothing. Tortilla Joe's shiny white teeth made noises on the crackers.

"One day she almost whupped me," the skinny man informed him.

"What for?" Buck asked.

"Overcharged her a thin dime on her monthly bill. Now what can I do for you, sir?"

The partners and Clair had just ridden into Buckskin. They had created quite a sensation, especially because Clair was with them, and gossip was buzzing. Where was that fat sheriff named Henry Potter?

Kids peered in the window. Elders sauntered by the store, casually glancing inside. A few of the bolder women, thirsting for gossip, even entered the store. They made a pretense of looking at articles they apparently wanted to purchase. One old dame, complete to sunbonnet, stood at a counter a few feet away, looking at some yard goods, running the gingham through her fingers, her head cocked to hear any possible conversation.

"She get her earful of cuss words eef she leesens too close," Tortilla Joe said, grinning widely.

The woman glanced at him. Her face reddened and she walked away without a word, her back poker-straight.

The merchant repeated, "What will it be, sir?"

Buck asked, "Have you got any black blastin' powder?"

The skinny man's big eyes studied him. "Yes, I have some, sir. I suppose you are taking it out the dam sight for blasting purposes, huh?"

"That's it," Buck lied.

The man had the powder in a cellar on the edge of town. Buck ordered very little. The merchant said it was hardly worth the trouble of going out to the storeroom to get such a small amount. Buck said, "I need other stuff, too," and this pleased the man, who sent his assistant to the powder house, warning him not to smoke in the cellar.

The boy said, "Do I look that nutty, pop?"

The boy left. The storekeeper sighed. "Oh, for the chance to be a boy again, and to know more than my parents. . . ." He squinted over his specs at Buck. "What else does you crave, cowboy?"

Clair McCullen kept watching the window. She seemed very nervous, Buck noticed. Discreetly the tall Texan grinned.

Tortilla Joe swiped two more crackers from the barrel.

"I want some steel drills," Buck said.

He bought four drills—all in the three-quarter-inch size. By now the merchant was scowling in puzzlement. What would a cow-puncher do with steel drills? He was bursting with curiosity that courtesy required he not voice.

"Anything else, sir?"

"One fuse," Buck said.

"That's in the powder house. I'll send my other son out to get it."

Buck nodded.

Tortilla Joe munched crackers. Clair watched the window. Buck asked, "Have you got a breast drill?"

"No, but I have a carpenter's brace," the merchant said.

Buck had no other choice but to buy the brace. He inserted a drill into it and tightened it down. A man who had just entered watched him. Buck shot this man a quick glance.

"Howdy, Banker Halloway," he said jovially.

Tortilla Joe smiled widely, cracker crumbs on his bottom lip. "Well, the banker," he said in greeting. "How are you todays, *señor?*"

From the tone of voice the two partners used one would never imagine Buck had once knocked the banker down. They seemed happy and good-natured, as though the past were dead forever. Some of this infectious feeling must have gripped the banker.

"Howdy, men."

"Nice days," Tortilla Joe chimed.

Buck noticed that Halloway sent a sharp glance toward Clair McCullen. The seamstress merely nodded her head; she did not speak. Halloway looked down at Buck's purchases. He seemed agreeable and forgiving.

"Going to do some blasting at the dam, Mr. McKee?"

"I am."

Halloway picked up a drill. He turned it between thumb and forefinger. Buck noticed the man's nails were clean, his hands had no callouses.

"Sort of a small hole to put powder in, eh?" the banker asked.

"We'll pour it in," Buck said.

"Oh." The lips formed the word almost silently.

Tortilla Joe spoke around a mouthful of crackers. "We had better get the wreckin' bar, too, Buckshots. An' we need more .45 bullets for our gons, no?"

"That's right," Buck agreed.

Scowling, the merchant got a wrecking bar, laid it on the counter. Halloway also scowled as he watched Buck inspect the bar. Finally Buck announced the bar had passed his inspection.

"How much for the mess?" Buck asked.

The boys had arrived with the fuse and the powder. The merchant did some figuring on a piece of wrapping paper. One of the boys waited on Banker Halloway, who wanted some cigaret papers. Buck paid the merchant, and he and Tortilla Joe and the seamstress left, going to their horses at the livery barn. The hostler was out. Buck saw to it that their broncs had lots of hay. He gave them all a measure of oats in the feed-boxes, too.

"We'll need fresh, fast horses for our get-away," he told Clair.

The woman spoke in an uncertain tone. "You mean, Buck, we still will rob Halloway's bank?"

"We sure do," Buck returned.

"But why?"

Buck studied her. "Why does anybody rob a bank?" he demanded.

"Well, for the money, of course."

Buck winked at Tortilla Joe. Clair did not see the wink. "There's lots of *dinero* in that bank. Lawrence keeps his dough there. We get the whole caboodle and turn the money over to Fiddlefoot Garner. Then him an' his farmers can build their dam and canals. And they can build them on Lawrence money. . . ."

Tortilla Joe grinned. "We no keep the *dinero,* savvy? We geeve eet away. We be like the Robin Hood, no?"

She asked slowly, "Have you boys ever robbed a bank before?"

Again that wink, unseen by Clair. "We sure have," Buck said seriously. He gave her a hard and long look.

"Why are you staring at me?" she asked.

Buck grabbed her thin shoulders. He shook her violently. She gasped, tried to break his grip, and failed.

"What's the matter with you, McKee?" she panted.

Buck spoke in a harsh tone. "You're gettin' cold boots. If you ever think of squealin' on us, sister, we'll cut out your purty gizzard, savvy. You're going out of this town with us. And you're going to keep your mouth shut all the time, understand?"

"Buck—you hurt me—"

Buck gripped her savagely. "You heard me, sister! You even think of squealing, and you'll not live long, even if you have got a purty face and a nice figure. You won't get away from us now. You know too much, young lady."

"That ees righto," Tortilla Joe chimed in.

Slowly she got Buck's fingers loose. "I heard you, Buckshot. Yes, I'm with you boys . . . to the bitter end, or however the end turns out. They lynched the only man I have ever loved. I'm sick and tired of this stupid town and its stupid, prying people. You can count on me, gentlemen."

"Now she ees call us gentlemans," Tortilla Joe said. "First time she meet us, she call us cuss names."

"I didn't know you then like I do now," Clair McCullen said.

Buck said, "Come dark, we'll lead our horses up the alley behind the bank. Get them ready for a fast getaway out of this burg. Like we did when we sprung that bank up in Wyomin', Tortilla Joe. We got to get some chuck packed and some blankets, too. We got blankets for us but we need some for Clair. You got a long, hard ride ahead of you, honey. We head south into Old Mexico. Loaf around there for six months or so until things quiet down, and we'll live like two kings and a queen."

"Then what?" she asked.

Buck was getting warmed up; his imagination was running on fast hoofs. "We slip north acrost the Border and stick up another bank. Over in Texas, maybe. Then we drift into Ol' Mexico again."

"Good," she said.

Buck said, "Now we go to your place, Clair. Spend the day there—what is left of it—loafing and getting ready for tonight. Too bad that blasted banker came in when I was buyin' that black powder and thet fuse."

"He hasn't got brains enough to be suspicious," she said. "He's too dumb to count marbles."

"Bet he can count the *dineros* though," Tortilla Joe said.

"All bankers kin do thet," Buck said.

They went to Clair's house. Tortilla Joe promptly kicked off his boots and flopped on the bunk. Clair busied herself getting some clothes packed and ready for the getaway trip. She would take just an extra pair of levis and a shirt. Buck said they would have to travel light. An extra pound on a bronc might slow him down to the point where a posse could catch him.

He put it on thick and scary. He noticed, at times, that her eyes would grow small and scheming, but those were the times when she thought nobody was watching her.

When they looked at her, she was always smiling. But the smile, Buck noticed, was forced. He had been all wrong in judging these two women. He remembered watching pretty Sybil Lawrence standing on tiptoe and kissing Halloway, there in the bank.

She had been playing a game—and she had been playing it because she loved her husband, Curt Lawrence. Sybil, Buck thought, was a good actress, one of the best he had ever seen. He com-

pared her with Clair McCullen. Mrs. Lawrence
stood head and shoulders above the seamstress.
Buck shrugged it off, blaming it on fickle fate.
He was a little jittery inside. He hoped his plan
would work. It had to work. He and Tortilla
Joe had to leave this town. Tomorrow there
would be the inquest, for the coroner had come
over from the neighboring county. Sheriff Potter was gone; he could not sit as coroner. Rumor
had it that the body of Jack Perry would go into
the fill of the dam, and the dam would be his
grave. A fitting memorial, Buck thought. Jack,
whom he had never seen, would lie forever in
the dam he had constructed, had planned, had
died for.

Buck said, "I have to get some bull durham
and papers."

Clair said, "Be careful, Buck. This town has
Lawrence gunmen in it."

Buck said, "I'll be careful, child."

He went to the saloon. Thick Neck looked at
him, sold him durham and wheat straw papers,
looking as if he were full of advice. But Buck
did not give him a chance to talk.

"Nice day," Buck said.

"Good day," Thick Neck said.

Buck walked toward the bank. The eyes of
Buckskin town were on him. Clair did not know
that he had ridden over to the Hammerhead and

had talked with Curt Lawrence and his wife. He had reported his conversation back to Tortilla Joe, but that had been on the side—Clair had not heard them talk.

Buck felt the desert heat hit him. He felt also a sort of relief that this would soon be over. Neither he nor Tortilla Joe had as yet written to old Sam Perry about his son's untimely death. Later they would write, but by then the killing would be solved.

Or maybe they would not write. Maybe they would both be dead. . . .

Buck smiled tightly. This was an odd deal. Here they were battling for a man they had never met, and that man was dead—a lynch mob had hanged him. But an old man—a good old man—a sick old man—was up in Colorado, and the hanged man had been the old man's son. . . .

Buck turned into the bank.

Halloway looked up from his desk. "Hello, McKee," he said. "Some favor I can do for you?"

Buck dug in his pants pocket. He came out with a gold piece. "My last twenty bucks," he said with a grin. "A man's summer wages go a-kitin' fast, eh?"

"That they do."

Buck said, "I'm driftin' out come daylight. Some of these small places ain't got change for a twenty, so guess I'll change it here—if you'll give me some silver for it. Darned sorry I hit you, Mister Halloway."

The banker smiled and rubbed his jaw. "Still a mite sore." He got patronizing and genial. "Maybe I asked for it, McKee."

He opened a cash drawer and got some change. Buck and he talked for a while. Both seemed congenial enough; still, inside of each, despite their friendly talk, was a guarded stiffness.

Buck got the impression that the sleek banker was feeling him out. Halloway was jabbing here, probing at this point. Buck had a definite purpose in talking to the banker, and in entering the bank. It had not been because he wanted a twenty-dollar gold piece cashed, either.

He said, "So long, sir, and continued good luck."

"Glad to have met you, McKee."

Buck walked down the main street. He met Clair and said, "Thought you'd stay close to the home wigwam. Figgered you was afraid of Mrs. Potter."

"She's home sick with the grippe," the girl said. "Even if she wasn't sick, I'd walk the street with complete indifference. I'm a citizen and a taxpayer."

"I've said that a few times, too," Buck reminded her. "Didn't keep me from gettin' beat up, honey. Take care of yourself."

"Where have you been?" she wanted to know.

Buck said, "First, to the saloon for tobacco. Then I cased the bank—cashed a twenty-buck gold piece as a blind to get inside and look around."

"Will it be easy to crack?"

"Like openin' a tin of bakin' soda," Buck said. "All we need is a can opener and a screwdriver . . . and some black powder for the safe."

"Oh. . . ."

Buck said, "Where are you going?"

She said she was going to the store. Buck said he was going back to her room. They left. She crossed the street to the Mercantile. Buck went between two buildings and came out on the alley. The thought came to him that this alley had seen a lot of excitement in the last few days. Will March had died in the alley, his blood soaking into Arizona sand. He remembered Sitting Bull Jones knocking out Hawkins. The gunman had come to, and he had been sitting in a garbage barrel in this alley. Buck had heard that Lawrence had run Hawkins off this range.

Buck watched, saw what he wanted, and then went to Clair McCullen's house. Tortilla Joe sat on the bed and chewed a tortilla in noisy excitement. He rolled his brown eyes and looked at Buck.

"What you find out, *amigo?*"

Buck sat on a chair. He shoved his long legs out and seemed interested in his unpolished and scuffed boots. He remembered the fine polished boots of Banker Halloway. The difference between the man who worked and the man who did not work was a quarter, he had heard somebody say.

And the gink who did not work was the one who had the twenty-five-cent piece, so the joke had run.

"How we rob thees bank, Buckshots?"

Buck said, "The bank roof has a skylight. I'll get in the back door. You stay up on the roof and watch through the skylight. I'll be the pig in a poke. The piece of human meat in the trap. The bait for the whole thing."

"Eef thees work right, I come down through the skylight, no. Weeth my *pistola* out, eh?"

"That's it, Tortilla Joe."

The Mexican felt of his teeth. "I steel got them all," he said after a while. "I bite into a rock in thees *tortilla*. How far ees eet from the roof to the floor?"

"Eight-foot ceiling."

"Long way for a fat man to drop," the Mexican said.

"I'll bring some pillows," Buck said sarcastically. "Put them on the floor to break your fall."

He told about meeting Clair McCullen.

Tortilla Joe nodded.

Within a few minutes, Clair entered. Tortilla Joe chewed on what seemed an endless chain of *tortillas*. His jaws crackled on them like the jaws of an Ohio hog eating corn. Clair sat on the bed beside Buck. Dusk came and turned into night; they sat there in silence. The night held its sounds of dogs and burros and people, and then these grew faint. Clair now dozed, and Tortilla Joe dozed beside her, but Buck McKee did not sleep.

He had moved over to the rocking chair. Despite his raw nerves, he sat with his legs out in front of him. The room became pitch dark.

Tortilla Joe started to snore.

Buck waited another hour or so. Then he lit a match and looked at his watch. He said, "It's time, folks."

Tortilla Joe came awake. "Time to rob a bank, no?"

"Yes," Buck said.

CHAPTER SEVENTEEN

Buck picked up the crowbar. He got the powder in a sack, saw that the fuse was in the bag also. Then he put a drill into the brace.

He gave last minute instructions.

"Tortilla Joe, you go across the street. Stand in the shadows in front of Thick Neck's saloon."

"Si, Buckshots."

"Watch the door of the bank. The front door."

"Si, amigo."

Clair asked, "What's my job?"

"You watch the back door. I jimmy it and go inside. You cover my back, and Tortilla Joe covers my front."

Her voice was a little unsteady. "You think you can crack the safe, Buck? It's a big safe."

Buck's voice oozed a confidence he did not feel. "I've cracked them afore . . . an' I'll crack them again. The bigger they are the easier they are to bust into. Thet safe looks like a tin can. A little hole an' some powder an' the fuse and then a little bit of a *boom* ... and the door'll pop open as fast as the eyes of an ol' maid comin' upon some kids in a swimmin' hole plumb naked!"

There was a moment's pause. Outside, Buckskin town slept. There was a sliver of a moon, but it shed little light as yet. The lamp sputtered and spat. Buck looked at Clair. Her thin face was set, her lips tight. Tortilla Joe's wide dark face was an emotionless expanse of human flesh.

"We all know our jobs?" Buck asked.

"I do, Buckshots."

Clair said, "Let's go. . . ."

They slipped out into the night. Buck carried the safe-cracking equipment. Within the tall cowpuncher was the fervent hope that this would work out all right. He was taking a big chance. He was making himself a human guinea pig in this experiment.

They went down the alley, Buck in the lead. The girl followed, and behind stumbled fat Tortilla Joe. He seemed to fall over every can on the strip. Buckskin was silent and Buckskin was asleep. Buckskin was seemingly lazy and tired and under the dark cloak of slumber. But it seemed to Buck McKee that, under this cloak of indifference, lurked a great and subtle danger.

They came to the rear door of the bank. Black and ugly, the building reared against the moon, which had gathered strength quickly.

Tortilla Joe whispered hoarsely, "I leave you two at thees point, an' I go across the street, no?"

"Okay," Buck said.

"I watch the front of the bank," the Mexican said.

He lumbered into the night, dark and heavy. Buck and Clair stood and looked at the rear door of the bank.

"What are we waiting for?" she shivered as she whispered her question.

"Wait till Tortilla Joe gets stationed," he said quietly.

He counted to fifty; then he stationed her in the alley. The dark shadows hid her. He went to the back door. With a hard, vicious jab, he drove the sharp end of the wrecking bar down, smashing it between the edge of the door and the jamb. It made a dull sound against the dried wood.

He drove it in further.

Again the sharp end cut pine wood. He laid his weight against the bar, but the door held.

Again he jabbed the crowbar into the slot. Again he laid his weight against it.

The wood creaked. The door gave in slightly; then the lock held. Buck put everything he had against the crowbar. The steel bent. The latch left the lock.

The door silently swung in.

Buck dropped the crowbar to the sand. It fell with a soft sound. He thought, Here it is, and he went inside the dark bank. He closed the door behind him. But because of the broken lock, the door would not latch shut.

For a moment he hunkered there, dark against the wall. He listened. He heard the dull slide of something across the roof. To the average ears, it would sound as if a bird had a nest on the roof, and were stirring around.

Buck thought, Good old Tortilla Joe.

He had spotted a long window-stick in the corner. He got this and he opened the skylight, finding the catch and pushing upward. A hand came down, found the end of the window-stick, and released it from the prong.

"I am the ready, Buckshots," Joe's voice came from the roof.

Buck lit a lamp. He left it turned low. He turned his attention to the safe. Strangely, he was remembering old Sam Perry's whiskery, pain-filled face. Sam had had but one joy in life— and now that joy, that pride, was dead. Hanged by lynchers from the jutting beam of the court-house. . . .

Buck had never opened a safe before. He did not know where to begin. Logic told him to act as if he were going to drill a hole. He put his tools on the floor. He looked at the bit in the brace.

He had expected the man to come in from the alley.

Instead, the man came from a side room. He came silently and he came in behind Buck, who had had one eye on the door.

The man held a .45 revolver. His face was grim, and his voice was a tough snarl as he said, "Turn around, McKee. And with your hands up high, too."

Buck had placed his own .45 on a nearby chair. He turned, and his belly had a tight knot in it. Wouldn't anything work out right? He wondered if the man had heard him open the skylight and had heard Tortilla Joe's hissed words from the roof?

The man had silently opened a door leading to another room. The thought came to Buck that, when the door had been closed, the sounds made by Tortilla Joe had not entered the room, and therefore this man did not know the Mexican was on the roof, poised over the open skylight.

That was a factor in his favor.

But there was one thing definitely not in his favor. He had hoped to get the drop on this man first; instead, the fellow had his .45 on him. And it was level and tough-looking, with the lamp-light glowing on it.

Buck spoke clearly so Tortilla Joe would be able to hear. "Halloway, eh?" he said.

"The end of your trail, McKee!"

"Well," Buck asked, "What have you got to say in your defense, banker?"

The banker's eyes widened with surprise. "What have *I* got to say?" Surprise blunted the hard edge of his voice. "You're the gent that should have something to say . . . and say it damned fast. You're robbin' my bank. A serious offense, McKee, and one for which you'll get killed."

Halloway cocked the .45.

The click was a loud sound. He looked big and tough, standing there with the big .45. Buck glanced at his own Colts. It was only five feet away, but it looked as if it were a half-mile away in the distance. The thought came that he might get killed here in the bank.

And that thought was not pleasant.

Buck spoke as clearly as he could. "You and the woman played it close, Halloway. She played up to Jack Perry. Fiddlefoot Garner's conversation with me put me wise."

Halloway asked, "Wise to what, McKee?"

Buck was stalling for time. Tortilla Joe should drop through the skylight any moment now.

"She pumped Perry for inside information about the dam. She then turned this over to you.

Then Sybil Lawrence played up to you. You hold notes on Hammerhead. The Lawrences told me that today."

"You talk smart, McKee."

Buck watched the .45. He would go out fighting, he decided. Why didn't Tortilla Joe drop down through that skylight? Surely the Mexican could see and hear. . . . Buck again glanced at his own .45.

"Go on," Martin Halloway ordered.

"You didn't record the notes. That left Potter in the lurch. He never knew Hammerhead owed you money. So Sybil played up to you—tried to get inside dope—but you were too slick. You already had one woman."

"Did that darned woman talk—did she tell you this?"

Buck said, "I got a promise from the Lawrences that might interest you, Halloway. They said that if I cleared this up, they'd not bother Cinchring any more."

Halloway's tongue darted out. He wet his thin lips. His eyes were on Buck—beady, scheming eyes.

"Go on, McKee. I'm curious."

"You and Clair McCullen came into Buckskin at the same time. You two saw your chance to hit something big. You both wanted Hammerhead. So you've had a gang stealin' Hammerhead cattle. You tried to break the ranch that way. You laid the blame on young Perry's construction workers."

"That's right, McKee."

The back door opened. Clair McCullen silently entered. Halloway glanced at her.

"Did you talk, woman?"

"Not a word, Martin."

She had a gun and her eyes were steel-hard. They glistened in the lamplight. She was not soft and feminine now. She was a female killer, with her lips peeled back and her gun in her hand.

Buck said, "Clair, you killed Old John Lawrence. Shot him down on open range, and laid the blame on Perry. You bawled when you mentioned Perry's name to me. You loved him, you said. You loved him enough to lead him to a hangman's noose."

"What do you mean?" she demanded hoarsely.

Buck said, "You deliberately led that Lawrence posse out of town so your lover here could get a mob and lynch Perry. Lawrence really didn't want a lynchin', but you two engineered it, knowing the blame would be laid on Lawrence. You worked Cinchring against Hammerhead."

Her eyes glowed. "Buck, I never killed Old John. Halloway shot him—from behind—from the brush. . . ."

Halloway snarled, "Close your mouth, woman!"

But Clair kept on talking. And her gun was rigid. She spoke out of the corner of her mouth and she directed the words to Halloway.

"I'm going to get rid of you. You got your will made out leaving everything you own to me. Now is my chance to get rid of you. If McKee goes down—then I shoot at you. If you go down, then I kill McKee. And when it is over, I'll kill the Mexican, and everybody will be silenced. And I'll own this and the notes on Hammerhead."

Buck gave her plan quick thought. She was right . . . if Halloway's will were made out to her.

"You'll never get Tortilla Joe," he said.

She said, "I'll just walk up to him, across the street, and I'll kill him. Or when he runs in here I'll waylay him. Two dead would-be bank robbers, and a dead banker."

She stood directly under the skylight. Suddenly the Mexican fell down. He came down hard and he hit her on the head and shoulders.

Buck heard her surprised gasp.

Then the tall Texan was going for his gun. He hit the chair and snagged the .45 and he rolled over, crashing against the wall. One glance showed him that Tortilla Joe was on the floor. Clair McCullen was on her feet, though.

And she was shooting.

Halloway shot at Buck, and he missed because Buck was rolling. He screamed, "I got you, Mc-Kee!" and he swung his gun on Tortilla Joe. Just then Clair McCullen shot the banker in the chest.

Tortilla Joe had rolled to the far wall. He sat there with his .45 out. Buck shot him a glance and said, "He got confused. He missed me, *amigo.*"

Tortilla Joe did not shoot.

Buck did not shoot, either.

There was no need for them to fire their pistols. This had simmered down to a battle between a banker and an unscrupulous woman. Halloway and Clair McCullen had eyes only for each other. Buck watched in horrified fascination. Back to the wall, Tortilla Joe stared, lamplight on his level .45.

He saw a quiver go over Halloway's big body. He went to his knees, bending at the waist; Buck saw blood on the white silk shirt. But as he went down, he fired twice.

His first bullet hit Clair McCullen. The second missed, but the first did the job.

Halloway looked at her, lying there on the

floor. He dropped his gun, and his fingers drew in and made his hands hard fists.

He looked at Tortilla Joe. "Come in through the skylight, eh? Thought I heard a sound up there—but pack rats run across the roof. . . ." He looked at Buck. "She warned me today of your plan. I aimed to pull a double-cross on her, but she beat me to it. . . ."

Buck watched, his throat dry.

Tortilla Joe lowered his gun.

Halloway's dark eyes touched the Mexican. They swung over to Buck McKee. Blood was coming down the white shirt, soaking into it. Buck had a moment of sorrow for this man who plainly was dead on his knees.

"We've been married seven years," the banker said slowly. "We worked this game—and it went sour on us. They want us both back East—bank embezzlement. They can come after us . . . now."

Halloway looked at the dead woman. Buck saw a tender feeling come over his face. He heard the slow, hesitant words.

"I'm sorry, sweetheart, I killed you. . . But wait just a minute, and I'll be with you, Clair. . . ."

Halloway lay on the floor then. He put his head on his arm, and Buck could see his eyes.

The eyes went blank.

Buck got to his boots, his knees shaky. "Never got to fire a shot," he murmured. He got Clair's wrist. Warm, but no blood pulsing through it. He looked at Halloway's body.

"You know the secret now, Halloway," the Texan drawled. "But you won't come back to tell about it."

Tortilla Joe crossed himself.

They went down the alley toward the livery barn. Buckskin had come awake. People were going toward the bank. Some were pulling on their clothes as they hurried.

Somewhere a dog howled.

Suddenly Buck remembered the body of young Jack Perry, swinging slowly in the wind. Then a dog had howled, too.

Maybe it was the same dog that now howled.

They rode out of town. "We settled a whale of a lot in a few days," Buck said. "In one way, they got their just deserts, for they ambushed John Lawrence, hung Jack Perry."

Tortilla Joe nodded. "Where we go now?"

"We ride to the Lawrence ranch. Lawrence sent that gunman, Will March, against me, remember? I aim to work the big son over a little with my six-shooter barrel, if I get a chance."

"Then where we go, Buckshots?"

"We head for the Gallatin spread. We gotta

write that letter to ol' Sam Perry, too. But now
we can tell him his son sleeps in peace, Tortilla
Joe."

The Mexican nodded. "Jack he sleep in
peace," he said solemnly.

THE TALL TEXAN

One

Five gun-hung Texans leaned against the bunk-house wall and watched Jim Parker ride into the Circle N, their slitted eyes sharp as Bowies. Not a man spoke or nodded.

Jim rode to the hitch-rack in front of the long stone house and dismounted, tense and tight inside. He looped his reins around the rack and walked up the flagstone path. A harsh voice asked, "What'd you want, stranger?"

Jim had not seen the man because the long porch was covered with thick morning-glory vines. The man sat in a rocking chair, his right foot on a stool in front of the chair – the foot in a plaster-cast.

Behind him, crutches leaned against the wall and beside the crutches was a Winchester.

Gaunt, bony, his tall body was living rawhide, toughened by saddle and rope. He wore no hat. His hair glistened like blue steel, matching the color of his emotionless eyes.

"I came to see your boss," Jim Parker said.

"Circle N's hirin' no riders. 'Specially no drifters."

The word *drifter* was an insult. A drifter was a rangebum riding from spread to spread mooching

225

free grub and a bunk.

"Who t'heck are you?" Jim asked.

"Matt Smith. Circle N ramrod."

"Where's the woman?" Jim demanded. "Owner of Circle N. Your boss. Clara Davis."

"You can talk to me."

"I'm Jim Parker. The new nester down on Turtle Crick."

Matt Smith nodded shortly. "I'll give you your answer: Get out and stay out! Circle N won't stand for farmers cuttin' up Circle N grass!"

"You don't say," Jim said cynically.

Without being asked he stalked into the house. Matt Smith cursed softly as he reached for his crutches.

The room was huge. A long oak table was in its middle. At the far end was a big stone fireplace, front smoked by soot.

She stood behind the table, plainly awaiting him, and Jim Parker tried not to stare.

First, he noticed her red hair.

She had it tied in a bun. It was the reddest red hair Jim had ever seen.

She had a short nose with a trace of tiny freckles. She wore a buckskin riding skirt and a pink blouse. She was an inch over five feet. A man could span her tiny waist with both hands.

Her green eyes flashed fire.

"I take it you're Jim Parker," she said. Her green eyes studied him. "You don't look like a farmer to me."

Jum shrugged. "A man can't make money ridin' for the other man."

"You think he can make more money hanging

onto the handles of a plow, huh?" Her voice held cynicism. "I guess you're here because of that sign?"

Jim pulled the sign out from under his sun-faded shirt. He threw it face-up on the table.

This is Circle N Grass, Sodbuster!
Get Out
And Stay Out!

"You taking my orders?"

Jim shook his head slowly. "I'm not moving."

Anger flared across her eyes, giving them even greater beauty.

Matt Smith had crutched his way into the room. Jim knew that Smith had broken his leg three weeks ago when a bronc had hit a dog hole and rolled over on him. He had learned all he could about Circle N before moving in on Turtle Creek.

Matt Smith had been foreman of the immense Big Bend country ranch for fourteen years. This proud ranch had been handed down from one generation of Davises to the other.

"Then Circle N will move you!" Clara Davis stated.

She stood straight and proud, breathing deeply.

"You people here are living in a fool's paradise," Jim said slowly. "The Civil War has been over twenty years. The Congress of the United States years ago passed what is known as the Homestead Act. Under its qualifications a man can file on a quarter section of land, free. And you own not a foot of Circle N range legally."

"This is Texas," Clara Davis pointed out angrily.

"And part of the Union," Jim added.

"So say the history books," she returned, "but some Texans think differently."

"I'll give up my homestead on one condition. That you put me on Circle N payroll."

Matt Smith shook his head slowly. "The drouth," the foreman said.

For eight years, this country had been held in the grip of the longest period of drouth ever registered in the memory and records of the white man.

Grass was almost non-existent. Many of the old time cattlemen in the Southwest Texas area had gone under. Cattle had died by the thousands from starvation. Frontier banks had closed their doors.

Circle N's losses had been tremendous. Eight years ago at the start of the drouth Circle N had run about thirty thousand head of cattle. Now its immense range held less than ten thousand longhorns.

Circle N hadn't sent a trailherd north for three years; the reason, no cattle with enough beef on their bones to be worth the trip.

And no cattle sold, no money.

But somehow Circle N hung on. Either the huge spread was using reserve capital or was making operating expenses some other way.

Jim pressed the point further. "I'm settled on Turtle Springs, right at the start of the creek. From what I hear, that spring never dries up. I got my first homestead papers filed. With them, Miss Davis, you'll own Turtle Springs, and own it legally."

"A Davis makes no deal with a plowman," Clara Davis said tersely.

Further argument was useless. Jim had ridden into this spread holding the homestead and job trade as his ace card. Now he held a worthless hand. He remembered the hawkeyed gunmen leaning against the wall of the bunkhouse.

"Get out of two places!" Clara Davis ordered. "Out of my house and out of this country!"

Matt Smith opened his mouth to speak, then closed it. Jim got the impression he didn't see eye to eye with his boss.

Jim went out on the porch. The gun wolves had left their den beside the bunk house. Two of them loafed to the nigh side of his horse.

One leaned again the big live oak tree beyond Jim's horse. This one held a rifle, the barrel nonchalantly pointing upward.

One short downward swoop and that rifle would cover him.

The remaining two stood directly back of Jim's horse. Heart pounding, Jim unlooped his reins, threw them over his cayuse's neck, and his left boot was lifting toward stirrup when one of the gunmen behind his horse said, "Just a minute, sodbuster!"

Blood freezing, Jim glanced toward the ranch house door. Clara Davis stood there. He couldn't see Matt Smith.

Clara Davis had given them the signal!

The gunman ambled forward. He was not over five six but he weighed two hundred, Jim guessed, and none of that two hundred was suet. He stopped a few feet from Jim.

He had a wide, cowish face. His heavy nostrils flared.

"I don't believe I know you," Jim said.

"My name's Nelson. Widespan Nelson."

Jim glanced over Nelson's shoulder at the rifleman. The rifle covered him now.

He started his boot toward stirrup again. Widespan Nelson kicked his boot down.

"Don't be in such a rush, sodbuster!"

Jim's only hope was to make a good fight of it. And his right, arcing up, slammed into Widespan Nelson's huge jaw.

He'd never hit a man so hard in his life.

Widespan Nelson went backwards, arms flailing. He had a surprised look on his wide ugly face. Jim pivoted, fists up, to meet the next gunman moving in.

From the corner of his eye, he saw the other two leave the hitchrack. Widespan Nelson was sitting down, facing him.

They came in like wolves pulling down a young steer. Hard fisted, ruthless, they made a punching bag of him. He remembered staggering from one to the other, rocking under their blows. Blood was salty in his mouth. His lips were cut, his nose bleeding.

Then something hard crashed across his skull.

And he slipped into blackness.

Two

When Jim Parker came to he was lying out on the prairie.

He sat up, head aching. Memory came surging back. He saw his horse standing a few feet away.

His first sensible thought was bitter. Clara Davis had surely out-bargained him. His plan had sure backfired.

His eyes focused and he saw Widespan Nelson's huge face.

"What're you doing here?" Jim asked.

"I brought you out here. Boss ordered me to. Guess she didn't want you to stink up the ranch buildings."

Jim got slowly to his feet. "Nice of her."

He staggered over and leaned against his horse. Nausea passed and he felt his head. He had a lump there the size of a big egg.

"Six shooter ... or a club?" he asked.

"Not that it makes any difference, but it was a six shooter," Widespan Nelson said. "Well, guess I'll ride back to the ranch."

"Just who are you on Circle N?"

Widespan Nelson wet his thick lips. "Right now I'm actin' foreman seein' Matt Smith is crippled up. You'd best get off Turtle Crick," he added. "This is only a beginnin' of what the boss will do to you."

"She can't do anything more than kill me."

Widespan Nelson shrugged. "Guess that's about the last thing that can happen to a man."

"Just for curiosity – who slugged me?"

"I did."

"I'll remember that," Jim promised.

"I won't lose no sleep." Widespan Nelson swung his huge bulk into saddle. "I won't forget you, either. You got the toughest skull I ever laid a six-gun barrel over!"

Nelson turned his grulla-colored horse and headed west toward Circle N. Jim noticed that his holster was empty.

A glance told him his Winchester was still in his saddle-holster. He jerked it out, jacked the lever.

They'd unloaded his rifle.

He noticed his off-saddlebag had a big bulge. He opened it. His six-shooter was in the bag. He saw the brassy cartridges, too – bullets for his rifle and Colt .45.

Slowly, grinning crookedly, he got on his horse. He pointed the animal south toward the *pueblo* of Cardenas, five miles away.

His head was clearing. What's my next move? he thought.

Right now he needed a breakfast. He'd not eaten that morning at his so-called farm.

His homestead entry filed on Turtle Creek was perfectly legal. But the purpose behind it had failed miserably.

He wasn't on the Davis payroll.

Thinking of Clara Davis, he also thought of another woman. His younger and only sister, Margaret.

Margaret's beauty had not been the flaming, fire-like beauty of Clara Davis, but dark, sombre, thoughtful.

A month ago, his mother had died.

He'd come home to Alpine for the funeral. He hadn't been home for four long years. A Texas Ranger was always on call, always on duty.

His father had been dead for more years than he could remember. Margaret had kept house for their ailing mother.

And in four years, Margaret had changed. Her dark, fascinating beauty was gone. She was thin, pale, wan.

She had periods of deep dejection and weeping, but wouldn't go to a doctor.

He'd intended to stay a week. He asked for three weeks and grudgingly got it.

She'd be morose, mean – and then she'd go down-town. She'd come back gay, laughing.

One night he crashed through her room's door.

Margaret was inserting a needle in her bare thigh. He tore the hypodermic syringe from her. He threw her roughly on the bed.

Horror stricken, he saw the ugly scars of other needles.

He'd hammered questions at her. She'd stared at him, anger writhing her mouth, and said nothing.

He'd taken her forcibly to Houston to a sanitarium.

Then he'd gone to the Capitol. "I want to be transferred to Narcotics, Captain."

He stopped being Jim Watson, and became Jim Parker. Dope was coming across the Rio Grande at Cardenas. Signs pointed to the smuggling being carried on by the Davis Circle N ranch. Or somebody working for that big spread.

Before taking this assignment, Jim had returned home from the Capitol. By detective work, he'd learned the name of the dope-peddler who'd got his sister on heroin.

He'd beaten the man unconscious. He'd broken his nose and his jaw. The dope-pusher was now in the state pen, facing thirty years sentence.

But it was over five hundred miles from Alpine to this Big Bend of the Rio Grande sagebrush country.

Here he was just Jim Parker, a stupid nester.

Which was just the way he wanted it.

A mile out of Cardenas he met a lone rider, a short, muscular man of about twenty-two. Jim recognized him immediately by his red hair: Carter Davis, Clara's only brother.

Carter Davis rode a prancing midnight-black stallion. He sat a silver-mounted thousand dollar hand-tooled saddle. His black stetson was of finest beaver.

He said, "You're Parker? The nester on Turtle Creek?"

Jim nodded, eyes narrowed.

"See the sign I tacked on your gate post this morning?"

Jim nodded. "I rode into Circle N with it."

Dark eyebrows arched. "You got a nice reception, eh?"

"It could've been pleasanter."

Carter Davis shifted his weight to his left stirrup. That made the white-handled six-shooter tied to his hip closer to his hand.

Jim knew the trick. He'd used it himself.

Suddenly Jim's old .45 was in his hand. The bore of the big weapon pointed directly at Carter Davis' silver belt-buckle.

Davis' breath caught. He stared at the weapon.

"You know how to handle that thing," he said dryly.

Jim flipped the gun, caught it, shoved it into holster. "I've been around a little," he said. "You were mentioning a sign?"

Anger rimmed Carter Davis' voice. "Circle N means just what that sign said, Parker! No sodbusters on Circle N grass, savvy!"

They studied each other for a long tension-filled moment, two bulldogs circling each other.

"I tried to deal with your sister," Jim said dryly. "Homestead rights for a job on Circle N."

"Why should we deal for something we already own?" Hard lines suddenly edged his mouth. "Be gone from that homestead by tomorrow night, Parker!"

"And if I'm not gone?"

"Circle N heel-tromps its own snakes!"

He gave the black stud his vicious star-rowelled spurs. The stallion leaped and Carter Davis was gone around the toe of the hill.

Jim grinned, shrugged, rode on.

Cardenas was a small town, situated on the sage-brush-covered flat where the Cardenas River, now dry because of drouth, entered the now shallow Rio Grande.

Most of its population was Mexican. It was the country-seat and therefore had a courthouse, a long adobe building. Already intense morning heat held the town in its sullen grip. Jim dismounted behind the Concho Cafe.

Jim had eaten here a couple of times before. He was alone in the cafe. He took a stool at the corner. His head still ached dully.

A fat, enormous Mexican woman waddled out of the kitchen. She spoke in Spanish.

"Breakfast or a beer?"

"Breakfast."

Her sharp dark eyes studied him. "You are the farmer who settled on Turtle Creek," she said.

Jim nodded. Word got around fast here in this immense country.

"I'm the man," he said.

She said but one more word. "Fool!" She waddled back into her kitchen. He heard cooking utensils bang. When she came out she carried a plate of hot-cakes and two fried eggs and a cup of coffee.

He was mopping up the last of his eggs when he heard the boots enter the door behind him.

"So you're still on this range, eh?"

The harsh voice took Jim spinning off his stool. He landed spraddle-legged on the adobe floor, hand splayed over his gun.

Widespan Nelson blocked the doorway. Jim wondered how the man had got to town so rapidly. But perhaps the man had headed for Cardenas to check that he, Jim, was leaving this area.

Widespan Nelson's hand rested on his gun-butt.

"I'm still here," Jim said.

"But you're through with your grub, fella. And now it's time to ride out, savvy?"

"I might ride out," Jim said, "and then again I might not!"

Cold anger twisted the heavy face. "No, you won't ride out," the thick lips intoned. "You had your chance to pull stakes! So now it's too late to ride out. They'll tote you boots first to boothill!"

And Widespan Nelson started his draw.

Three

Jim heard the fat Mexican woman scream. Her scream became lost in the sudden roar of guns.

Jim Parker moved with the liquid speed of a leaping cougar. Widespan Nelson had the edge, logic told him. Jim used an old trick he'd learned as a Texas Ranger.

First, you pulled your gun. And, as you made your draw, you moved to your left, sprawling to the dirt floor. It was this sudden, unexpected lunge to his left that saved his life.

For Widespan Nelson's six-shooter had already spat lead. The bullet whammed harmlessly into the counter where Jim had been standing. Jim Parker was a rolling ball of human muscle. And out of this ball came twice the liquid stab of gun-flame. His first bullet missed, smashing into the adobe wall at Widespan Nelson's shoulder.

But the second found its living mark.

Widespan Nelson shuddered. His gun exploded, throwing a bullet into the floor, bringing up a patch of dust. The force of Jim's bullet took the heavy man out of the door and out of sight outside. But Widespan Nelson's pistol lay just inside the doorway, smoke idly trailing upward from its long barrel.

Jim scrambled to his feet. Two jumps took him to Widespan Nelson's .45. He scooped it up, jammed it inside his gunbelt. Then, gun in hand, he lunged out of the cafe.

For the second time in a few hours, Widespan Nelson sat bottom-down on the ground – only this time from Jim's bullet, not his fist. A huge hand clutched his left shoulder, blood seeping around the fingers.

Jim said angrily, "Clara Davis – She sent you to town with orders to kill me? Or did you take on the chore of your own accord?"

"That's my – business …"

Suddenly the fat Mexican woman broke through the cafe door and ran down-street toward the courthouse.

Already the sound of shooting was bringing people on the run. Widespan Nelson got to his feet, lurched over and leaned against the trunk of a live-oak tree, face down and lips twisted as he fought pain.

The thought came to Jim that he'd not yet met the local sheriff. His orders from Headquarters had been to work alone and not reveal his identity to anybody, not even the local lawmen.

He wondered if somehow word had got around, through the grapevine, that a Texas Ranger was working this area, and that he was that Ranger. These dope-smugglers would be suspicious of each new man on this range.

The doctor, a short heavy-set Mexican, came through the crowd, recognizable because of his black bag. He made Widespan Nelson lie on his back, unbuttoned the Circle N man's bloody shirt and carefully removed it from the wide chest. Widespan Nelson lay with his eyes closed, thick lips compressed.

The doctor's fingers explored. "The bone is not broken," he told Jim in Spanish. A thin, tall man stood now beside the medico. This man wore a tarnished law-badge on his greasy vest. He turned suddenly and looked at Jim.

"You shot Nelson?" the sheriff asked.

"He came into the cafe. I was just finishing my breakfast. He drew and fired first." Jim gestured to the fat Mexican cafe-owner. "She'll bear me witness on his shooting first."

"I say nothing!" The Mexican woman came over, shaking her brown fist under Jim's nose. "Somebody will have to pay for the bullet hole in my counter and it'll be you, stranger!"

The sheriff growled, "Get in your cafe, you fool!"

The woman glared at the lanky lawman, then swung dark angry eyes onto Jim, but without another word went into her restaurant.

"What's your name and occupation, stranger?"

"Parker's my name. Jim Parker. I took up a homestead the other day out on Turtle Creek." Jim figured he was telling Sheriff Harkness nothing new. Circle N was the political power here. Harkness held his job on the good graces – and votes – of the Davis spread.

"Turtle Crick, eh? No wonder Nelson jumped you. That's Circle N grass, mister."

"Mine now," Jim corrected. "Legal homestead entry filed with Uncle Sam's land officials."

"One thing to file a homestead entry. Another to hold the homestead, Parker."

"You're the elected Law in this county. If Circle N bothers me, I have the right to appeal to you for law and justice."

He had the sheriff pinned down and Sheriff Clem Harkness' face showed this.

"Circle N's big," the sheriff pointed out.

"Not as big as the Law *should* be," Jim reminded.

Sheriff Harkness' thin face flushed. Jim's home-office had furnished him a complete file on this lawman.

"What sent Widespan Nelson against you?" Sheriff Harkness carefully changed the subject.

Jim told him about the trouble at Circle N that morning. Harkness listened carefully. "You taking Clara Davis' advice and driftin' out, Parker? the sheriff asked.

"I'll think it over."

Harkness smiled slightly. "Don't wait too long," he warned. "Clara Davis had a temper that matches that purty red hair of hers. And her brother ain't too long on patience, either."

The doctor had made a temporary bandage over Nelson's shoulder and had him on his feet. "I'm taking him to my office," he told the sheriff.

Harkness nodded shortly. Jim could guess at the uncertainty roiling inside the lawman. For the first time in many years of loafing in his well-paid office, Sheriff Harkness was facing trouble – real trouble.

Jim figured the sheriff would stay with Circle N, his only logical move. He, Jim Parker, was one man alone, a man without political power, and Circle N had political power. Circle N was this county's biggest taxpayer. And Harkness would not take a stand against the Davises, for they paid his salary.

"What if this Nelson bucko files a warrant against me, sheriff?" Jim enquired.

"Nelson won't file a complaint. The Davises won't let him. Circle N handles its own problems."

"Then to me you're admitting that Circle N is so big it walks around the Sheriff's Office?"

Anger colored Sheriff Clem Harkness' face. "You talk too damn' much," he said shortly.

"Thanks," Jim said dryly.

Harkness stalked away, back straight. Jim entered the cafe.

"You go against Circle N," the Mexican woman snapped. "Circle N keeps me in business. You get out!"

"Never paid you for my breakfast," Jim reminded.

"You pay and go! And never come back! Two *pesos*!"

Jim dug out his wallet and laid two silver *pesos* on the counter. He turned toward the door, then stopped. A young woman stood there – an American girl he judged to be about twenty. She had coal-black hair and a pretty, dark-skinned face.

"Seems like you're not popular around here, stranger," she said.

Four

He found himself comparing her to Clara Davis. Both were little beauties, one red-headed, the other dark-haired. But this girl was taller than tiny Clara. She wore a man's blue chambray shirt and levis. Her boots were brush-scarred.

"And you get out, too, Martha Worthington!" the heavy Mexican woman said angrily. "I do not want you, either!"

Martha Worthington smiled. Jim shrugged. "Looks like we're not welcome, Miss Worthington." He introduced himself. "I'm Jim Parker."

Jim and the girl went outside. "You the *Americano* who plugged our good friend Widespan Nelson, eh?" she asked.

Jim grinned. "I'll have to plead guilty." He found himself wondering about this girl.

"Nelson had been looking for it, Parker. Somebody had to call his hand sooner or later."

"He'll be up and around right pronto. Bullet in his left shoulder – no bones broken."

"Then you'd better watch the big son of a gun. He shoots with his right hand, you know."

"Well do I know that," Jim said earnestly. "But

245

he won't do any shooting until I give him his weapon back."

"Understand you filed on a homestead," Martha Worthington said. "Out on Circle N's best water-hole – Turtle Crick?"

They were walking down Cardenas' main street.

Jim nodded. "News travels fast," he murmured. "You a homesteader, too?"

She smiled. "No, you're the first nester, Parker. My father and me have a little medicine show."

"Medicine show?"

"We travel up and down the river from one Mexican town to the other. We work both sides of the border. I dance a little and my father sells the coloured-water to the suckers." Her smile widened. "Cures anything, you know – snake bites, rheumatism, gout, all that stuff."

"Where's your show now?"

"Across the Rio Grande in Bravo."

Bravo was directly across the Rio Grande. It was bigger than Cardenas, Jim understood. He hadn't ridden over there yet.

She said, "You'll drop over and see me perform? We'll be in Bravo at least another week."

"I'll be over," Jim promised.

Her hand touched his lightly. "I'd like that, Jim." She'd stopped in front of a store. "Well, I came over for a few things and here's where I leave you. It has been nice meeting you, Jim."

"And the same to you, Miss Worthington."

Her dark eyes touched him. "Martha," she said quietly.

Jim Parker grinned. "Martha," he repeated.

Jim walked down-street toward the Court House.

The Court House was a rambling adobe building and the county office he wanted was at the far end, door open. Painted on the door, both in English and Spanish, was the sign, *Sheriff Office*.

Sheriff Clem Harkness sat behind an old desk, boots on the desk, bare from the waist up, sweating it out.

Clara Davis sat on a chair against the south wall. She wore a riding-skirt made of finest yellow buckskin and her white silk blouse set off her flaming red hair.

Jim nodded at her. She gave him a slight nod in return.

"You want somethin', Parker?" the sheriff said tersely.

Jim dug the pistol out of his belt. He laid it on the desk. "Property of one Widespan Nelson," he said.

He glanced at Clara Davis.

Her face was frozen. Her tiny mouth was set. Her eyes were lifeless. They were on Nelson's gun lying on the sheriff's desk.

But the implication showed in the rigid tenseness of her body. A man – a stranger – had shot down a Circle N man.

Jim looked at her. "How is Nelson?"

Her cold lips moved slightly. "None of your business, Mr. Parker."

Jim shrugged. He looked at Sheriff Harkness. "I'll put the same question to you, Sheriff."

Harkness said gruffly. "He's on his feet now. He's rather mad. And he's still got his right hand good."

"I hope I don't have to kill him," Jim said. His hard eyes probed the girl's stubbornly beautiful face. "But the deal still stands – my homestead entry for a riding job on your spread."

"It can stand forever," she said stiffly.

Jim's brows lifted. "I take it you're going to swear out a complaint charging me with the attempted murder of Nelson?"

Before she could speak Jim said, "If you do, you're putting your sheriff here in a bad position."

Harkness cut in with, "What're you drivin' at, Parker?"

"You'd have to serve the warrant, Harkness. And I might not submit to arrest, you know. Nelson drew first."

Harkness started up out of his chair, jaw clenched. But the calm voice of Clara Davis cut through the tension.

"Circle N is filing no warrant, Parker," she said slowly.

Jim nodded slowly. "In other words, Circle N is bigger than the sheriff on this range?"

Now the snarling voice of Sheriff Harkness cut in. "What t'heck you tryin' to do, Parker? Get yourself killed off?"

"I came in peace," Jim said. "Just a would-be dirt-farmer, that's all. But Circle N won't let me be only a dirt-farmer, is looks like." He looked squarely at Clara Davis. "Did you order Nelson to lift his gun against me, Miss Davis?"

His eyes held the green eyes of Clara Davis. There was a long moment of tense silence.

Then she said slowly, "No, Parker, I didn't."

For some reason, Jim felt better – and he didn't know just why. Then doubt surged in. A Ranger rode alone. He trusted nobody but himself.

She rose to her feet. "For many, many years Circle N has lived in peace. Now let's look at this sensibly, Mr. Parker."

Jim nodded.

"This country cannot be farmed. The land is rocky and first you'd have to clear off the thick *manzanita* and *chamiso*. Clearing the land alone would be an almost impossible chore."

Jim could only silently agree.

"Then there is not enough rain for head-crops. And with this drouth – Really, Mr. Parker, I cannot understand you, at all."

She was correct. The Office's idea about coming in as a nester was all wrong. No sensible man would attempt to farm this land. It had been a big mistake. The Home Office did not know the contour and brush-surface of this land.

Anybody who filed on a homestead here had to be one of two things – either crazy or very stupid.

"I took up that homestead for only one reason, Miss Davis. That was to use it as a bargaining-lever to get on your payroll."

Her green eyes narrowed. "That is very hard to believe. I cannot imagine a man going to such lengths just to get a steady job."

"Jobs are scarce, Miss Davis."

She said, "My answer is the same. You'll find no job at Circle N. I have a feeling, Mr. Parker, that this will be the last time I see you."

"I don't figure the same."

She sighed quietly. "What a stubborn young man. ... You know, Mr. Parker, I sort of like you, if for no other reason than your stubbornness." She turned and walked out.

They listened to her bootheels click out of hearing down the covered walk.

Harkness said, slowly, "At long last, I do believe I've met a perfect fool."

"You – or me?"

Harkness's teeth clenched. He gritted his words. "Get outa my sight, Parker!"

Jim smiled. "With pleasure!"

Five

Carter Davis strode back and forth, the rowels of his silver-inlaid Mexican spurs chiming. He glared at Widespan Nelson, seated on the bunk in the foreman's shack.

"So he's fast, eh?"

Nelson moved a little and the gesture brought pain, compressing his lips.

"Fastest man I've ever pulled against, Carter."

A thin smile touched Carter Davis' thin lips. "An' you've always shot off your big mouth about how fast you can pull a gun ... Wonder this Parker gent never killed you!"

"He could of," Nelson admitted. "I got in first shot but he hit the dust, rollin' over – an' I missed."

"And he plugged you," Davis said sarcastically.

"He missed the first shot, though," Widespan Nelson said. He leaned forward, lips again showing pain. "Lissen, Carter, just who is this Parker gent?"

"He's a dirt-farmer, remember?"

Nelson shook his bull-thick head slowly. "That I jus' can't believe, Carter. No man with a lick of salt in his head for brains would try to farm this worthless country."

Carter Davis stood silent, staring at Nelson. "I don't know," he said slowly. "We got to be suspicious of every stranger. He might be. And he might not be."

Nelson lifted slow ox-big eyes. "A bullet from the brush, maybe? Some moonlit night?"

Carter Davis thumbed his bottom lip. "No," he finally said, "not that. Not at this stage of the game, anyway."

"Why not?"

"We might be wrong – way off base, Nelson. He might be as stupid as he acts. We'll watch him a few more days. Then, if he doesn't leave, you can use your Winchester."

"Think he'll go on with his farming idea?"

"What's he got out there?"

"He come in with an old wagon loaded with a plow an' a few other farmin' things. He's got three hosses – two he had hitched to the wagon. He built a brush *ramada*, nothin' more."

Carter Davis smiled thinly. "His camp is hid back in the brush. He ain't put up no fence yet – jus' put down corner-posts markin' his homestead, looked to me."

Hate suddenly contorted Nelson's wide, ugly face. "I gotta kill him, Carter!"

Carter Davis crossed the room in two strides. He slapped the thick-set man hard across the jowls.

"I'm boss here, Nelson! An' don't ever forget that! I never ordered you to pull against this nester! You took that on yourself – lookin' for a little glory! We got something big here – danged big! An' you're not foulin' it up by lookin' for revenge, *sabe*?"

Nelson's lips trembled in anger. His huge right

paw came up and slowly rubbed blood back into his face.

"You slap me again, Davis, an' it'll be you I gun down!"

Suddenly Carter Davis' gun was in his hand, the movement so fast it beat the accuracy of the eye.

"You'll gun *who* down?"

Fear flamed across Nelson's big eyes. He stared at the big .45, mouth opened slightly.

"For the love of mike, Carter! Put that gun away, please!"

The gun slammed down into its holster. And Davis' smile was ice-thin.

"He'll move," Davis said sharply. "He might be what we think he is. If I find proof that he is, Parker's good as dead already!"

Carter Davis strode outside and up the walk, bootheels angry. Matt Smith sat in his rocking-chair on the vine-covered long porch.

Davis nodded absently. "My sister in?"

"She is."

Davis entered the house. His thoughts played with Matt Smith for a moment, probing the character of the old foreman for danger – but he found none, not at the present time, anyway.

Clara Davis was doing book-work at the big table in the living room. She raised her red head and said, "What's on your mind?" Her voice held impatience.

Carter Davis let a grin hide his annoyance. He moved over and looked at the ledger. "Well, we haven't got into red ink yet, anyway, eh?"

She sighed.

"No, but it won't be long, the way I figure."

"The drouth will break soon. We'll have rain again."

She slammed her pen on the big table. "That's all I've heard for eight long years! Amateur weathermen!"

"What we got to kick about? North of here Bar S is out of business. Cattle wandering around unbranded, what few there are. Ride further north to Quarter Circle Nine on the Pecos. Or west to the Big Loop. The story's always the same. But we're still out in black ink."

"Not for long." Clara Davis mopped her brow again.

"We got Turtle Crick back again. That's our main water hole."

She debated that, lips pursed. "Only a fool would try to farm this desert country, 'specially so since this long dry-spell set in. He couldn't even get a plow in this dry ground." Her eyes narrowed slightly. "I can't understand him."

"He told you his bargain. His homestead for a ridin' job with Circle N. That's all there is behin' it."

"Jobs are scarce," she said calmly, "but surely not that scarce. And what do we pay our riders – ten dollars a month and beans, nothing more."

He shrugged, said, "You figger it out," and turned to go, but her next words stopped him, whirling him to face her. "Say that again, please?" His voice was dangerously low.

"You heard me the first time. This drouth doesn't seem to affect your spending money."

"What're you drivin' at, Clara?"

"You hang around that gambling den in

Cardenas. You're in the big one across the river in Bravo when you're not gambling in Cardenas. You ride a two thousand dollar silver-mounted saddle. You could sell that saddle, ride an ordinary cowpuncher kak, and throw the money into saving this ranch."

"You forget one thing, Clara."

She waved a hand impatiently. "Sure, we're right back on the same old subject. The will. When mother died six years ago, she left the ranch in my name. But she never cut you off completely, like you seem to imply."

"Oh?"

Impatience grooved her smooth forehead. "She made the stipulations in her will that way for just one purpose – give you a chance to grow up and act like a man. I was nineteen when she died. You were sixteen. But five years from now, when I'm thirty, you'll automatically become half-owner of Circle N."

"If there's anything left by that time!" Anger twisted his thin lips. "So I'm supposed to grow up, as you say – and become a man, eh? Two females – a man's mother and sister – plotting against him, nothing more!"

"Let's not argue again about it, Carter. The will stands registered and filed and no court in the world would throw it out."

He smiled crookedly. "Nobody's blabbin' about breakin' that danged will! Though I think it could be done in court."

"On what grounds, may I ask?"

"This is an old Spanish land grant. Under Spanish law property passes to the first-born son, not the oldest of the children." He shrugged, spread thin hands. "But let it go. But before I leave, Your Majesty, let me remind you that the Old Lady left me five thousand dollars in an account all my own."

"That saddle cost you two thousand. That's almost one-half of five thousand," she said significantly.

His smile was boyish, now. "You forget the card games, darling sister. And poker is one game I know."

"Good luck you know something. You apparently know nothing about the cattle business."

Red anger tore across his face. "I've ridden every danged foot of Circle N range. I've choused more than my share of thirsty stock down on springs for water. And I've shoved them into mesquite thickets, too, so they could strip down beans. Don't jump me on that, Clara!"

She said, wearily, "Please leave, Carter!"

He bowed ironically. "With pleasure, Your Majesty!"

He stalked out with spur-rowels chiming angrily and strode across the porch, fully aware of Matt Smith's eyes, knowing the foreman had probably heard every word passed between him and his sister.

Six

Jim Parker was frowning when he left Sheriff Clem Harkness' office. He found himself trying to evaluate the sheriff.

A Texas Ranger had to always be one thing – a Texas Ranger.

Suspicious of every person he met – until that person was proven innocent. And he had only one faint clue to work on, and then it was based mostly on rumor.

The Head Office hadn't been certain that Circle N was tied in with this dope running. Dope was apparently crossing the Rio Grande around the town of Cardenas. And the office map of this Big Bend section of Texas had shown that Circle N range ran about thirty-five miles down-river east of Cardenas and about forty-three miles up-river from the adobe town.

That left Circle N controlling seventy-eight miles of the north bank of the Rio Grande.

He wondered if the Head Office had contacted the Mexican rurales, telling that tough outfit that a Texas Ranger was working the Rio Grande at this point.

"This is mostly heroin and opium," his boss had

said. "Neither drugs are raised in Mexico, Jim. Marijuana is a Mexican product, yes – but too small a drug to be contrabanded – not enough money in it."

"Then where is this dope coming from?"

"We figure it's being unloaded from Chinese ships at some of Mexico's western seaports."

"But it's a lot of miles from the Big Bend to any of those ports," Jim'd pointed out. "What makes you think then it's coming across the Rio Grande in the vicinity of the Davis spread?"

Again a trip to the big wall map. "Uncle Sam has his boys pretty well scattered out along the U.S. – Mexican Border. Immigration, Customs, and Border Patrol. But Uncle just hasn't got enough money to hire men to patrol every foot of the Border. The Rio Grande runs almost fifteen hundred miles along the U.S. – Mexican frontier. That's a long, long distance, Jim."

"Has Uncle got a man stationed on the Rio Grande around Cardenas?"

"Not a one, Jim. I'll be truthful. Uncle's forces are so thin that he's left patrolling the Border almost alone to us Rangers. And you know danged well our men are scarce, too."

Jim'd nodded.

"You'll be on your own, Jim, with about twenty thousand square miles of mountainous-desert to patrol."

Jim has never been on a case like this before. This would be his first case calling for undercover detective work.

He'd given this matter long and serious thought. If he failed to get on Circle N's payroll, he'd have to play the game from outside the ranch. And he'd failed to get on the Davis list of riders.

Maybe Circle N wasn't even connected with this dope-running?

This would require patience, night-rides, and both eyes and ears wide open.

Logic told him a dope-runner made easy money. And those who made a dollar with the minimum of work usually spent that dollar freely. And one place to lose a buck fast – or win one just as fast – was at a poker table.

Where was the closest poker game in Cardenas?

A wizened, bent-over old Mexican man came hobbling toward him. Jim put the question to him.

The man answered in rapid, angry Spanish. "Are you blind, Americano? Have you no eyes? The Casino is right across the street!"

Across the dusty street he saw a squat and wide adobe building. It had high small barred windows in its thick walls. The door was wide and made of thick planks.

Across the front of the building he barely could make out a faded red bunch of letters: *Casino de Naipes*. The House of Cards.

The interior of the dive was dark. Kerosene lamps hung on the walls, giving a feeble yellow glow.

Another lamp hung from the ceiling, suspended over the table, its wide shade throwing light downward on the greasy green cloth. Five men were seated around it, cupping their cards, and Jim recognized one of them.

He was the short, tough man who'd leaned against the live-oak tree, back at the Davis ranch –

the man who'd held the rifle on him.

The man looked up. His flintly, slitted eyes moved slowly over him, and then returned to his cards. His slight smile angered Jim.

There was a long wooden bar the length of the joint's south side. A Mexican peon, dirty apron strapped to his fat belly, dozed on it.

Jim was the only customer at the bar.

Jim said, "Any beer? Cold?"

The head came up slowly. Big brown eyes studied him as though seeing him in a fog. Jim glanced at the pupils. This peon was brain-fogged by marijuana cigarets.

"*Cerveza,*" the thick lips said. "Oh, *si, Senor.* Beer, in *gringo.*"

Jim grinned. He spoke Spanish. "If it's cold."

"*Si, es frio, Senor.*"

The obese man waddled to the far end of the bar. Here they had a well and he slowly turned the windlass, coming up with a wooden bucket that held beer bottles dripping water. He ambulated back, bottle in hand.

"Nobody drinks much *cerveza* here," he grumbled. "Pablo sells about one bottle a day."

"How much?"

"*Peso.*"

Jim walked over to the card-table with his beer. The Circle N man looked up at him.

"I'm ridin' a lucky hoss, nester. Don't stand behind me."

Jim smiled. "Seems to me you weren't a bit superstitious out at Circle N when you held that big rifle on me. That was right brave of you Circle N buckos – if my adding is right, there were six of you brave gents on one man!"

The bony man slowly laid down his cards. His dull eyes bored into Jim's. The other four hurriedly shoved back chairs.

The Circle N man got to his feet. "You lookin' for more of the same, nester?" His voice was quietly dangerous. His right hand was splayed over his holstered gun. "You're not dealin' with Widespan Nelson now. You're facin' Bob Wiley."

"Nice to know a coward's name," Jim said dryly.

The other had carefully moved back along the bar out of possible bullet-range. The hot air wreathed with the insult of *coward*.

"You said the wrong word there, nester!" Bob Wiley's lips twisted with rage. "You pack a gun! Use it!"

And Bob Wiley started his draw.

But he never finished it.

Jim used an old trick he'd learned in the Rangers. He moved in quick as a rattlesnake striking. And, as he moved, he twisted his wiry body, grabbing Bob Wiley's left arm. He heaved the man over his left shoulder. Wiley sailed through the air. His gun flew out of his grip, landing on the adobe floor.

Wiley crashed, head-first, into the iron bar-rail. He rolled over, half-unconscious. Jim walked forward and got Wiley's gun. He automatically ejected the cartridges from it. He put the cartridges in his pocket. He tossed the gun aside.

The big pistol fell on the ground behind the bar. Jim turned his attention to Bob Wiley. His own .45 was out now.

Bob Wiley got in a crouching position, shaking his head dully. Sanity returned to his eyes.

"I'll get you if it's the last thing on earth –"

Bob Wiley came up like an uncoiling human spring. He lunged forward, intending to slam his head into Jim's belly.

Jim sidestepped with the ease of a matador dodging a bull's wicked horns. Wiley lunged by. Jim's .45 came smashing down on the man's skull. Wiley landed in an inert unconscious heap ten feet away.

Jim holstered his gun. He picked Wiley up, holding him over his head. He carried the man to the door and heaved him out on the street. At that moment Sheriff Clem Harkness happened to be walking by.

Wiley hit the sheriff. The lawman fell into the street in a sitting-down position, the Circle N man's body across his thighs.

Harkness' thin face first showed anger. Then the anger changed to surprise. "What t'heck is this?" he blurted.

Jim grinned. "We're going to play some poker," he said.

Seven

Rage twisted Carter Davis' thin lips.

"So you tangled with him, eh, Wiley? And he buffaloed you down and threw you out of the cantina?"

Fear rimmed Bob Wiley's words. "For the love of mud, Carter, put that danged gun down, man! You even got the hammer eared back! That thing's got a hairtrigger!"

They were in the Circle N office, a small adobe building set behind the long bunkhouse.

Widespan Nelson said placatingly, "Bob's right, Carter. He done his best. This nester just outguessed him, that's all!"

Carter Davis turned on the balls of his boots with cat-quickness. The big .45 covered Widespan Nelson. Nelson's face paled beneath his tan. Never had he seen such livid anger in Carter Davis' thin, clean-shaven face.

"You keep your big mouth outa this, Nelson! You took a whack at this gent, too – and he trimmed your horns! What t'heck is Circle N gettin' to be? The laughin'-stock of the Big Bend!"

Bob Wiley put his head in his trembling hands. "I never met a man who moved so fast before,

Carter! I went for my gun – and then I was sailin' over his head!"

Carter Davis now studied Bob Wiley. Suddenly the rage left his lips to become replaced by a twisted smile. Lamplight glistened on the blue-steel of his Colt as he flipped it once and holstered it.

"I might be wrong, but there seems to be something more behind this than that nester working this homestead scheme to merely get on Circle N payroll."

"He's the Law, maybe?" Wiley ventured.

Carter Davis shrugged. "Who knows ... except the nester? Only thing I can say is he needs watching. But one good things came out of it, anyway."

"An' that?" asked Widespan Nelson.

Carter Davis smiled. "Sheriff Harkness won't love him now. Not only because he threw Bob out on him, but he's keeping Harkness from enjoying his siesta – and the sheriff's been on a siesta ever since he got that star!"

"What about Harkness?" Nelson asked.

Davis studied the brick-built man. "Now what do you mean by that?"

"Hell, Carter, you know what I mean! These *peons* are dirt-proof. Time was they could make a year's livin' ridin' roundup for Circle N. But times has been so bad we ain't run a round-up wagon out for five years."

"Get to your point!" Carter Davis said hurriedly.

"You know the point as well as I do! Times are tough in Cardenas. Those Mexicans that used to ride our roundups are the ones who voted the way Circle N wanted. Circle N has controlled county offices through their votes, because they were beholden to Circle N. But ... no longer."

Carter Davis rubbed his bony jaw thoughtfully. "Go on, Widespan," he encounraged.

"They ain't happy with the county officials. They claim the county bunch should get some money in from the State – if not money, ship in some beans and flour. There's even talk about running their own men for county offices this fall election."

"They can elect their own bunch, too," Bob Wiley put in. "Then Circle N's got no political pull."

"You talk like fools," Carter Davis said angrily. "Let them vote as they please, dang 'em! I'll see that the votes are counted to suit Circle N. Or that ballot boxes suddenly disappear!" Suddenly his face lighted. "I got a better idea. Tomorrow drive ten Circle N beefs into town for butchering. Allot the meat out to the poor devils."

Bob Wiley laughed softly. "Boy, and what beefsteaks it will be, what with our steers only skins and bones!"

"It will look good, though," Davis said, "and that is all I want." He paused. "There must be some way to get the sheriff to knock off this nester for us. That way all blame will be out of Circle N hands."

"Swear out a warrant against him," Nelson said. "Either me or Bob here will sign it." He grinned grimly. "We got just grounds."

"Talk sense," Davis growled. "This nester can be got rid of easy, if it comes to that. A rifle bullet outa the brush! Wiley, ride out to Turtle Crick. Go through his belongings, if they're still there."

"What if *he's* there?"

"Kill him. Bury his carcass somewhere back in the brush. Turn his horses into our north pasture. We'll trail them to Mexico with the next herd and sell them below the Border."

Wiley reached out and got his rifle leaning against the wall.

"Here goes nothin'!" He left.

Widespan Nelson looked at Carter Davis. "This has been a good deal for four years," he said slowly. "But sooner or later the Law is bound to get wise. Only thing that has pertected us so far is that they ain't no U.S. men ridin' for Uncle Sam in this area."

Davis put a hand on Nelson's good shoulder. "Forget it, Widespan. Turn in and get a good night's sleep. Tomorrow is another day."

Nelson got to his feet. "When do we move them cows across the river into Mexico?"

"How many head you got gathered?"

"Aroun' three hundred, I'd reckon. I'd have had more but that sister of your'n – she's spendin' lots of time in her saddle of late. You don't figure she's a mite suspicious?"

Carter Davis laughed. "Don't overwork your imagination, Widespan! She knows nothing! You just leave her to me, eh?"

Nelson's good shoulder shrugged. "You're the ramrod." He walked into the night.

For a long moment Carter Davis stood in deep thought, chin in his hand. Finally he picked up his Winchester and went outside, heading for the horse-barn.

He saddled a line-back bucksin gelding. He jammed the Winchester .30-30 into the hand-stamped saddle-holsters.

He led the horse outside, swung into saddle, and at that moment his sister's voice asked, "And where is Sir Lochinvar riding this night?"

He stared into the shadows, anger roiling him. "What you doin' here? Spyin' on me?"

"Oh, yes, spying, beloved brother!" Her voice dripped cynicism. "If you must know, I'm walking around because it is so hot in the house – and sometimes a breeze comes across the prairie."

She wore a blue blouse. Her skirt was blue, too. She looked like a little girl. And something within him softened. He leaned from saddle.

"Did anybody ever tell you that you're a beautiful young woman?"

She laughed quietly. "There's no use throwing compliments around, Carter. They'll get you nowhere. Am I as beautiful as that little thing you got down in the Casino? That halfbreed female?"

The softness suddenly became hardness. He straightened, fingers gripping the fork of his ornate saddle.

"I can't say a decent thing to you any more," he said angrily. "If I do, you switch it around to something dirty. You go your way – I'll go mine!"

"That sounds brave, Carter. But it can't be true. As long as both of us are on Circle N, our ways are tied together."

"Then maybe I'll get off the danged spread!" He used his rowels savagely on the buckskin. The horse leapt into a hard gallop.

Common-sense replaced anger. He twisted in saddle, one hand braced on the fork, the other on the cantle, and he looked west toward the highness of the Big Bend Mountains. He let his eyes move from peak to peak, and a strange solace entered him.

Come morning he'd apologize to Clara.

He had to keep in her good graces. Her nerves were raw, he knew. The drouth, clinging and deadly, sucking the arid earth. Circle N cattle, bony, gaunt, drifting from *mesquite* clump to *mesquite* clump, searching for beans – anything to stave off starvation. And the water-holes and springs, so many dry now.

He looked up and searched the sky. Not a cloud in sight, only the blue fathomless Texas sky. Then suddenly his thin face hardened, sinking into a devilish mould.

He hated Texas. He hated the Circle N. He hated the cattle-business. He wanted only one thing – to flee from this barren, unhospitable land. And this he would do, soon.

Within a year, at least – maybe sooner. But this deal was, for him, a good deal, and would continue to pay him well. And anybody who stood in his way would die.

It was after ten o'clock when he rode into Cardenas. The town's only lights were the small yellow squares of the Casino.

Davis rode to the tie-rack and swung down. He noticed Jim Parker's cayuse was tied there with four others.

Men played cards at the only occupied table. Three were Mexican business-men from across the Rio Grande.

The fourth man was Jim Parker.

The fifth player was a woman. Her coal-black hair was tied into a severe knot at the nape of her neck. She was Martha Worthington.

She wore a yellow silk blouse and a buckskin split-riding-skirt. The red bandana, loosely knotted around her tanned throat, gave her a carefree, gypsy appearance.

She did not look at him. Her fingers cupped her cards.

"What'll it be, Carter?" the bartender asked.

Davis shook his head. "Nothing."

Booze had no place here. This called for a clear head. He did not want trouble with Jim Parker. But if Parker forced trouble –

Jim Parker shoved out two chips, both red. His face held the marks of the beating he'd taken in Circle N's yard that morning. Parker's left eye had a blue-black ring. One cheek was swollen slightly.

Davis walked over to the table. "Mind if I sit in, Parker?"

"I'm not running this game, Davis. Ask the house man."

"Wide open game," the house man said quickly. "Sky's the limit, Carter."

Davis' boot hooked a chair. He slid into it facing Jim Parker. Martha Worthington sat two chairs away at Davis' right.

Davis lit a cheroot. Jim Parker had a nice stack of chips in front of him, mostly reds – the ones that counted. Martha Worthington also was winning.

Martha raked in that pot.

Jim Parker had the next deal. His fingers worked swiftly. The game was dealer's choice. "Draw," he said.

This time Carter Davis was dealt in. He cupped his cards, catching two queens and a nine of hearts, six of hearts, and deuce of spades.

Jim Parker looked at him. "How many cards, Davis?"

"Three, Parker."

Parker dealt him three cards – another deuce, a five of diamonds, an eight of hearts. Davis threw his hand into the discard.

Davis' eyes met Parker's. For a moment their glances held, then broke.

Carter Davis swung his over to Martha Worthington. Evidently she caught the imprint of his gaze. She lifted her head.

Her dark eyes met his.

Carter Davis smiled quietly.

Slowly her left eyelid came down in a wink. Then her eyes were again on her cards. Carter Davis let his gaze wander around the other players. All were occupied with their cards.

None had seen her wink.

Eight

The horseman came at a fast gallop, hoofbeats ringing ahead through the moonlit night. Jim Parker had pulled his horse off-trail into the high *chamiso* brush. His pistol was in his hand.

Now the rider came into view, slanting around a bend in the trail. He rode a sorrel horse. He sat his saddle awkwardly.

It was not until the horseman was a hundred feet away that Jim saw the white cast on the rider's right foot.

Jim spurred his horse into the narrow trail, gun on the rider. The man pulled in, horse kicking up dust, hand on his holstered gun. Then he recognized Jim and drew his hand back.

"You ride a late trail, Parker."

"I could say the same for you, Matt Smith. When I left the poker game down in Cardenas my watch said fifteen after two."

"Circle N range," Smith pointed out significantly. "And I'm ramroad of Circle N. I guess that gives me the right to ride anywhere on Circle N range any time I so want."

Jim holstered his gun. "I guess it does, Smith. But you came from the direction of my camp."

Matt Smith laughed shortly. "You can ride an easy saddle there, nester. I might've come from the direction of your camp but I never rode in. I take it you'll be headin' out soon?"

"You seem anxious, Smith."

Smith gestured. "Makes no never-mind to me, fella. But your plan to hitch onto Circle N payroll bucked you off. And you know – and I know – a man can't make a living farmin' Turtle Crick."

"I'm a stubborn man, maybe?"

Matt Smith shrugged blocky shoulders. "So you say, Parker. But many a man has been buried because of his bull-headedness." He yawned suddenly, shoulders sagging. "I'm a good ten miles from my bunk, fella. And this jawin' gets no ends accomplished."

Jim said merely, "So long."

Matt Smith put his horse to a lope, right foot hardly touching stirrup. Jim rode slowly onward to his Turtle Creek camp.

He'd had a lucky night … at least, with the cards. He'd come out around a hundred bucks winner. But the big pots had gone to Martha Worthington. She apparently was a born poker player.

She'd won around three hundred, by his reckoning.

Carter Davis had been the big loser. They'd dug into him for around five hundred, Jim figured.

The poker game had told Jim much about Carter Davis. First, he had money – and losing didn't hurt him. Secondly, he was composed of two opposite facets of character. One hand he would plunge recklessly, placing all upon bluffing out his opponents; the next hand, he'd play his cards cautious and slow, depending not on bluff but on the value of his hand.

Davis had found Jim rock-hard, not reckless, not too conservative. A man who had a good balance, who depended not so much upon luck as upon logic.

And each had found in the other a strong enemy, a tough opponent.

Jim had come to one outstanding conclusion. If dope was being smuggled by Circle N, Carter Davis was the real boss.

He did not ride openly into his camp. He left his horse in the brush and moved down Turtle Creek on foot, rifle in hand. He came to the edge of the brush circling his camping-quarters. There he paused, eyes searching, probing. But he saw nothing alien, so he walked boldly into the clearing.

His two other horses were safe. He's sneaked past them up-creek on their picket-ropes. His wagon stood in the same spot. He had driven four cedar posts into the ground, covering the area above them with brush – the Mexicans called it a *ramada*. He'd carried in an old Army folding cot. Under it he'd thrown his buckskin war-bag containing his few personal things – shaving soap, razor, and a bunch of letters, bound with a cord.

The Home Office had concocted this idea, the letters written in headquarters in Austin. They'd been stamped with fake cancelling from Amarillo.

They were supposedly letters from a fictitious father and brother. Each cancellation bore a different date. He had catelogued them according to cancellation dates.

He lit the lantern hanging from a scrub-cedar post at the head of his bunk, dragged his war-bag from under the bed. The two thick leather straps were in the holes he.'d left them in.

Nobody had ransacked his war-bag.

And if Circle N had sent a man over, the war-bag's letters would only more securely fasten in the mind of the looter that he had no connection with the Rangers.

According to the letters, he'd tired of punching cows, had decided to become a farmer, and had headed for the Big Bend country.

He unbuckled the bag and dumped its contents on his bunk. Nothing had been taken from the bag. He laid the articles in a row – shaving soap, straight-edged razor, razor-strop, three bars of toilet soap, other knick-knacks, and the letters.

He thumbed through the letters, flicking them between fingers like a man handling cards, glancing at the dates – then suddenly he stopped and went back three letters, comparing dates.

His breathing stiffened.

The first letter was dated September 14, 1884. Last fall. The next was dated March 5, 1884. Last spring. The third was dated January 9, 1885. This winter.

He checked dates again to make sure. But he was not wrong – somebody had taken these letters out from under the cord, and had put them back in wrong order.

He checked further on. He found another letter filed incorrectly. That clinched his suspicions.

Somebody had searched his camp while he'd been at the poker game, for the letters had been in proper sequence yesterday morning.

Circle N?

Tense, tall, deadly, he stood there, limned by yellow low lantern-light. There was no danger in this, he reasoned. Whoever had read these letters would be convinced he was only an errant cowboy, who'd headed south to turn into a plow-man.

Suddenly his body froze, muscles ice. He'd heard the scrape of a horse-hoof north in the brush. He blew out the lamp in one explosive gesture, leaving the area bathed in cold Texas moonlight.

Two strides and he was across the clearing, body bent over – expecting any time to feel a bullet tear into his screaming muscles. He slammed into the protecting brush on the dead run, but no bullets came.

He heard it again – the sound of a horse's hoof. Closer this time. Then logic came into his brain; no raider would come so noisily.

A hundred yards from his camp ran a dim trail. The same trail Matt Smith had ridden.

The thought came that Matt Smith, despite his declaration, had pilfered around his camp. But this thought did not fit into the character of Matt Smith.

The hoof-sounds grew louder. No, this rider – whoever he was – was merely riding past his camp, not riding into it.

He came to the trail the instant the rider passed. Gun jutting, he said sternly. "Who goes there?"

The rider pulled the horse to a sliding stop. For a long moment tension spun its steel-web, with Jim peering upward at the rider in the uncertain light.

He said quietly, "Clara Davis ... And at this time of the night, too, riding range?"

Her flat-brimmed black stetson lay on her back,

held by the throat strap. Moonlight glistened on her glowing red hair. Moonlight showed her face, too, just clearly enough that he could see surprise drain out, becoming replaced by a hasty anger.

"This is my Circle N range, Parker! Why the gun on me, nester?"

He holstered the gun. "My camp's back in the brush. I heard a horse – and a man never knows, Miss Davis!"

She spoke with metallic stiffness. "I don't bush-whack, Parker!"

Jim laughed shortly. "Don't play the high and mighty with me, Miss Davis! I remember a few things – my swollen face won't let me forget! You might not bush-whack – but you gave a signal to turn six men onto me in your yard yesterday morning, remember?"

She hesitated, eyes on his. The beauty of her struck him with stunning force. The red, glistening hair, the small, sun-tanned lovely face with the tiny freckles across her nose – and the thin waist a man could cup in both hands. His breath caught.

Then she said, "I lost my temper, Mr. Parker."

He softened suddenly. "Yes, I guess we all lost our tempers, Miss Davis." Their eyes held for a long silent moment. Then he said, "But I'm wondering why you're in saddle out here at this early hour."

"You just wonder, Parker."

He tried a shot in the dark. "Maybe because of your foreman, Matt Smith?"

"What about – Matt Smith?"

He shrugged. "I played poker in town until about two. Your brother was in the game. Coming out here I ran into Smith. Now I run into you.

Somewhere it seems to tie in, Miss Davis."

She didn't answer that. Instead she said slowly, "You know, Mr. Parker, I sort of like you, much as I hate to admit it – and shouldn't admit it. I take it you're giving up this homestead idea?"

"I think so, too. It didn't get me on your payroll."

He saw her smile slightly. He liked that smile. He liked everything about her – her wealth of red hair, her green eyes, even the freckles marching quietly across her small nose. He liked all except the fact they were on opposing sides.

Perhaps he was looking at the person who smuggled this destroying dope across the Rio Grande? Perhaps his work would put her behind bars in a federal penitentiary?

These thoughts were terrible.

"I take it then you're going to leave, Mr. Parker?"

"I might, and I might not. The state pays a buck apiece for killing coyotes. This range seems to have a lot of coyotes. I'm thinking about turning coyote-hunter. A man can kill two coyotes a day and make living wages."

"I'd not advise it." Her voice was stiff now. "Circle N can kill its own coyotes and wolves. The fact of the matter is: Circle N wants only Circle N riders to move across Circle N range."

He grinned. "What do you advise?"

"Just one thing – you get off Circle N, and stay off!"

She was gone then, horse lunging into a dust-choking lope. The last he saw of her was her gleaming red hair as she went around a bend.

For a long time Jim Parker stood there, thinking.

As a Ranger, he'd never had to move against a woman before. Always it had been gun-hung, tough men – never a woman. Was she involved in this smuggling? He hoped not. He prayed not.

He saw her in a federal pen behind bars. He lowered his head in his hands, emotions tearing at him.

And then he thought of Margaret. His sister.

The vision of Margaret flashed across his mind, etched in lines of fire. Of her dark, vibrant Spanish beauty, of her enormous drive as a child and a young woman – filled with energy, always smiling, working, laughing, playing, enjoying life.

And he thought of Margaret now.

Wan, sick, pale, thin – a living mockery to the former Margaret. Margaret, with the ghastly needle-wounds on her shrunken, thin thighs. This tore at him, ripped through him, giving him nerves of steel.

He raised his head, eyes cold.

Maybe Clara Davis was involved in this terrible tragedy. Maybe she wasn't. But if she were, one thing was certain.

Clara Davis would pay.

Nine

False dawn streaked the east when Clara Davis rode into Circle N, horse sweaty. She unsaddled, threw her kak over the rack, led the horse to pasture, slipped free the bridle.

The wind was slowly turning the windmill's big fan. She wondered if the piston was pulling up water

She saw a trickle of water coming from the pipe into the trough. She turned, shoulders sagging, and hooked her bridle over the horn of her saddle.

What was this all about? Why had Matt Smith, bum leg and all, headed out late last night?

Sleep had been slow in coming. She'd been sitting beside her window, her room dark so no mosquitoes would enter, looking out over the Circle N yard. And she'd seen Matt Smith leave his foreman-house, back of the bunkhouse, and go to the barn.

She'd thought he'd gone to the barn to gossip with Old Windy, the holster.

For fifteen minutes, she'd watched the door.

But Matt Smith hadn't come out.

That hadn't made sense. Old Windy wasn't in the barn, apparently. She'd gone to the barn. Matt Smith's saddle was gone from the rack. So was his top-horse, gone from its stall.

Apparently he intended to stay in his saddle for his crutches leaned against the stall partition.

That meant he hadn't headed for town. For if he'd gone to town, he'd surely need his crutches.

The fact that Smith had ridden out the back door – and not the front – further added to her curiosity. Plainly the foreman rode on some secret mission, or was her mind being too active?

Ten minutes later she sat her horse in the brush on a high ridge two miles north of the ranch. Although the moonlight was not bright, it showed the tumbling range rather clearly.

This was the thick brush country of Texas. Here they used dogs to run out cattle, for in some places the brush was so dense a man and horse could not penetrate it.

So deduction had told her that Matt Smith would do no brush-breaking. He would stay to trails, not head into the brush.

She thought she detected a rider ahead, moving toward the level country around lower Turtle Creek. Because she thought of Turtle Creek, she also thought of Jim Parker.

Tall and tough. Yes, and handsome, too, her woman's heart said. Her mouth twisted; the fool! Trying to farm Turtle Creek! And with this eight year drouth, too!

Surely a man like Jim Parker couldn't possibly be that stupid? And if he'd filed that homestead entry just to try to trade it for a job at Circle N –?

That just didn't seem logical.

She wanted to trail Matt Smith. But this, she

knew, would've been almost impossible even in broad daylight.

She sighed quietly, letting weariness seep into her. What was wrong here on Circle N? Day by day she and Carter were drifting further and further apart. Not that they'd ever been close. Carter had always built that stiff, high wall around him.

She had wished many times the will had given them each one-half of Circle N. Then perhaps they could have worked amicably together?

She'd talk it over soon with Carter. They could ride to the courthouse, their lawyer could draw up the necessary papers, and she would of her own volition give her brother control over one-half Circle N.

What there was left of it …

She headed toward the spot where she thought she'd seen a rider. She rode at a running-walk, letting her horse take his time. Within thirty minutes she came to a wide mesa. Here the thick brush had played out, leaving an area about a mile square. Cattle were bedded down under live-oaks.

She reined in, studying the Circle N cattle. Why had so many head drifted to this one spot? There was no water here, for the spring was dry.

Perhaps they'd come to this clearing to be safe from lobo-wolves and coyotes. Prairie wolves were dragging down Circle N steers and cows. The cattle were weak from lack of grass and water; therefore the wolves were brave. And coyotes were hamstringing spring calves. The only animals that were fat on this range were the wolves and coyotes.

Yes, that had to be the reason.

She'd been in saddle over an hour. Maybe Matt

Smith hadn't been able to sleep, either, and so had tested his bum leg in saddle? By this time her foreman might be back at Circle N. She turned her horse east, looking for the trail that led past Turtle Creek back to Circle N. She found it and Jim Parker jumped her. And Parker had reported Matt Smith riding ahead of her back to Circle N.

Now she turned slowly and walked to the house. Suddenly weariness struck her, sagging her square shoulders.

She was crossing the dark porch when Matt Smith said, "You're gettin' to be like your brother, Clara. Comin' in at daybreak ..."

His voice startled her. She went over and faced him, leaning against the porch railing.

"For some reason I couldn't sleep, Matt. So ... I took Sonny Boy and went for a short ride."

Silence spun its thin web. He broke it by leaning forward in his chair. His voice was very low. "Clara?"

"Yes?"

"Don't worry, Clara, darling. Everything will work out all right."

She laughed shortly. "Look at the sky, Matt! Not a cloud in sight! Day after day, year after year – no rain!"

"Rain will come, Clara."

"And look at Carter. Running around with that halfbreed gypsy, or whatever she is! Away from home nights at a time. Gambling down in Cardenas or Bravo. And that expensive saddle, and all that!"

Matt Smith nodded somberly. "His money doesn't come from the ranch. You know that; so do I."

"Then he must be darn lucky at poker. And this would-be farmer ... this Jim Parker."

Matt Smith dropped his hands. "Parker? And what about him?" The foreman's voice seemed suddenly to be very sharp.

"I rode past his camp. He jumped me in the brush. He told me you had ridden in ahead of me."

"Yes? ..."

"Something is wrong here, Matt. Something phony. Parker is the first man who ever tried to homestead anywhere on Circle N. And even an idiot knows it can't be done."

"What do you think, then?"

She stood straight. "I don't know, Matt. But somehow I can't believe him when he said he'd homesteaded to have something to trade for a job at Circle N. I just can't put a man like Jim Parker into such a role."

"Then where would you peg him?"

"I don't know, Matte. But for some reason I have a strange, empty feeling."

"Your imagination, maybe. This drouth – cattle dying –"

She shook her head slowly. "No, Matt, it goes beyond that. I don't seem to be able to shake it. It's nothing new, Matt. I've had it now, off and on, for a couple of years, maybe longer."

Matt Smith sighed deeply. He took both of her small hands in one big one.

His voice was very low. "Don't give up, Clara. You've always got Matt Smith, you know."

His gnarled right palm stroked her glorious red hair. Her hair was soft and fine and clean. Wisely he said nothing but he kept on stroking her hair.

And his blue-steel eyes, narrowed slits, stared into the gathering dawn.

Ten

Jim Parker broke camp that same morning. He loaded his grub and personal things in the wagon, hitched up the team, and headed west.

Gradually the country grew rougher. Savage deep canyons cut down from the foothills of the Big Bend mountains.

He drove as far as he could with the wagon and then abandoned it in a gully, loading his meagre supplies onto one of the extra horses. Nine o'clock found him making a camp at the toe of Lightning Mountain on a sandbar on the north bank of the Rio Grande.

Logic told him to stay close to the river. For the heroin and opium, he knew, came from the south out of Old Mexico. And to reach the United States, it had to be transported across the Rio Grande.

But at what point? And who was moving it?

Anger touched him, hardening his tanned, wind-battered face. This anger was directed toward himself. He'd made no progress toward finding out who was moving this ugly dope. The only thing he'd done on this range was to make enemies.

Carter Davis, for one. Widespan Nelson. Bob Wiley. And maybe Clara Davis? He didn't like this latter thought one bit.

Fatigue pulled at his sinews. He'd been up all night. Yesterday morning had been a rough one – that terrible beating he'd taken in Circle N's yard.

He put two horses out on picket. Then he saddled the third, a big bay, leaving the cinch slack, and tied the horse to a small sapling. He kicked a circle of rocks together on the sand. Twigs were around and soon his coffee-pot was boiling. His big skillet came out. He fried bacon and made hotcakes. Then, hunger satisfied, he unrolled his bed-roll under the shade of a live-oak and lay down. And the next thing he knew he was coming awake, body drenched with sweat.

He glanced at the sun, reading it at about two o'clock. Then he lay in silence, listening, but he heard no alien move. Dense heat clung to the Texas soil. Live-oak trees drooped in waterless exhaustion.

Here the Rio Grande was dry except for a small pot hole of water. He led his horses to it and watered them. The water was muddy but it was water and the horses drank despite the mud. He gathered his grub and belongings into a piece of canvas, pulled in the four corners to make it a bag. He threw a short length of rope over the limb of a live-oak. The other end he tied to the top of the canvas bag. He pulled the sack up into the tree and tied the loose end around the tree's trunk. No marauding bear would get his grub-supply.

This done, he mopped his sweaty forehead. Heat or no heat, he had a job to do, and it was time to get about it.

He checked his rifle. A bullet in the barrel.

He mounted and rode down-river.

Occasionally he came to a pot-hole of stagnant water. Invariably these were surrounded by bony Circle N cattle. He saw the carcasses of Circle N cows and steers that had died of starvation.

Tracks showed that cattle passed back and forth between the American side of the Rio Grande and the Mexican side. These tracks told him nothing else.

He judged his camp was about ten miles upriver from the towns of Cardenas and Bravo, on the Mexican bank.

He rode down-river about six miles, then swung north into the brush. Within a mile, he'd shot his first coyote. The coyote had been trotting along the base of a hill. One shot had sent him rolling and dead.

Jim hung him by his spread hing legs to a tree limb and skinned him out. From what he'd heard Sheriff Clem Harkness paid the bounty money.

Suddenly, he tensed, knife poised. South in the brush a horse had moved. Quickly he was in the deep brush. He stood with his back against a tree, rifle half-raised to cover the dim trail.

The rider came into view. He lowered the rifle, staring at the rider, now about a hundred feet away.

Martha Worthington wore a flat-brimmed black stetson. Her blouse also was midnight-black, as was her split riding-skirt. Black well-polished boots. And she rode a black horse.

Jim said, "This way, Miss Worthington."

Surprise made her set her horse on his haunches. She whirled him, faced Jim, anger in her face.

"What're you tryin' to do! You scared me half to

death, Parker!"

Jim grinned. He went forward, rifle under his arm.

She had no reason to be here – or had she? Something definitely was out of kilter; the pieces of the puzzle didn't fit.

"It's a hot day, Miss Worthington. Too hot to ride out for pleasure."

"I was looking for a clean swimming-hole in the Rio. I heard a shot and rode this way out of curiosity.

"I killed a coyote. Was just skinning him out."

"Then where to?"

"Cardenas. Turn in the pelt and get my dollar."

"I'll ride back with you," she said. She frowned. "But why this sudden desire to become a coyote-hunter? Seems to me you got out of that poker game last night with some extra change?"

"I'll prob'ly lose it tonight … if I play." He studied her for a moment. She was, he decided, a beautiful young woman, but for some reason she did not appeal to him very strongly. He judged her to be somewhere in her early twenties, but the lines around her mouth and eyes, it seemed to him, were a little too pronounced, and her eyes sometimes held a strange hardness.

She remained in her saddle, watching him finish his skinning-job.

"How's the medicine-show business?" he asked.

She gestured. "Not too good. With this drouth there isn't much money floating around. My dad and I might move south deeper into Mexico."

"More money there?"

"Yes. Grass down there. Higher elevation and

more rain. The dry area runs out about a hundred miles south in Mexico."

Jim played momentarily with this fact. Why didn't Circle N move its weakest stock south into Mexico until the drouth broke? But perhaps the cattle were too weak to make the trek?

"I'll cross the river this evening and see your show, Miss Worthington."

She flashed a nice smile. "I'd be happy to have you, Mr. Parker." White teeth gently nibbled a nice lower lip. "But it seems to me we decided yesterday when we met to drop this Mr. and Miss business."

Jim grinned. "Okay, *Martha*."

"Okay, *Jim*."

On the ride into Cardenas, she chatted gaily – but said nothing of importance. She gave the impression of being just an ordinary young woman. Then Jim remembered her in the poker game, and he decided she was no *ordinary* young woman.

She had brains besides beauty.

"Do you know Clara Davis?" he asked.

He thought her lips stiffened slightly. "Oh, yes, I know her, but not well! I go with Carter, you know!"

Jim didn't remember hearing this.

"Clara doesn't like me. She's not woman enough to tell me to my face, though. According to her I'm just a *halfbreed* Mexican girl out to snag Carter for his part of Circle N!"

Jim merely nodded.

"For almost a century Circle N has ruled the roost here, they tell me. Marriages have been arranged, I understand – Davis men have married high-class Mexican women. No *peons*. *Hidalgas* only. Mexican women with pure Spanish blood. Carter's mother was such a woman."

"I didn't know. But somewhere an ambitious Irishman must have crossed blood with the Davises, to give Clara and Carter that red hair."

She laughed quietly, the laugh scattering the hard lines about her mouth. "That is a joke!" Her anger was gone now. "I shouldn't have told you that, Jim. I just lost my temper for a moment, so please excuse me?"

They were in Cardenas now. Jim pulled his horse to a halt in front of the adobe court-house. "Here's where I collect my dollar."

"You'll be across the river in Bravo tonight?"

"I'll be there, Martha." He smiled crookedly. "But Carter might not like it. I want no more trouble with him."

"You imagine things." She rode on.

Jim swung down, looped his reins around the tie-rack and took down the coyote pelt. Clinging heat hung to the dust-covered street. Peons dozed in the shade. Siesta time.

Under the court-house's arcade it was a little cooler, but not much. For some reason he thought of the words of a general who'd fought the Civil War in Texas.

"If I owned Texas and Hell," the general had said, "I'd rent out Texas and live in Hell!"

Jim grinned.

Eleven

Sheriff Clem Harkness slept in his swivel chair, runover boots resting on his old desk, his head back as he snored. Carter Davis slept on the office-bunk on his back.

Jim looked at Davis. Then his eyes moved back to the sheriff. And a heavy anger surged into his muscular, saddle-tough body.

Clem Harkness was *supposed* to be a lawman. A man of the badge, the sworn sacred oath – a man whose job it was to be on the job all hours, night or day. The anger changed to rank disgust.

Jim coldly studied the sleeping sheriff. Unshaven, dirty-clothes, a rusted badge pinned to his open, greasy vest. Thin nose jutting from the weak face, the mouth sagging open. The disgust surged back into anger.

He threw the bloody coyote hide, blood-side down, over Harkness' sharp-featured face.

The sheriff came alive with a jerk. Both arms flew up, pawed the pelt from his face; his boots thudded to the floor. Jim caught the coyote pelt as it fell.

For a long moment, Harkness stared at him, a streak of blood across one cheek. A claw-like hand went up and wiped the blood away. His angry eyes took in the coyote pelt.

"What'd you think you're doin', Parker!" His voice was harsh, grating. It brought Carter Davis suddenly sitting upright, hand on his holstered gun.

"You owe me a dollar," Jim said.

Harkness started out of his chair, eyes blazing. Jim backhanded him across the face with his free hand. The blow knocked Harkness back into the chair. Jim pulled the sheriff's gun from holster.

Jim's blow had brought blood to Harkness' hawkish nose. His angry eyes stared up at Jim. He said clearly, "I'll kill you for that, Parker!"

"I'll be waiting," Jim promised.

Carter Davis' wary eyes moved from the sheriff to Jim. "What broke loose?" he finally asked.

Harkness spat the words. "He threw that bloody coyote pelt across my face! When I was sleepin'!"

Davis broke into loud laughter. "The boys in the Casino," he choked out. "What a story!"

Harkness had his breath now. "Why t'heck you do that, Parker?"

"Just because I wanted to. You still owe me a dollar."

Harkness pulled open a drawer in his desk. Jim tensed, thinking perhaps the lawman had another gun there – but the drawer held only scattered papers and a cigar box. The cigar box held some Mexican *centavos* and *pesos*, a five dollar gold piece and some American coins along with a few one dollar bills.

Harkness' trembling dirty fingers picked out two silver *pesos*. He threw them on the desk.

"That's a buck," Harkness said.

"*Americano* money," Jim said.

Harkness slid the two *pesos* back into the box. He threw Jim an American dollar.

"*Gracias*," Jim said dryly.

Harkness leaned back, himself again. "You're only lookin' for one thing, Parker – somebody to kill you!"

"You're a disgrace to your badge," Jim said. He looked at Carter Davis, who'd stopped laughing. "Is this the best Circle N can get as its own private tin-badge?"

Carter Davis came quickly to his feet, hand splayed over his holstered gun.

"Don't rub Circle N's hair the wrong way no longer, Parker!"

Jim shrugged, eyes boring into Davis'. "Circle N is getting rather low, Davis. Somebody ransacked my camp while we were playing poker last night. Stealing is *low down*. But pilfering behind a man's back is *real low down*!"

The insult was there, hanging between them.

Suddenly the sheriff reared out of his chair, barging between them. His bony right claw snaked out, jerking Davis' .45 from leather. He made a lunge for Jim's gun, but Jim quickly stepped back, leaving the sheriff holding only Carter Davis' weapon.

Carter Davis grinned satanically, eyes locked with Jim Parker's.

"You talk like a fool, Parker! Circle N never pilfered your camp! But take a bit of advice, huh?"

"Shoot!"

"I don't know why you're here in Cardenas! I know nothing about you except that you tried to muscle in on Circle N payroll. But I do know one thing, and that for sure ..."

"Yeah?"

"Keep on acting the way you are and we'll be havin' a funeral soon in Cardenas – an' you'll be the gink in the wooden box!"

"Your opinion, and yours alone," Jim said shortly.

Davis walked over and sat on the bunk. "You disturbed my siesta," he said quietly. He swung his legs onto the bunk and lay down and closed his eyes.

Harkness sat down again. He said, "You got your buck. Now why not get out, Parker? Not only of my office – but clear out of Cardenas?"

"Yeah," Jim said, "I'll leave. I'm going across the river to Bravo." He backed to the door, hand on his holstered weapon. "I don't trust either of you skunks the distance I could throw a bull by his tail!"

Davis lazily opened one eye. "Thanks."

Jim grinned as he walked down the shaded porch, bootheels ringing on the ceramic-tile floor. He felt better, now.

He'd made an enemy of the sheriff. He shrugged that away. To him Harkness, and his inefficiency in office, was less than dirt.

He moved out into the blazing sun toward the Casino, for his experience as a lawman had taught him that a saloon was a good place to gather information.

He was walking past the town's only store when Clara Davis came out, carrying something in a gunny-sack he judged to be supplies. "You get around, Mr. Parker."

"A habit of mine, Miss Davis. For your information, I've abandoned my homestead."

"Oh ... You saw the light, then?"

He shrugged. "You could call it that. If you're looking for your brother he's in the sheriff's office, sleeping."

"But I'm not looking for him, thank you."

"Just a thought, nothing more."

Her green eyes held his. "You're an odd man," her red lips murmured. "I don't quite understand you."

"There are times when I don't understand myself, Miss Davis."

Anger touched her lips. "You talk in riddles. Sometimes I dislike you very much. Then other times I feel sorry for you."

"Sorry?"

"Because of your ignorance."

He lifted his hat slightly in arrogance. "Thank you for the compliment." Suddenly his voice was flint-hard. "But if you move your hired hands against me again – like you did yesterday morning on Circle N – somebody is going to die, and I don't think it is Jim Parker!"

"You're a homesteader no longer, you tell me. Therefore Circle N has no reason to use force against you."

"I'm hunting coyotes now. That means I'll move across land claimed by Circle N."

"Coyotes?"

"And wolves, too," he said.

"Circle N can cure that very easily and quickly," she said angrily. "Circle N puts up the bounty money. It can cancel the bounty payments."

"Do you hate me that bad?"

"I don't hate you, Mr. Parker. I dislike your arrogance and cock-sureness. You've thrown the red flag into Circle N's face! And that means there is no place for you in the Big Bend country!"

He studied her for a long moment. "Thanks," he said quietly. He turned to go. She caught his arm.

"Why don't you leave? Why do you ask for Circle N to kill you?"

Before he could answer, a dozen head of bony Circle N steers trotted onto Cardenas' mainstreet. Two riders hazed them. One was Widespan Nelson. The other was Bob Wiley.

"What's this, Miss Davis?"

"For your enlightenment, I'll tell you – though it's none of your business. Circle N is giving those cattle to the local townspeople to butcher."

Jim grinned. "I get the drift, Miss Davis. You got to control the *peons* because the *peons* have the votes to keep your Circle N hand-picked county officials in office. So Circle N has decided to bend over backwards and fill the bellies of the *peons* – for a few days, at least."

She made no reply, lips trembling in anger. Her green eyes were stormy, locked with his quiet gaze.

"You're using the right tactics," he continued. "A man with a big belly never led a mob, you know. And you want inefficient men like Sheriff Harkness to remain in office. Circle N will then retain its slipping power."

"What business is it of yours?"

"None." He spoke truthfully.

Cattle were moving past them now, heading for

the skinning corrals down along the Rio Grande. Widespan Nelson saw him and said, "Bob, you take the dogies down to the chute," and Jim saw Bob Wiley nod. His eyes were on Jim Parker.

Nelson rode an iron-gray big stud. He reined the horse close to the hitchrack. His thick lips moved. "This nester pesterin' you, Clara?"

Anger flared across Clara Davis' eyes. "I don't need your help, Nelson! Don't get out of place! You're just a hired hand on Circle N!"

Nelson's lips twisted. "I see ..." he murmured. He turned his horse sharply and galloped after the cattle.

Jim said, "I've got just one thing to say, Miss Davis?"

"And that?"

"You're a beautiful woman, I think you are the most beautiful woman I've ever seen. And you're still more beautiful when angry!"

Her eyes softened. She said quietly, "That was a very nice compliment, Mr. Parker."

Their eyes met, held. And Jim thought he read something in her sea-green eyes; he figured that what he had read there had only one name: loneliness.

He lifted his stetson slightly.

Then he continued down the street. As he entered the Casino, he glanced back.

She stood in the same spot, watching him.

Twelve

Cattle were moving through the brush, Circle N cattle. They smashed through *manzanita and chamiso*, wide horns back, running as though the devil breathed hot fire on their rumps, running under the silent Texas moon. Spilling over ravines, lumbering wild-eyed across gumbo flats, working always toward the Rio Grande.

Carter Davis pulled in his rearing, plunging black gelding, the animal fighting the cruel spade-bit. A rider had come in from his right.

Widespan Nelson rode a sorrel horse. His arm was encased in a black cloth sling.

"Ain't we runnin' them kinda fast, Carter? These cattle ain't got much strength, you know."

"Once they cross the Rio Grande, then they can take it easy!" Davis snapped. "Get back to your position and pound them hard over the trail!"

Nelson shoved back his black hat. "I don't quite foller you tonight," he said. "Usually we work these cattle south slow and easy so they'll have strength enough to trek the hundred miles to grass in Mexico."

"You're workin' for me!" Carter Davis snapped. "I'm not workin' for you, *sabe*!"

Nelson merely grinned. "You got a sand-burr under your tail. And it was put there by this fella Jim Parker!"

Carter Davis leaned suddenly forward.

"You just keep your big mouth to yourself, Nelson, or by hades I'll cut your wind short – with a .45 slug! No man's talkin' that way to Carter Davis an' gettin' by with it!"

"I meant nothing wrong, boss. Just a joke, nothin' more!"

"Why do you think this Parker bucko has the Injun sign painted on me, Nelson?"

"Damn it, Carter, I said it was just a joke!"

Carter Davis shook his head slowly. "You're craw-fishin' now, an' you know it! What was behin' your words?"

"Well, this Parker gent might be a lawman – a Ranger –"

"You're right on that angle. I still figure that homestead entry stuff was only a blind. But Bob searched his warbag – found nothin' pointing to him totin' a badge ..." Davis thumbed his bottom lip idly. "He's moved camp, too. Martha met him up-river today."

"He's a coyote hunter now, remember?" Nelson's voice carried heavy sarcasm. "Carter, we got to get shut of this Parker gent! We got to make sure, man! This thing pays us money – and lots of it. Selling Circle N cows to that Mexican dope-runner, gettin' dope to tote back to this side of the border – Shucks, man, they hang cow-thieves here in the Big Bend region!"

Carter Davis rocked in silent laughter. "Nelson, how dumb can you get, man? These are Circle N cattle! I'm Carter Davis. My ancestors built up this spread. Did you ever hear of a man dangling at the end of a rope for selling his *own* cattle?"

"But that will your ma left – They ain't your cattle, Carter. They're your sister's stock –"

"One thing you don't know, Nelson. Down in Cardenas today Clara said she'd give me half of Circle N, and break that danged will."

"Did she do it?"

"She would have, but that danged lawyer wasn't in town."

"Maybe she knew he was gone?"

"Maybe you're right, Nelson. But we got cattle to move – not set here jawin'!"

They had moved the Circle N cattle off Whispering Mesa, not knowing that last night Clara had ridden that part of Circle N range and wondered how so many head of cattle had happened to be bunched in that particular place. Nelson and Bob Wiley had discreetly headed Circle N cattle toward Whispering Mesa for a week now.

Now Bob Wiley rode out of the hanging dust, a black bandana shielding his mouth and nose.

"What's holdin' you boys up? We got stock to move."

Carter Davis grinned. "Widespan's gettin' cold boots."

Wiley laughed shrilly. "Ever since this Parker bucko outdrew you and put that slug through your shoulder, you been shiverin' in your boots, Nelson! I can't speak for Carter but if you get cold boots on me, I'll give you more than Parker gave you – and it won't be in your shoulder!"

Savage anger ripped across Widespan Nelson's

huge face. His right hand dropped to his holstered gun. Without warning Carter Davis leaned from saddle. The butt of his quirt cut down, smashing across Nelson's huge wrist.

"No gunplay, savvy!"

Nelson rubbed his right wrist with the fingers emerging from his shoulder sling. "I was goin' kill this Parker bucko," he said quietly, "but now maybe I'll kill you, Carter!"

Carter Davis laughed. He put an arm around the man's wide shoulders. "Look at it this way, Nelson. For four years now you an' me an' Bob has worked this deal, an' we all got a dang fine pile of gold down in the Mexican bank in Saltillo. We got to pull together, not apart."

Nelson softened, smiling suddenly. "Okay, men, no grudges. Time we hit into the dust again, eh?"

Davis' pocket-watch showed ten minutes to twelve when they came to the Rio Grande. They crossed the river at Soldiers Crossing. Here for about a mile the Rio Grande had a stream of water – not very wide, but wide enough. Half a mile downstream, the water disappeared and ran underground in quicksand.

Disappearance of water into quicksand was a habit of the Rio Grande. When the quicksand beds were moved, sometimes due to high flood waters when flash-floods hit the river miles away in New Mexico, the entire river bottom would be quicksand. And, after the flood had spent its fury, the Rio Grande would be dry for miles – with a strong stream of water hidden and flowing under the quicksand.

Therefore it was logical that where there was

flowing water there'd be no quicksand. Many herds had been completely swallowed up, across the years, by the quicksand bars, if the trail-boss did not understand and know this fickle river.

"Chouse them into it!" Davis ordered.

Widespan Nelson rode close, bullwhip coiled around saddle-fork. "They want to drink, man."

"Let 'em gulp water on their way across. Ain't good to get them belly-logged with water, anyway – seein' they got so many miles ahead of them!"

Nelson shrugged. "You're the boss."

Bullwhips popped savagely. Steers, cows and bulls lunged into the water, grabbing mouthfuls as they crossed. Nelson rode west flank; Bob Wiley rode right flank. Carter Davis took up the middle.

He rode back and forth, bullwhip slashing, horse splashing muddy water.

When the dregs of the herd had clambered up the Mexican bank of the Rio Grande, Carter Davis reined in and pulled off his boots, pouring water out of them.

Now that the Circle N cattle were on Mexican soil, they drove them more slowly – within two miles, they came to a huge lava bed black against the desert soil, a wide endless area of solid volcanic flint that left no tracks.

Three miles out on the lava bed they met four men. Carter Davis held his right hand high and Bob Wiley and Widespan Nelson rode in.

Bob Wiley said, "Just our Mexican friends takin' over the herd."

The riders moved in and one said, "Another herd through." He was a tall, bony-faced Mexican, apparently the leader of this group. "How many head, Davis?"

"Three hundred and twenty-six, Don Enrique. Want to run a tally?"

Don Enrique ran an experienced eye slowly over the herd. "I'll take your word." He had a set of saddle-bags lying across the fork of his Mexican saddle. He tossed these and Carter Davis caught them. "You'll find the stuff in there, as usual, Davis."

Davis asked, "Any trouble?"

Don Enrique de la Vega laughed shortly. "The usual rumors, Davis. The boy that brought that stuff up from San Luis Potosi hinted that maybe the *rurales* had eyes on me." He shrugged nonchalantly. "But *rurale* eyes have been swung my direction many times."

Cater Davis knew full well what Don Enrique meant. Twenty years ago the *Emperor of Mexico*, Maximilian the First, had died before the firing-squad, down in central Mexico. Don Enrique de la Vega had been one of the ill-fated *Emperor's* generals. Somehow he'd escaped the Mexican firing-squad that had announced to the world, by killing Maximilian, that Mexico had no place for a Hapsburg dynasty on its soil.

Since then Don Enrique had lived in the pale of Mexican law, running in guns and stolen U.S. cattle, sending out dope in return payment for those rifles and cows.

But to Carter Davis, Don Enrique de la Vega had always been honest – always the saddle-bags had contained the correct amount of heroin and morphine. Don Enrique had a profitable business here. He would be the last to kill it by cheating.

"You know any Texas Rangers?" Davis asked.

Silent laughter rocked the bony *bandido* in saddle. "What a question to ask," he said in liquid Spanish. "Me, all my life I have fought the Rangers! Why do you ask, *muchacho mio*?"

Carter Davis described Jim Parker.

"I do not know such a Ranger," the Mexican said, shaking his head. "I think your fears are grounded on air, *hombre*!"

Relief surged through Carter Davis. "Thanks," he said quietly. "We'll have another herd ready for you a week from tonight. You'll be here?"

"With my men."

Soon the Mexican cowpunchers and the Circle N cattle were out of sight, absorbed by the dark lava beds, and Carter Davis and his two men were riding northeast, heading toward the Mexican town, Bravo. Now a lone rider came toward them.

Guns leaped into fists. Then the rider came closer and Davis said, "Martha."

Guns glistened, found holsters.

Davis asked surlily, "Why are you late?"

"That Texan – The tall one … Jim Parker."

Davis reached forward. His fingers were steel talons on her wrist. "What about this tall Texan?" His voice was a savage croak.

She stared at him, surprise in her black eyes. "Carter, what's wrong, darling? I was only going to say that Parker rode across the Border about nine this evening. He loitered around my father's medicine show. He seemed to want to be near me, talk to me all the time."

"You look at him twice, Martha – and I'll kill you both!"

Anger rimmed her words. "I'm not looking at him twice – or even once, for that matter! You talk like a locoed fool, Carter. But because of him, I had a hard time sneaking out of Bravo."

Carter Davis dropped his hand. "Are you sure he didn't trail you?"

She laughed shakily. "Trail Martha Worthington! Who knows every dog-trail in this section of Mexico and across the line in Texas! Of course, he didn't trail me!" Her voice softened. "Carter, you're afraid this Parker is a Texas Ranger, aren't you?"

Anger smashed into Carter Davis' words. "For four years, we've been workin' this cattle an' dope business – and it's paid off and paid off good, for all of us. I'm usin' what little brains God gave me! And it's only logical that somewhere along the line the Uncle Sam boy an' the Rangers an' even the *rurales* might get suspicious."

"Then you got to do one of two things," Martha Worthington said. "One is bury your stupid jealousy."

"What'd you mean by that?"

"Let me work on this Parker gent. He might be a Ranger. You're a man – you'd never find out! But a woman – playing up to him … Many a man has been tipped upside down by a woman."

Davis' eyes became slits. "And the other way?"

"Ambush him. Either in his camp or on the trail. Nobody would find his grave."

"She's got a strong point," Bob Wiley cut in.

"His camp would be the logical place," Carter Davis said. "But where t'heck is his camp?"

"Up the river, I'd say," Martha Worthington

Davis turned on stirrups and faced Bob Wiley. "Head up the Rio, Bob. Find his camp. Kill him from the brush. We don't know if he is a Ranger, for sure – but we got to get shut of him!"

Bob Wiley said slowly, "He's a dangerous man, Ranger or no Ranger. He can handle his short-gun. He showed that when he sent a slug through Widespan here. What's in it for me?"

"You're makin' money!" Carter Davis' voice was glacier-cold. "You never had so much money before in your danged life! Your bank account down in Saltillo runs into four figures!"

"One hundred bucks, Carter?"

Davis grinned and said, "Fifty, Bob."

"Okay."

Bob Wiley rode northwest, heading for the Rio Grande. Widespan Nelson shifted in saddle, stirrup-leathers creaking. "Me for the home ranch." He rode straight north, leaving Martha Worthington and Carter Davis alone. Martha reined her horse close. Her arms went around Carter Davis.

Their kiss was long, ardent.

Finally they broke.

"Better tie those saddle-bags onto the back of my saddle, Carter. I'll take the dope to our medicine wagon. Don't you think it's about time my father and me move the wagon north to Alpine and get rid of this stuff? We got quite a haul in that hiding-place under the wagon floor, you know."

"Let's make one more raid, Martha."

"And then, darling?"

Davis stood high on stirrups, gaunt face showing elation. "That stupid sister of mine! Her conscience is bothering her, I guess. Wants to give me one-half of Circle N, and Circle N is dead – out for good, unless rain comes danged soon. If she only knew –"

Martha Worthington laughed deeply. "One more raid then, darling?"

Davis settled back in saddle. "One more, then your medicine wagon moves north. We get our money from this stuff in Alpine. Then we'll head into Mexico. I'll buy you the finest rancho in Jalisco state. We'll live like a Davis should live – Mexican *hidalgos*. A huge rambling house, cattle over a hundred hills."

His voice trembled with savagery that sent a cold spear of ice through her veins, chilling her blood. His eyes swept hungrily across her immobile, darkly-beautiful face.

"What's the matter, *Querida*?"

She shrugged daintily. "I think it's time we headed for Bravo. We split a mile out of town, as usual, and ride in separately, darling."

Suddenly passion tore at him. He pulled her close with steely arms, smashed his lips down on hers.

Neither knew that a man watched them.

This man had left his horse two miles to the west, hidden in a gully. Under cover of the thin brush, he'd sneaked close on foot, limping on his right foot.

And his eyes were frozen steel.

Thirteen

Jim Parker had trailed Martha Worthington out of Bravo.

His logic had been simple. Martha Worthington had openly admitted she was going with Carter Davis. What meagre clues he had pointed toward Circle N. Carter Davis was a part of Circle N.

But so was Clara Davis, logic told him. Therefore if Circle N smugged in dope, Clara Davis would be involved. That thought brought him discomfort.

He tried to shrug it aside. He was a Ranger out on a dangerous mission, and had to be impersonal.

But the galling thought of Clara Davis, behind bars in a federal pen, brought a tightness to his muscles.

He was hiding in the shadows when Martha Worthington rode her horse out of the barn. Because of his police-training, he noticed immediately no saddle-bags were tied behind the cantle of her saddle.

She rode east. He knew the trailing would be difficult, for the *chamiso* brush was a high as a man on horseback. He lost her three miles east of Bravo.

He returned slowly to the town. The Worthington medicine-wagon was parked in the town *plaza*.

Martha had introduced him to her father, Hank Worthington, a bony-shouldered, middle-aged man. He looked like a man who'd spent his life in a saddle. He was the last person in the world Jim would pick out to give a carnival pitch-spiel.

While Martha had been at the wagon the young bucks had crowded around, lured by Martha's beauty. But, even then, sales of colored water and knick-knacks had been little, if anything. If the Worthingtons were eating off their medicine-wagon sales, then they must have been existing on Mexico's cheapest commodity – *frijoles*. Beans.

"Ain't you the hombre who shot down Widespan Nelson?" Worthington's sunken eyes had been sharp Bowie knives against Jim's face.

"Had to do it," Jim had admitted. "Either I'd knock him out of the fight, or he'd kill me."

"All over that homestead, eh?"

"Yeah," Jim'd said. "Over that homestead."

"How come you settle on such a worthless piece of land?"

Jim had shrugged. "Filed papers on the homestead up in Pecos. The boys in the office there said this was good farming country."

"No money in this danged town," Worthington grumbled. "Guess we'll have to move the wagon come a few days or a week."

"Head south into Mexico?"

"Dunno for sure, Parker. Might head up around Alpine an' the Fort Davis Mountains. Not much money in Mexico."

Martha had come over to her father. "Dad, I'm going home to bed. I'm tired." She'd turned a radiant smile on Jim. "So nice you came over this evening, Jim." Her touch had been light on his forearm.

Jim had taken her elbow. "I don't want to make Carter Davis any madder toward me than he is. Safe to walk you home?"

"Carter and I are not engaged, you know."

The Worthingtons lived in a small adobe house on the outskirts of Bravo. She quickly pressed his hand and went inside. He started back toward the *plaza* and the medicine-wagon. But once around the corner he ducked back through the alley and flattened against a building, watching the make-shift barn behind the Worthington *casa*.

Soon Martha Worthington came from the house's backdoor. She had changed in to a black blouse, a riding skirt, also black, and riding boots. She entered the barn and soon came out riding a dark sorrel horse.

Now, upon returning to Bravo, Jim hid his horse in an abandoned shed, down the alley from the Worthington barn. Again he took his station where he'd been hidden when he'd seen Martha ride out.

Gradually the town of Bravo became quiet. Only occasionally a dog barked or a *burro* brayed.

A shadow materialized on the walk in front of the house. He recognized the stoop-shouldered form of Hank Worthington. Then the house hid the man. Evidently Worthington left his medicine-wagon each night in the *plaza*.

He settled back again. Now a lamp showed dimly from the one high window in the back of the adobe *casa*.

Jim was just about to give up when a horse and rider came down the alley. Instantly he recognized the dark sorrel horse and Martha Worthington.

She rode on to the door of the barn. She unsaddled, throwing her saddle over the rack, turning her horse loose. The horse, glad to be free, trotted by Jim, smelled him for the first time, and snorted loudly.

Martha stood at the saddle-rack, taking saddle-bags off the saddle. The horse's trumpeting sound brought her tensely upright. Her eyes probed the dark area wherein Jim Parker was hidden.

Jim remained silent, muscles screaming, hardly breathing. For a long moment, she stared at his hiding place. Then she finished untying the saddle-bags. She threw them over one shoulder and entered the house.

One thought hammered on his brain. When she'd ridden out she'd had no saddle-bags. But now she'd just carried a pair of saddle-bags into her *casa*. *Somebody* had given her those saddle-bags.

Who?

He wondered if he could sneak into the house after both were asleep and get the saddle-bags. But that idea was illogical. The cabin was very small. The slightest movement would bring somebody awake.

And maybe he had the thing figured out all wrong. Maybe she'd crossed the Rio Grande to Cardenas ... But no, she'd ridden east, and Cardenas was across the Big River, to the north.

The light went out in the adobe house.

There was nothing he could do but return to his horse. The night was hot with high humidity. He'd stop in at a *cantina* and have a cold beer, if there was such a thing in this sun-baked Mexican town.

He dismounted in front of the *Cantina Real*, the Royal Saloon. Half a dozen horses stood dozing at the hitchrack. The inevitable poker game was running. Three men were at the bar drinking.

Two were squat, barefooted peons, nothing more.

But the third was a tall Mexican. Their glances met for a moment. Jim found himself looking into midnight-black hawkish eyes, stern and tough. Then the tall Mexican returned his gaze to his mug of beer.

This was no run-of-the-mill Mexican, no peon. The man's boots were brush-ripped, and he wore leather shotgun chaps that clung to his strong, long legs. His shirt was black, faded blue in spots by the blazing sun. He wore one gun, a Colt Frontier .45, tied low on his thigh, the broad hand-made leather belt glistening with cartridges.

Jim said, in Spanish, "You got a beer, *cantinero*? *Frio*."

"*Diez centavos, Senor, y gracias.*"

Jim threw the coppers on the bar. The beer, was rather cool; his throat welcomed it. He twisted a Bull Durham cigaret, watching the hard-faced tall Mexican in the dirty back-bar mirror.

He was surprised to see the Mexican pick up his beer and move down-bar toward him. Tension suddenly played along Jim's spine.

"You are Jim Parker, no? You are the man who shot Widespan Nelson?" He spoke rather good English with only a slight accent.

"I'm the man," Jim said coldly, wondering just what this man wanted. "News travels fast in this country. And who are you?"

Unconsciously, his right hand had dropped to his

holstered gun.

"My name is Juan Ferdin," the man said. "I rode up from the south. I thought there might be a job punching cattle on Circle N."

Jim nodded. "From what I hear, the Circle N is almost broke. The Davises are not hiring."

"You should know, no?"

Jim studied the hard-faced man in the dirty mirror. "I think you're talking about something that isn't your business, *Senor* Ferdin." He spoke in soft Spanish.

Juan Ferdin's eyes hardened momentarily, and the tension grew stronger along Jim's spine. Then the Mexican smiled quietly.

"I beg your pardon, *Senor* Parker." He also spoke in Spanish. "I did not mean to offend. But the beating that Circle N gave you – those six men on one – that does not sit well on either side of the Border, you know."

"My business, and mine only!"

"Again, my apologies. Our glasses, *Senor*, are empty. You will drink with me, perhaps?"

Jim thought of his long lonesome ride back to his desolate camp. "It will be my pleasure, Mr. Ferdin."

They drank that beer in stony silence. But beneath the silence there was no tension now. The two lobo-wolves had stopped circling each other, fangs glistening. They now drank at the common water-hole.

Jim ordered two more. He had to repay the courtesy. This beer was spent talking about irrelevant things – the drouth, how poor local cattle were, would the drouth ever end. Their drinks finished, Juan Ferdin offered to buy another, and Jim politely turned down the offer.

"We shall meet again, Mr. Parker."

Jim murmured, "It will be a pleasure, *Senor* Ferdin," and left. Outside he swung into saddle, turning his horse toward Cardenas.

But he did not cross the Rio Grande at Cardenas. He turned his horse west, riding along the Mexican bank of the Rio Grande. And for some reason, one image kept lingering in his mind.

The stony, rugged face of *Senor* Juan Ferdin.

Fourteen

The rider came from the south out of Old Mexico. Jim Parker saw him, a dot in the moonlit distance, and pulled his horse into the high brush.

Jim slid from saddle, gun in hand. Now who was this rider, hitting this trail at this hour of the night – heading for the American side of the Rio Grande? He walked through the willows and brush, finally squatting hidden beside the trail. He waited.

Again, time moved slowly.

He straightened, muscles aching, frustration surging in his tall, gaunt body. He did not like this way of attempting to gain his objective. A Ranger should ride in, Winchester in saddle-boot, Colt at his hip, and meet his enemy, face to face, gun to gun if necessary.

Without warning, the rider was limned against the southern moonlight – a gaunt, bent-over man, riding slowly, horse at a plodding walk, about two hundred yards away, too far for identification.

But still there seemed something familiar about him.

Jim's gun leaped into his hand again.

Gradually the horse plodded closer. When the man was about forty feet away, recognition stabbed at him, bringing him into the trail, big Colt pistol rock-hard in his fist.

"Going somewhere, Matt Smith?"

Matt Smith pulled his horse to a sliding halt.

He said hollowly, "By golly, if it isn't the nester, Parker!" He reined in, leaning from saddle. Suddenly soft laughter raked him.

"Two nights in a row," he said. "Each night, Jim Parker comes out of the brush and stops me, gun in hand!" His next words were edged with steel. "Is this a game, Parker! Or are you trailin' me, dang you?"

Jim holstered his weapon. "Just accidents, Smith, both times. But I'm wondering why, two nights running, you're out riding this late at night."

Matt Smith's eyes were live coals under grizzled heavy brows. He seemed to be debating something.

But when Smith spoke he merely said, "Figgered for sure that by this time you'd drifted out of the Big Bend country, Parker. Clara Davis told me you'd abandoned your homestead."

"A man can make a living shooting coyotes and wolves for their bounties, you know."

Smith studied him. "I can't fit you into that job," he said shortly. "But … the night's wastin'. So long, Parker."

Matt Smith's horse leaped ahead, scattering sand. Within moments, brush hid him. Jim'd noticed no crutches tied to the man's saddle. That meant that Smith could hobble around now under his own power.

Smith's hoofsounds ran out. Jim sighed and went to his horse. Why had Matt Smith been riding south of the Border?

Last night there'd been meetings with both Smith and Clara Davis. And tonight Smith had again been in saddle, and Martha Worthington had ridden out, too.

Was there a connection here? Had Martha ridden out to meet Matt Smith?

He mounted and rode west along the river. A feeling of danger played along his spine, grabbing his belly. He did not ride openly into his make-shift camp. He never rode openly into any of his camps. A Ranger, in many cases, was a marked man, and this, he felt, was one of those times.

Accordingly he crossed the sandy river-bottom about two miles below his camp, heading north a mile or so into the Texas brush, then he swung east toward the Big Bend mountains.

Within ten minutes, he was stationed under the dark shadow of an over-lapping live-oak tree. As he dismounted, he pulled his rifle from saddle-scabbard.

He tied his horse to a low branch on the tree, removed his spurs and tied them to the saddle, and started climbing the ridge, rifle in hand.

His camp was in the gully on the other side of this spiny ridge. The moon was rapidly disappearing. He hoped it would last until he made sure his camp was unwatched. But here fate ran against him. The moon sank rapidly.

Breathing hard, he gained the ridge's summit. Directly below him, about two hundred yards, was the location of his temporary camp.

There still remained enough moonlight to reveal his two extra horses, dozing on the end of their picket-ropes. For a long moment his eyes searched the area, finding no sign of danger – but because of the falling moon the scene below was very dark, rapidly becoming one big black shadow.

If his camp were being watched, the watcher – or watchers – would hide their horses in the deep brush in some ravine, and come in on foot.

He moved cautiously down slope, careful to dislodge no small boulders. By the time he reached the base of the cliff, the rangelands were dark as pitch. He worked methodically, coming in from the east, rifle at the ready-position. He judged he was east of his camp by a hundred feet or thereabouts.

Suddenly one of his horses snorted.

The sound crashed through the stillness, loud and ominous. Jim settled on his haunches, giving this matter some thought. There was a slight wind but it blew in from the west, blowing his scent away from the animal.

Perhaps a stray wolf or coyote had moved through the brush? Or the horse had smelled a lumbering bear, high on the slopes of the mountains?

Jim listened, ear cupped.

But he heard nothing but the slow wind moving across the wilderness. He moved forward silently again. His intention was to entirely circle his camp.

Suddenly his boot hit a half-buried boulder.

He caught himself in time not to fall down. But he was sure the sound had been rather loud. He moved to his right, squatting under the darkness of a live-oak tree.

He listened. For three minutes he remained crouched, hearing only the jarring pound of his heart. He was getting to his feet, when he heard boots moving toward him.

His blood quickened. His heart was a pounding machine.

Head canted, he listened again. He heard no other sound. Surely his ears, keenly on edge, had betrayed him – manufacturing a sound that did not exist?

Silently he got to his feet, standing with his back against the live-oak. Then, without warning, a man came out of the brush, about ten yards away. But now his eyes had grown accustomed to the darkness. He could see the outline of the man but the darkness did not allow for recognition.

He saw a rather short man with a six-shooter in his right hand. He stood for a long moment, keening the night, looking this way, then that.

Jim watched, hardly breathing.

Suddenly the man turned, back to Jim. He started to move out of the clearing. Jim stepped silently forward, rifle jutting waist-high.

"Looking for Jim Parker, ambusher?"

His harsh words froze the man in his tracks.

"If you are," Jim said, "your search is ended. Jim Parker's standing right behind you!"

Without warning, the man pivoted, body a rigid, tight ball. And from this ball came the flashing stab of gunfire.

Because of his speed, the man got in the first shot. But because of his haste, he shot to Jim's left, bullet whamming harmlessly into the bole of the live-oak. And then Jim's Winchester boomed.

Jim had no time to bring the rifle to his shoulder. To do so would take a valuable second and, in that second, this man would get in another shot.

So Jim shot from the hip.

The Winchester kicked back, ugly and savage. The Winchester's high whine cut into the rear of the man's six-shooter. Jim had spent long hours – and many cartridges – perfecting his rifle hip-shot. And now that practice paid off by saving his life.

For the man stiffened suddenly, bringing his body up straight. He screamed, mouth open, head back. His pistol fell from his loosening fingers to the ground. And he stood like that for a long, terrible moment, tense and frozen.

Jim watched, rifle ready for another shot. His mouth was sand-dry. His belly was a tight, hard fist.

Then tension broke the man's muscles, and he plunged ahead two steps. His knees gave out and he lunged forward, falling face-down on the ground.

The only sound was made by the horses, circling on the ends of their picket-ropes.

Then they quieted. He circled the area, carefully keeping to the brush. This man might have an accomplice. Jim moved with cold sureness, muscles on his back tight. Any minute a bullet might snap his spine.

For thirty minutes he scouted, the thought of the man lying in the clearing bitter gall in his thoughts. He'd not wanted to kill that man. He did not like the idea of taking a human's life.

Sure that no other ambusher lurked in the brush, he returned to the clearing. The man lay as he had fallen on his belly.

Jim rolled the man over, body limp and heavy. He peered at the dead face but the darkness was too thick. He dug in his pocket, got a match, thumbed it into sharp life.

He stared down at a bloodless, silent face. The lips were sagging, loose. Dirty tobacco-stained teeth. He stared down at the face, and then the match burned his fingers.

The face of Bob Wiley.

Fifteen

A harsh fist hammering the door brought Matt Smith out of a broken sleep. "Who's there?"

"Nelson."

"What'd you want, you fool?"

"This gink Jim Parker! He jus' rid into the yard!"

Matt Smith fumbled for his pants, still half asleep. The alarm clock on the table read seven twenty.

"What about Parker?" he growled.

"He rode in leadin' a Circle N horse. An' he's got a dead man acrost the saddle!"

Smith froze, one leg in his pants. "An' who's the dead gent?"

"Bob Wiley!"

Matt Smith cursed under his breath. He dressed hurriedly and walked out buttoning his blue chambray shirt. Jim Parker sat his horse in front of the long Circle N ranch-house. Matt Smith's tired eyes swung over to the Circle N horse Jim Parker had led into the ranch. The body of Bob Wiley was jack-knifed across the saddle.

"Where's Carter?" Smith asked.

Widespan Nelson shrugged. "Not on the ranch, best I know."

"Prob'ly down in Bravo with that Worthington gal of his," Matt Smith muttered. "Where's Clara?"

"Dunno. She ain't in the house or she'd be out by now, I figure."

"What happened between you an' Wiley?" Matt Smith asked, approaching Jim Parker.

Jim told him in terse words. Matt Smith listened, nodding occasionally. He did not seem mad or excited, Jim quickly noticed. Jim had the feeling that something was amiss here. "Miss Davis home?" he asked.

"She might be sleepin' late." Smith spoke to Nelson. "Go in an' see if she's in the house."

Nelson ambled across the porch. When he shut the door behind him, Matt Smith looked up at Jim Parker. "You killed this bucko after I seen you down along the Rio, eh, Parker?"

Jim nodded.

"Glad you didn't mention meetin' me in front of Nelson."

"Why?" Jim shot the question.

"Jus' personal reasons, no more. Well, if Wiley here tried to kill you I don't blame you for killin' him."

"Who sent him out to watch my camp?"

Matt Smith spoke quietly. "I can tell you one thing, Parker – I never sent Wiley out to scout your layout!"

Jim found himself believing this grizzled foreman. "Maybe Carter Davis sent him out?"

Smith shrugged heavy shoulders. "I can't talk for

Carter. He isn't on the ranch. Prob'ly down in Bravo. He's rushin' that black-haired gal with the medicine wagon, you know."

Jim remembered seeing Martha Worthington ride in last night. Carter Davis might have been the one who'd given her those two saddle-bags.

There was nothing he could do but watch his back-trail, work patiently ... and hope.

"This Wiley watchin' your camp don't make sense to me," Matt Smith said. "You've given up your homestead. To me that means you're no longer a danger to Circle N."

Jim remembered throwing the bloody coyote pelt into Sheriff Clem Harkness' leering face. Had not Harkness forced his bulk between them there in his office, Jim and Carter Davis would have fought it out. Had Carter Davis sent Bob Wiley out to kill him because he'd rubbed hard against Carter Davis' stubborn pride?

Memory also brought back the outlines of his fist-fight with Bob Wiley down in the Cardenas saloon. The day he'd thrown Wiley out the door and knocked down Sheriff Harkness walking by.

He remembered Bob Wiley's hissing, angry words. "I'll get you if it's the last thing on earth –"

Wiley might have decided to try to kill him without taking orders from anybody on Circle N. From what he'd heard, Bob Wiley'd had a big reputation as a rough-and-tumble fighter on this range.

Widespan Nelson ambled out of the house. "She ain't in her bunk or in the house, Matt."

Matt Smith rubbed his whiskery jaw. "Anybody see her ride off the ranch?"

"Not that I know of. I'll go to the barn and see if Sonny Boy is gone."

Nelson went toward the barn.

Jim leaned his weight on his off-stirrup. "Well, I delivered this stiff to Circle N, so my job is over." He threw the reins of Bob Wiley's horse to Matt Smith, who caught them in one hand. "To keep things legal I should go down and report this to Sheriff Harkness."

Suddenly Matt Smith asked, "Jus' what you doin' on this range, Parker?"

Jim studied the man. The thought came that this grizzled foreman might be an honest, law-abiding man. Then this was smothered by the fact that he did not know Matt Smith well.

So he merely shrugged. "Hunting coyotes now, Smith," was all he said.

Nelson came out of the barn. "Her hoss ain't here," he hollered.

Jim turned his mount. He had to meet Widespan Nelson as he rode out of Circle N. He drew in opposite the thick-shouldered, ambling man.

Quietly he said, "Take a lesson from this, Nelson. You crossed my trail once and I let you live. But the next time you pull a gun against me you'll be just a dead as Wiley is, *sabe*?"

Jim saw a tremble come into the man's thick fingers. "And that goes for Carter Davis, too," Jim finished.

Nelson's thick lips moved. "Sure looks to me like you're hankerin' for Circle N to kill you off, Parker. An' for the life of me I cain't see why, either."

Jim grinned.

He rode on, a tight spot on his spine. Then the

spot left him as he thought of Matt Smith's level blue-steel eyes. He had the impression that the Circle N foreman was an honest man, not a bushwhacker.

A mile down the trail, he swung his bronc north into the *chamiso*, heading for a high hill about a mile ahead. The crest of the hill was dotted with big limestone boulders. Here he dismounted, horse hidden, and he went to the lip of the hill, field-glasses in hand.

The buildings of Circle N were hidden beyond the rise of another hill. But he could clearly see the trail leading south. He was playing a hunch, nothing more.

Actually he'd expected trouble upon taking Bob Wiley's corpse into Circle N. But he'd run into none. Possibly this had occurred because Carter Davis was not on the ranch. Nor was his sister.

Had Clara Davis been on her ranch, she might not have caused trouble. He remembered his brief talk with her yesterday down in Cardenas. He had gotten the impression she'd seemed a little confused and uncertain.

He figured that neither Sheriff Harkness or Carter Davis would tell about the scene in Sheriff Clem Harkness' office. His actions had thrown the lawman clearly on the defensive. He'd made a fool twice out of Harkness.

Now a rider came from the direction of Circle N. Jim recognized Matt Smith. Perhaps Smith was headed for Cardenas to notify Sheriff Harkness that he, Jim Parker, had killed a Circle N man.

But Matt Smith swung north off the trail, riding along the toe of the butte where Jim was hidden.

Within half a mile, brush and the rolling hills hid the grizzled Circle N foreman.

Matt Smith had found out from the old hostler that Clara Davis had ridden north. Fear pulled at the foreman, setting his face into stern lines. He rode hard despite the heat and his bum leg. Within an hour, he found her.

Clara Davis sat her horse in the clearing called Whispering Mesa. She turned her horse to face him, a puzzled frown on her lovely face.

"Jim Parker just rode into Circle N. About a hour ago. He shot down Bob Wiley. Had his carcass tied across Wiley's saddle."

Clara Davis stared at him. "Tell me about it, Matt?"

He could only repeat what Jim Parker had told him.

She spoke hollowly. "Bob Wiley was a proud man. He rode out to kill this Parker because of their fight in Cardenas. Good luck Carter wasn't home. He and Bob were good friends." She looked at Matt Smith. "What shall we do, Matt?"

"We could ride to town. Swear out a warrant charging Parker with murder."

She laughed shortly. "And get Sheriff Harkness to serve it ... That would be a laugh, Matt. Harkness would never serve it. He's yellow to the tips of his old boots."

Smith shrugged. "You're right, Clara. But Carter might pick up the fight."

"He's twenty-two years old. I can't shield him all my life."

Again Smith was silent.

"There's one thing that bothers me, though.

What is this Parker doing on Circle N range?"

"Huntin' coyotes and wolves, he says."

"That seems a foolish excuse to me. I'm pulling off the bounty on coyotes and wolves. Then he'll have no logical excuse to stay."

Smith changed the subject. "Why did you ride out here to Whisperin' Butte, Clara?"

"There seemed to be too many Circle N cattle bunched here a few days ago. But they sure aren't here now." She scowled. "Where did they go?"

Matt Smith spoke gently. "Cattle move a lot during a dry spell like this. Lookin' for water an' mesquite beans and what little grass there is. They've just drifted away, that's all."

She said, "I guess that's it."

"Let's head back to the ranch," Smith said. "You haven't had breakfast yet, have you?"

They rode toward Circle N. Neither said much. Matt Smith rode slouched in saddle, thoughts bitter gall.

How did you tell a sister that her brother was stealing her cattle? That he was running these rustled cattle south into Old Mexico?

And trading them for dope …

He rode in silence.

There was no way …

Sixteen

When Jim Parker strode into Sheriff Harkness' office that morning, the sheriff's hand went toward his holstered gun.

But already Jim's .45 covered him.

"What'd you want, Parker?"

Jim moved around the desk. He snaked Harkness' gun out of leather. He threw it on the bunk. He holstered his own gun. "Now we can talk better," he said quietly.

Harkness' eyes showed more than anger, Jim read it as *fear*.

"I had to kill Bob Wiley this morning," Jim said tonelessly.

Harkness' dull gray eyes studied him. "Where did it happen – and how?"

Jim told him.

"Why come an' tell me?" Harkness demanded. "You claim it was self-defense. No witnesses were there to testify for you or against you. Everybody knows Wiley swore to kill you. Even if Circle N wanted to file a warrant against you, neither me or the county attorney would let them." Harkness pulled in a deep breath. "An' I know Carter Davis an' his sister. Like I said before, Circle N kills its own snakes!"

Jim said, "Just wanted to make it part of the legal record, nothing more."

"Carter Davis won't take this," Harkness said.

"I'll chance that."

Their eyes locked. Harkness saw a tall, trail-dusty young man, hard lines etched around his eyes, mouth a tight, stubborn line. Then Jim scooped Harkness' .45 off the bunk. He walked to the door, Harkness' hot eyes on his wide back. Just outside the door he dropped the gun. It made a loud metallic ring as it hit the glazed tile floor of the long porch.

Sheriff Clem Harkness remained welded to his swivel chair.

A one-man plague had hit this once-peaceful range. One man alone – a tall tough Texan – was challenging the might of Circle N. And for what reason?

Was it because of the beating Circle N gunmen had given Jim Parker there that morning in the dusty yard of the huge *rancho*?

This was possible. But it seemed far from probable. Perhaps Bob Wiley had ridden out to ambush Jim Parker *not* because of the fight with Parker in the *cantina*.

Somebody might have ordered Wiley to kill Parker.

Widespan Nelson had a reputation on this range as a fast gun-fighter – possibly the fastest man on Circle N with a gun. Yet this same Parker had let Nelson shoot first. And then had sent a bullet that had sprawled Circle N's top gunhand into the dust.

Surely Bob Wiley, who'd been nowhere as fast a gunhand as Widespan Nelson, wouldn't move of his own accord against this Jim Parker.

A tight steel band seemed to gather around the sheriff's chest, choking him and stifling him. Suddenly it seemed that somewhere out on this brush-choked sea of *chamiso* and *manzanita* lurked a deadly, silent enemy.

Harkness leaned back in his chair. He'd never married. He'd sat on this chair almost all his adult life. His hardest work had consisted of getting his county-warrant every month.

Now the long honeymoon apparently was over.

He had a nice bank account in the Cowmans State Bank at Austin. He had only a few personal belongings. He owned no property in Cardenas. He'd boarded with the Widow Ramirez for years.

Suddenly he grew sick of Cardenas. Weary of its dusty ugly streets, its conglomeration of unpainted adobe shacks.

He was picking up his gun outside when Carter Davis came around the corner. Davis wore a beaver Stetson that cost at least a hundred bucks. His shirt was of blue silk. And his black, hand-tooled boots glistened with high polish.

Davis grinned, boyish face clean-shaven. "Playin' ball with your .45, Clem? Bouncin' it up and down?"

Harkness jammed the weapon into leather. "Was checking it and it dropped," he said.

"Lucky it didn't go off," Davis said.

Harkness went into his office, Davis following him. Harkness sank into his chair, head in his rough hands.

"What's the matter, sheriff?"

Harkness lifted heavy eyes. His jowls sagged grayly. "This Jim Parker bucko. He was in here about fifteen minutes back. He shot and killed Bob Wiley last night, Carter!"

Blood receded slowly from Carter Davis' face. He sank down slowly on the bunk, staring at Sheriff Harkness.

When he spoke his voice was hollow. "Where did this happen – and at what time?"

Harkness dutifully recited the information given him by Jim Parker. "And he rode openly into Circle N, too. With Wiley's body across the saddle of Wiley's own Circle N horse!"

Blood had returned now to Carter Davis' handsome face.

"What'd you want to do about it?" the sheriff asked. "Swear out a warrant an' get me to throw the handcuffs on this Parker bucko?"

Davis laughed shrilly. "That is a laugh! You couldn't handcuff a four-year-old child!"

Anger touched Harkness' cheekbones, making them white. He stared at Davis, hate naked in his glistening eyes.

Davis got to his feet. "Where is this Parker now?"

"I don't know. He might still be in town."

"Came across the river from Bravo. Never saw his mount at any tie-rack. But he might still be in town."

Davis started toward the door. Harkness' tired words stopped him, turned him. "Carter, in the name of God – what is this ruckus all about?"

Carter Davis' lips twisted. "I wish I knew – for sure." Then he was walking down the tiled patio toward the arched main entrance of the courthouse. Two hours later, Harkness left the office.

Evidently Jim Parker had left town. Harkness figured Carter Davis had gone out looking for Parker. And had Jim Parker been still in Cardenas, there would have been a shoot-out. Or at least a fist-fight, Harkness reasoned.

Apparently neither had taken place.

A glance at the hitchracks along mainstreet showed no horses. That meant then that neither Davis or Parker were in Cardenas. Sheriff Clem Harkness sighed lustily.

He turned into the *Casino*.

Only two men were in the saloon. One was the bartender, dozing in his chair. The other was a tall, hard-faced Mexican wearing brush-scarred shotgun chaps, run-over Mexican boots, and an old shirt.

Harkness had never seen this Mexican before.

Cold black eyes, glistening like polished bits of coal, swept over Harkness from head to toe, and for some reason the sheriff's blood chilled.

The obese bartender lifted his shaggy head. "Somethin', sheriff?" he asked in Spanish.

"Beer."

Harkness asked, "Carter Davis drop in here some time back this morning?"

"*Si*. He asked about this man, Jim Parker."

"Evidently he didn't find the *Senor* Parker?"

"I think Parker left town before Carter came in. Parker had one beer, earlier this morning, and then he rode out."

Harkness nodded, lifting his bottle. The lukewarm beer felt good in his parched throat. He wondered just how much courage Carter Davis had.

Then his memory went back two years. A poker game here in the *Casino*. And a drifter moving through, gun tied low on his thigh. And words with Carter Davis, accusing him of cheating.

They'd toted the drifter out feet-first for boothill. Yes, Carter Davis knew how to handle a gun, and would use it if circumstances demanded. The stranger had been Black Jack Newcombe, the famous gunman from up around El Paso way.

Harkness killed his beer.

Now the hard-faced Mexican said quietly, "Have one on me, sheriff."

Harkness didn't want to drink with any Mexican except a Mexican friend, and then on rare occasions. A man in public-office had to adhere to the strict cleavage of the color-line. But something in the bony man's eyes made his say, "Well, now, stranger – thank you heaps."

The man's lips smiled. But there was no smile in his glistening eyes. He'd caught the sheriff's hesitation and had read it correctly.

Harkness tipped his bottle. "Don't reckon I've ever seen you around Cardenas before, *Senor_*"

Shoulders shrugged. "First time in town. Came up out of Durango. Times are tough down there. Heard maybe Circle N was hiring."

Harkness shook his head. "No chance of a job there. You'd just waste your time making the ride. By the way, what's your name?"

"My name is Juan Ferdin."

The name meant nothing, but the beer hit the right spot. Harkness hadn't been drunk for about a year now. Suddenly he wanted to get drunk.

The tall Mexican drank beer with him, but the

Mexican didn't seem to get drunk. That was because he killed one bottle to Harkness' half-dozen. As the day progressed the alcohol loosened Harkness' tongue.

"I'm goin' kill this Parker gent," he told the bartender.

The bartender stared through round brown eyes. He glanced along the bar. Other peons and *Americanos* were drinking to escape the outside heat. To a man they'd heard the sheriff's words.

"Next time I see him, I'm going to kill him," the sheriff repeated.

Now a cold voice came from the back door. Jim Parker had just entered. "Well, here I am, sheriff."

Sheriff Harkness tried to turn fast, but his knees almost let him fall. He grabbed for the rim of the bar, not his gun. He stared at Jim. Evidently he had trouble focusing his eyes.

Juan Ferdin said, "He's purty drunk, Parker."

Jim nodded. He came toward the bar. "I can see that, *Senor* Ferdin."

"He is a good man," the bartender soothed, "but he is drunk now, *Senor*. Should I serve him no more?"

Jim shrugged. "That's your business." He stopped beside Ferdin and ordered a beer, watching the sheriff in the dirty back-bar mirror. Sheriff Harkness stared straight ahead, lips bloodless. When he raised his bottle his hand trembled. Jim killed his drink and went outside, leaving by the back door.

Somebody laughed, "You had your chance, sheriff!"

Harkness wheeled on the speaker. "Close your

filthy mouth. I'll kill him ... or he'll kill me!''

About six that evening, Carter Davis dropped in. By this time Sheriff Harkness was stupidly drunk, mouth drooling.

Juan Ferdin saw the bartender beckon Davis to the end of the bar. They held a long, close conference. Davis tossed down a slug of whisky and left by the back door. Harkness had not seen him enter.

Harkness kept on drinking. He set up drinks for the house. His mind was made up – tonight he'd drift out of Cardenas. He'd just swing into saddle and ride north. And never return.

He looked for Juan Ferdin, but could not see him.

Well, it made no never-mind – just another good-for-nothing Mexican, nothing more.

He did not know that Juan Ferdin had searched for Carter Davis in every possible place the man could be in Cardenas. He had not found Davis. Accordingly he rode across the Rio Grande. Davis was not in Bravo, either. Then Juan Ferdin had recrossed to the American side. He circled Cardenas *pueblo* to the east unnoticed. He cut west and watched the trail leading to Circle N.

About ten that night, two riders came from Circle N. One was Carter Davis and the other was Widespan Nelson. Nelson stationed himself and horse in the brush on the west limit of the adobe structures. Carter Davis rode openly into town. He tied his horse in front of the *Casino* but did not enter.

Juan Ferdin was lying on the top of the town store. He saw Carter Davis slink into a dark slot on the north end of main street. Ferdin waited patiently. About eleven, Sheriff Harkness lurched out of the saloon, a jug in his right hand.

A young Mexican boy was with the sheriff. Ferdin heard the lawman say, "Get my horse, Pablo. Bring him here."

The Mexican disappeared.

He returned in a few minutes leading Harkness' saddled and bridled horse. He helped the sheriff, jug and all, into saddle.

Now the lawman was in saddle. "I'm ridin' out to hunt down this Parker," he mumbled. "He cain't make a fool out of Sheriff Clem Harkness."

The sheriff turned his horse, whooped wildly, fed the animal the spurs. The horse's lunge almost dislodged the drunken man from saddle. Ferdin watched, eyes cold.

Harkness rode around the corner. Then came a shot – smashing across the hot night. A shot that came from the hiding place of Carter Davis.

Instantly the town came alive. Mexicans ran toward the spot, jabbering and calling in wild Spanish. Ferdin went to the back of the store and dropped to the ground. He walked toward the corner Sheriff Harkness had just ridden around.

The sheriff lay on the ground, sprawled-out, a bullet-hole in the back of his head. Men and women were gathered around him.

Juan Ferdin knew the man could be nothing but dead. Carter Davis was a crack shot, placing a bullet so accurately, his victim on top of a plunging horse in the moonlight.

Suddenly Carter Davis pushed through the group. He said, "Listen, men!"

They heard the hoof-noises then. A rider drifting

out fast, somewhere in the brush, heading east.

"There he goes, the murderer!" Carter Davis hollered his words. "Ambushed the sheriff, and now he's headin' out!"

"Who did it?" a man asked harshly.

"I saw him shoot him down," Davis said. "I was walkin' along the street. He hid in the alley there. The sheriff never had a chance."

Juan Ferdin listened, hiding his thin smile. He remembered seeing Widespan Nelson hide his horse in the brush. Now Nelson was riding out fast, playing his role in this tragedy.

"Who – shot – him, Carter?"

"I saw the man, I tell you! And it was nobody but this danged would-be farmer – this Jim Parker!"

Seventeen

After leaving the *Casino de Naipes*, Jim Parker rode across the river to Bravo.

He wanted no trouble with Sheriff Clem Harkness. Harkness had the courage of a chicken. Booze in him had been talking, not man-courage.

The Worthington medicine-wagon still stood in the town *plaza*, sides boarded up.

He rode openly to the Worthington *casa*. Hank Worthington was taking his *siesta* in an old canvas hammock hung in the shade between two live-oak trees. He uncoiled his limber length and sat on the edge of the hammock.

His surly voice asked, "Somethin', Parker?"

"Your daughter around?"

Hank Worthington's faded eyes studied him. "You must be hankerin' to get shot, fella? The last two days you've done nothin' but curry-comb Carter Davis' hair the wrong way. Now right in broad daylight you come a-callin' on Carter's woman. Reckon you just wanna get killed an' –"

"That's enough, father!" Martha Worthington's harsh voice came from the adobe shack's front door. "I'm not Carter Davis' *woman*!" She smiled up at Jim. "Won't you come in, Jim?"

Jim wanted just one thing: to get in the house and see if the saddle-bags were still there. And here was his open invitation! "Just riding by, Martha. Thought I'd stop in and say hello."

"This house has thick walls, and it is a little cooler inside. I've made some lemonade, too."

Jim dismounted and went inside.

The floor was packed adobe. A rickety table stood against one wall. The stove was an open hearth. The pottery was clean and the floor swept dustless. Two bunks were at the far end.

Jim could see under both beds. The saddle-bags were not there. Nor were they apparently in any other place in the *casa*. They might now be in the makeshift barn in the rear.

He decided to forget the saddle-bags. He finished the lemonade and got up.

"Well, guess I'd best be riding on, Martha." He laughed softly. "Or else Carter Davis will really be out to nail my hide on his bunkhouse wall."

She stood close to him. Her hair had a nice aroma. He looked down on her well-built form. Her red lips were parted slightly. Her dark, glistening eyes smiled up at him.

"I don't think Carter bothers you too much, Jim ..." Her voice was a soft caress.

She put both her hands in one of his. Her fingers squeezed and a crinkly smile wrinkled her pretty nose.

"I like you, Jim," she said quietly.

Jim's heart pounded. But he didn't put an arm around her and this made her frown slightly. He took his hand from her grip. "That goes for me, too," he said. "*Adios,* Martha."

He went outside and swung into saddle. Hank Worthington dozed on his back, mouth open. Martha waved to him and he lifted his hand in reply.

He crossed the Rio Grande on a sand-bar about three miles up-river from Cardenas. Then, once across the river, he cut at a sharp angle through the brush, heading toward the Circle N ranch.

There were many ways to get dope from Mexico into the United States. A man on horseback, crossing the Rio Grande at almost any point. Or hauling it hidden in a buggy or wagon ... something like the Worthington medicine-wagon!

He thought of the medicine-wagon, sitting in the *plaza* in Bravo. He wanted to look that wagon over. But it might just as well have been in the U.S. mint. It was that well protected. Out there in plain sight with peons moving night and day along Bravo's dusty street, searching the wagon was out of question.

Martha had been putting on an act, he knew. She wanted no part of him. Carter Davis was a dandy, well-dressed, apparently wealthy – from the local leading family, a family of much power that had been, before the drouth, very wealthy. Yet she had played up to him, there in the adobe *casa*. There'd been in his estimation only one reason for this: she suspected him of being a lawman?

What few clues he had, meagre as they were, pointed toward Circle N. Matt Smith had had no reason for riding into Mexico last night. Maybe Circle N cattle had strayed across the Rio Grande onto Mexican soil? But a man didn't hunt down stray cattle at night.

And Clara Davis, too …

There was only one thing to do: keep a close eye
on Circle N. So he rode that direction, taking his
time through the deep brush.

He decided to circle the ranch and come in from
the north. He reached the hill he'd occupied once
before, tied his horse hidden in the shade, then,
field-glasses in hand, he went among the high rocks
and settled down with his back against a granite
boulder.

Because of the hill between him and Circle N, he
could not see the big *rancho*. But he could see the
wagon-road leading to Cardenas. He moved his
glasses in a slow circle.

His glasses moved northwest, then were suddenly
jerked back a few degrees. For a rider had come out
of the brush about a mile away, hazing three head
of cattle ahead of him.

The rider put the cattle into a big clearing. Then
he turned his horse to ride back again into the
brush. And it was at this moment that the glasses
showed him fairly clearly.

Jim could not clearly make out the man's face.
But the way the man rode his saddle, the way he sat
the kak, showed him to be Widespan Nelson.

Nelson now did not wear his sling. He rode easily
in saddle, a cowman working cattle.

The brush swallowed the Circle N rider.

Carefully, Jim swept the glasses over the range
trying to determine if another Circle N man rode
with Nelson.

He saw none.

He searched for green spots that would tell him a
water-hole lurked among the greenery. He lowered

the glasses and frowned. Plainly Widespan Nelson was not hazing cattle close to water. For no water apparently existed.

With difficulty he picked out cattle lying in the shade of live-oak trees. Quite a herd was gathered on the mesa. He wondered if Nelson had driven the cattle there so he could brand the calves. But apparently the man was not doing this. For time after time he hazed more cattle into the *mesa* clearing.

At sundown Nelson returned to the *rancho*. Jim moved silently on foot to the brush behind the barn.

It was about a hundred feet from the edge of the brush to the barn's open wide door. He walked across the clearing, back tight, muscles screaming. Smoke came up from the cook's stove, blue against the dusk. Lights were beginning to come into life in the bunk-house.

The horse-corral was attached to the barn's west wall. Suddenly the broncs must have smelled his alien odor for they circled the corral, snorting and pounding the earth with shod-hoofs.

Jim darted the remaining ten yards to the rear of the barn. He'd just flattened himself against the barn's wall when he heard the bunkhouse door open.

A harsh male voice hollered. "What's bitin' them broncs, Windy?"

"Danger if I know, Nelson!" The words came from inside the barn.

Jim knew then a hostler or somebody stayed in the barn.

"Go check on 'em, you ol' fool! Might be a cougar

sneakin' in for some hoss meat!"

Jim heard boots coming toward the barn's back door. Hurriedly he glanced around. To his right was a big *mesquite* bush growing flush with the barn wall. He leaped into it. Harsh thorns tore at his clothing. One hook-like thorn ripped his right cheek enough to bring blood.

A man came out the door with a lighted lantern. A wizened, bent-over old man, who paused, stood and looked around. His eyes roved over the *mesquite* slowly.

Jim's breath froze.

For what seemed eternity, the seamed eyes studied the *mesquite*, then slowly moved on, landing on the horses in the corral. Jim started to breathe again. His legs ached, thigh muscles tight from crouching.

Then the hostler moved on again, circling the corral. The corner of the barn came in and hid him and his lantern from view.

"What'd you find, Windy?" Widespan Nelson's voice again.

"Not a thing, you dang fool! These cayuses are all right."

At that moment the cook hammered on his triangle, the bell-like notes smashing across the dusk. Jim slowly eased his way out of the thorn thicket. He rubbed the slight blood from his face as he moved along the barn wall to the corner.

Men were streaming out of the bunkhouse toward the cook-hall. The old timer with the lantern was legging it toward the mess-hall, too. That meant the barn was empty, which was just what Jim wanted.

Cautiously, he slipped into the barn, flattening against the wall. Two lanterns were hung on high ridge-beams, dimly lighting the interior.

He saw nothing suspicious. The saddle-racks, now lined with empty saddles; the horses, standing in the half-staffs, some munching hay, others just standing hip-humped, lazy and dozing.

Although he'd made a mental note dismissing the saddle-bags, he found himself wondering if they were here in the Circle N barn. He went to the saddle-rack. Carter Davis' gaudy saddle was missing.

Suddenly he heard a door slam somewhere. He tense against the wall, close to the ladder running up into the haymow. The boots came toward the barn. The owner of the approaching boots would enter the front door before he could clear the back door.

There was nothing to do but climb into the haymow.

He scurried up the ladder. Dust and loose hay covered the floor. He threw himself prone on his belly over a wide crack. The barn below him was clear.

A cowpuncher bowlegged into the barn. Jim recognized him as a Circle N hand. He'd been one of the Circle N men who'd jumped him that morning he'd ridden into Circle N.

The man dug into a saddle-bag. He came out with a whiskey bottle which he uncorked, raised, and drank deeply. Then he replaced the bottle and went out the front door.

Darkness came sweeping in. Jim ached with weariness. He wondered when he'd last had a night of good sleep. He reasoned that his horse was safe, hidden in the brush. Gradually sleep came over him. About two hours later, words below jerked him awake.

He peered down through the crack.

Carter Davis was talking to the old hostler. "Go get Nelson," Jim heard him say. "And you stay in the bunkhouse, savvy? I want to talk to Nelson alone."

Carter Davis saddled a fresh horse, a dark sorrel. He was slipping the bridle on the animal when Widespan Nelson stalked in, scowling.

"Was ridin' a lucky hoss in the poker game, Carter! What's on your mind, fella?"

"Saddle your horse. And come with me."

Eighteen

They were a tough compact group of riders. They plunged along the trail, riding fresh broncs.

Hidden in brush, Jim Parker watched them come.

He counted eleven riders.

Carter Davis rode the big sorrel, solid in saddle.

"One hundred to the gent that kills this Parker bucko!" he hollered.

A pace behind Carter Davis' lunging horse rode the Mexican, Juan Ferdin. Now Ferdin snarled, "Killed the sheriff right under our nose, the lowdown skunk!"

"He'll pay for that!" Davis hollered.

Then they were gone, slanting around a bend in the trail. Brush hid them now. Jim stood for a moment, tall and silent, remembering the conversation he'd heard bewteen Widespan Nelson and Carter Davis, back in the Circle N barn.

"We don't know whether or not this Parker gent really is a Ranger," Carter Davis had said, "but he's waved a red flag in front of Circle N too danged long, the long drink of water! Time we got shut of him, for good. And at the same time, we can get shut of that loud-mouthed sheriff, too."

After they'd gone Jim had scurried down the haymow ladder, got his horse and had trailed them toward Cardenas.

Carter Davis had called upon Widespan Nelson and not Matt Smith to aid him in this nefarious scheme. He could come to but one conclusion.

Matt Smith did not ride with Carter Davis.

Matt Smith rode alone. But still, he rode plenty – covering many miles of desolate brush, and he rode at night. And then Jim remembered Widespan Nelson bunching cattle on the *mesa* that afternoon.

All signs pointed one way: Davis and Nelson were stealing Circle N cattle. He remembered hearing about the will that had left Clara Davis boss of Circle N. Her brother was hitting back at her.

Now where would the cattle go ... after being rustled?

There was only one answer to that: south into Old Mexico. There they would be sold or traded – and traded for what?

Dope, of course!

Matt Smith ... last night, along the Río Grande. Riding north toward Circle N ...

Had Smith trailed a stolen herd south? And there was the case of Martha Worthington, riding out *without* saddle-bags and coming back *with* saddle-bags? Had those saddle-bags contained dope received by trading Circle N cattle?

The whole thing dove-tailed together.

He knew that Carter Davis would take the posse to the west and look for his camp along the foothills of the Big Bend Mountains. Bob Wiley had found that camp. Carter Davis and his drunken riders would also locate it.

He'd look up Matt Smith. He'd throw a gun down on the Circle N ramrod. And he'd make Matt Smith talk.

Smith was probably at Circle N. To see the foreman, he'd have to risk riding into the ranch. He'd use his field-glasses and catch Smith somewhere out on open range.

By killing the sheriff, Davis had made him, Jim Parker, a wanted man – an outlaw. From here on every rifle on this range would be against him.

To stay alive he needed three things: eternal vigilance, plenty of cartridges, and some grub. Carter Davis would not find his war-bag. He had buried it under a boulder back of his camp. In it he had cartridges and a slab of bacon and some flour.

The best thing he could do was remain here until the posse returned. He moved his bronc further back into the brush. Then, rifle leaning against a live-oak, he squatted at the base of the tree, and dozed.

The posse returned about three in the morning. Horses plodded wearily. Riders rode slumped in saddle, whiskey-glows gone. Jim grinned at the woebegone lot.

Carter Davis still headed them, but Juan Ferdin was not behind him. That spot was now held by Widespan Nelson. Nelson had evidently doubled-around and joined the posse.

The last rider led Jim's two extra saddlehorses.

Again, Jim mechanically counted riders.

This time – even with Nelson – there were only nine. That meant that three had left the posse somewhere. Jim guessed they would be watching his camp. Juan Ferdin was not now in the posse, he saw quickly.

The first streakings of dawn were smearing the eastern cloudless sky as Jim neared his camp.

Anger grew his mouth into hard lines. These three men guarding his camp-site would pay, even if it meant taking their lives.

A half-mile from his camp, he rode his horse into a coulee. He tied him there and snaked his Winchester rifle out of saddle-scabbard. He moved silently through the thick brush, rifle in hand.

Within twenty minutes, he was in the brush directly east of his camp. He leaned against a tree, listening. There was no sound.

He wet his lips carefully. Suddenly he spoke in coarse Spanish. "The *gringo* – I think I saw him – in the brush –" He levered a bullet into the air, the sound savage in the dawn. "He went that way –"

"I am coming," a voice said in Spanish. Within minutes, a heavy form ran into view, crashing through the brush. The form kept on crashing. Jim had come in behind and slugged the man hard with the barrel of his heavy Winchester.

He lay silent.

"What is it, Pablo?" The voice came from Jim's left.

"The gringo –"

Jim shot again. Then, bent over, he hurried toward the man who'd spoken.

Now the man slanted around the bend, rifle raised and moved past, peering into the dawn. Jim snaked in behind him. The man heard him, turned, and his rifle roared. But already Jim's Winchester's barrel had come crashing down across the man's skull.

The man's wide sombrero went one direction. His

rifle fell from his hands. Then the man landed in a heap, lying motionless in the trail.

Now Jim had two rifles. He snaked the six-shooter out of the holster. Now he also had two six-shooters. He jammed both under his gunbelt, handles protruding. He threw the rifles into the brush. Then he froze, muscles ice.

For something round and hard had been jammed against his spine. He knew without looking that it was the barrel of a rifle. His brain screamed, Two down, and one to go – and the third is behind me!

A soft voice said, "*Senor* Parker, *no es verdad?*" And instantly he recognized the voice of Juan Ferdin.

He stood stock-still, expecting any moment to feel a bullet thud through his back. Fear left quickly, logic replacing it.

The man had the rifle against him. Ranger training had taught him this was a dangerous thing to do. The proper method was to stand a few feet back of your victim, rifle on him.

For with a rifle barrel directly against a man's body, the man could turn sharply, batting the rifle to one side as he whirled.

Jim prepared to make his twisting motion but, to his surprise, the rifle quickly left his back. He heard the rifleman step back a pace, chuckling softly.

"Now you can turn, *Senor* Parker," Juan Ferdin said quietly. "Sometimes a man forgets, you know. I almost forgot a part of my training when I put that barrel directly against your back. But, *hola*, I remembered in time, *no es verdad?*"

Jim turned, rifle sagging under his arm. Juan Ferdin stood on wide legs, hat pushed back. Dawn lighted the craggy seams of his dark, handsome face. A smile played on his lips, revealing white teeth. That smile angered Jim Parker. And he snapped out, "What's so danged funny, Ferdin?"

"The fact that I forgot, *Senor* Parker. I forgot that you'd gone through much training, a rifle against your back. You twist suddenly, bat the rifle aside, and the bullet plows into the ground! Ah, you learned that, did you now, in school?"

"What school?" Jim's voice was hoarse.

"The school for Texas Rangers, of course."

Jim stared at the swarthy, grinning face. "Now who are you?" he demanded.

The smile widened. "I am Juan Ferdin, of course. Do you not remember me introducing myself, *Senor* Parker?"

"And what *else* are you?"

Juan Ferdin shrugged nonchalantly. "Nothing much, *Senor* Parker. Only a Mexican *Rurale!*"

Nineteen

Huge Mexican spur-rowels made clanking, ugly noises. Carter Davis stopped pacing and pounded one fist against the other.

He stared wordlessly at Widespan Nelson, sitting on the unmade bunk. Nelson seemed interested in studying his scuffed old boots.

"I don't understand this," Davis muttered thickly.

Widespan Nelson raised his big eyes. "You're not the only one who don't, Carter. You got lotsa company!"

Carter Davis whirled. He stared at the huge calendar on the shack's wall.

"Six days since this Jim Parker disappeared. And not a trace of hide or hair seen of him since on either side of the Rio Grande!"

"And it ain't because everybody ain't been lookin' for him," Nelson said. "That hundred buck bounty you put on his scalp for *ambushin'* the sheriff has pulled every peon out of his adobe shack."

"I can see that part of it, Nelson. Everybody alive around here wants that hundred bucks. They don't know that I sent that bullet through Harkness' worthless skull. Only three people in the world know that Parker didn't do it."

"What'd you mean by that, Carter?"

"Use what little brains God gave you, you danged fool! You know and I know – and so does this Parker bucko!"

"I get the drift now," Nelson said slowly. "Parker knows he's framed. And you figure he won't run out until he gets the gents who put the double-cross on him?"

Carter Davis whirled, looked around. He went to the door and went outside. Nelson heard his boots pace around the Circle N's office. Then the door opened and Davis entered, hand on his gun.

"There's nobody around at this hour," Nelson said calmly. "Your sister's in bed – her room has been dark about a hour. Matt Smith is asleep in his shack. The other punchers has all turned in."

"Parker must've got cold boots and skipped the country," Davis said. "That's the only answer I can see."

"He ain't been seen in Mexico, either. No, he's read the handwritin' and drifted, Boss."

Carter Davis bit his bottom lip in thought. "And we've had all our Circle N boys ridin' the brush for him, too. An' nobody's seen his shadow, even. Yeah, he must've left."

Widespan Nelson hesitated visibly. Davis growled. "Okay. Out with it!"

Nelson chose words with extreme care. "Don't figure me for a yeller-belly, Carter. But this thing – well, it's got me worried, Boss."

"What's got you worried?"

"I just cain't lay my hand on it, Carter. But

things has been too danged quiet since that tall gink pulled out. I been chousin' cattle outa the brush to build that Black Butte herd. I ain't seen nothing suspicious but ..." His voice trailed off.

"You feel like the walls are closing in, eh?"

Nelson mopped his forehead with a dirty blue bandana.

"That's the way I feel, Carter."

Davis had had the same feeling for some time now but pride would not permit him to admit this. To the best of his knowledge Clara had been off the ranch twice since Jim Parker had disappeared, and both times she'd gone to Cardenas, not out on the range. He knew because he'd seen to it he'd ridden with his sister.

Matt Smith, to the best of his knowledge, hadn't left the ranch all week, for the foreman had suffered a relapse with his leg.

A week to the night had elapsed since he and Widespan Nelson and Bob Wiley had choused the last herd across the Rio Grande. Tonight was the night due for the present Circle N herd to swarm across the Big River to the rendezvous with Don Enrique de la Vega.

But this ignorant, blundering oaf was right, he now thought. Things were getting too hot here on Circle N. This would be his last raid. But he wouldn't tell Widespan Nelson. Nelson would help him deliver the herd to Don Enrique de la Vega. And that would be the end of Widespan Nelson.

A bullet through the head. From behind, in the broiling dust. His mind flicked across the brush to Bravo and gangling, ugly Hank Worthington. Worthington had served his purpose, too.

But before getting shut of Hank Worthington, the dope in the medicine-wagon would have to be delivered safely to its outlet in middle Texas. Then, with the money ready to be split, would be the time to get rid of Worthington.

Sudden savagery tore across his face. And if Martha objected, there'd be a bullet for her, too, somewhere out in the brush. He was already tired of her. He'd sampled her wares and now his appetite was sated. There were a million Marthas in Mexico.

When he rode south, he'd ride alone.

But he needed Hank Worthington and his daughter until the last of the dope had been peddled. After this raid tonight, he'd drift northwest toward Alpine, and somewhere he'd get rid of Widespan Nelson.

Carter Davis jerked back to reality. "How many head you think you got bunched out there, Nelson?"

"Biggest we've ever got, Carter. Must be all of seven hundred head; mebbe closer to eight. An' that Mex had better have double the amount of junk to pay for them, too!"

"He'll have it."

Nelson glanced at the old alarm clock on the desk.

Twelve-thirty.

"We got to play this safe," Nelson said thickly. "For all we know, Smith an' your sister might be wise. I've got two saddled horses tied in the brush back of the bunkhouse. Both black horses. I've covered the silver on your saddle with black shoe polish so it won't shine. I'll go to the bunkhouse like

I'm turnin' in for the night."

Davis nodded agreement.

For a long moment, he stood silent in the darkness, running over his plan for possible errors, searching each corner carefully. He could see no flaws. Accordingly he went outside. Everything was dark on Circle N except the two lanterns hanging in the barn. He paused for a moment against the wall of Matt Smith's foreman-shack. But he heard nothing so he moved on to where Widespan Nelson awaited with the horses.

An hour later he and Nelson were chousing sleeping cattle to their feet. This night they did not use bullwhips to bring the cattle lunging upward. A blacksnake whip made a popping noise that could be heard for a long distance. They'd agreed to beat the cattle to their hoofs with the ends of their lariats. These made no noise.

Terrified native steers leaped to their hoofs, eyes wide in the dim moonlight. By the time they made the contact with Enrique de la Vega the moon would be bright, Carter figured.

The herd bunched, they pointed the lead-steers southwest, heading for Solider's Crossing on the Rio Grande, about nine miles away.

With only two men to handle the herd, each rider had to ride flank and drags both. Now out of the dust came Widespan Nelson, big as an ox in saddle.

"We got them headed right, Boss. There's that big roan steer on point. He's headin' for Soldier's Crossin' like it was a magnet pullin' him that direction."

"I'm going to drop back a half-mile or so and scout our back-trail."

"Good idea."

This manoeuvre was nothing new. One of them had done this each time a herd had been moved.

The Circle N cattle were wild. Despite their bony condition, they were savage and rough, wanting to fight. Nelson hazed them skilfully, a man born to the saddle, who'd cut his eye-teeth on the butt of a quirt.

Dust rose from the parched earth. It hung in a yellow cloud to mark the passing of the herd. There was no wind.

He'd worked the herd to the north bank of the Rio Grande before Carter Davis materialized out of the dusty moonlight. Widespan Nelson sat his horse on a sand-bar running out into the river, now almost dry.

"You was gone a long time, Boss. I druv these critters alone for at least six, seven miles." He glanced at Davis. "Find anythin' suspicious?"

"Not a thing. Just another drive."

Nelson looked down at the cattle, bunched around a water-hole. "Goin' let them drink a little, eh?"

"There ain't much water in that puddle. They can drink it dry."

Nelson moved in saddle, leather creaking. Davis smiled quietly. This giant was nervous. Well, he'd never see this side of the Rio Grande again, Carter Davis thought wryly.

Finally Nelson said, "Don't you figure we'd better get 'em headed south again, Carter?"

Davis jammed spurs angrily into his horse. Squealing in pain, the horse leaped off the sandbar, racing toward the cattle.

Widespan Nelson followed suit.

Twenty

Three riders headed north, led by a bony, hard-faced Mexican. They spilled across a hard-pan flat, pushing tired broncs hard.

The bony Mexican rode a Zatecas saddle and over its sloping fork hung two saddle-bags. The leather bags bulged with their contents.

Don Enrique de la Vega sighed. Within a few miles – just beyond the toe of yonder long sloping hill – he would rendezvous with Carter Davis and the Circle N cattle. Then would come the long trail back to his rancho, thirty miles south of Saltillo, and the job of changing the brands on the cattle.

Usually he carried three men with him but he figured now two would be enough. And his hawkish eyes stabbed into the moonlight, darting this way and that. He saw nothing out of the ordinary.

Just another delivery, nothing more.

Now he and his riders had reached the toe of the long hill. The black lava bed stretched ahead – sinister and dark in the night.

Then a harsh voice spoke from the shadow of a huge boulder. "That's far enough, de la Vega!"

The words were spoken in rough Spanish. They dragged Don Enrique de la Vega's horse to a sliding halt on his haunches. They brought de la Vega's right hand to the ornate pistol on his right thigh. They pulled his two riders to a dust-scattering stop.

For a long, tense moment, there was no sound – only the labored breathing of leg-weary horses. Many thoughts flashed through the Don's active mind. The man had spoken in Spanish. Had some other Mexicans learned about his trading dope for Circle N cattle?

The Don's voice was a savage croak. "Who speaks there?"

"A Texas Ranger."

Tension left de la Vega. He leaned back in saddle and laughed roughly. "What is this, Senor? A joke? A Ranger has no authority this side of the Rio Grande. And why are you stopping innocent travellers?"

His dark eyes probed the shadow of the boulder but could not make out the form of a man. There was only the rock-rigid voice.

"You are not an innocent traveller, Don Enrique de la Vega."

This man knew his name, too! A cold spot grew on the Don's spine.

"Why do you say that?"

"Because you carry dope, de la Vega. Heroin and morphine in the saddle bags in front of you. And you intend to trade this tonight to Carter Davis for Circle N cattle."

The Don stared. *Madre de Dois*, what was this? This hidden man knew all about his dope-running!

Don Enrique de la Vega's voice was a crow's croak. "You talk as mad as the wind, Senor! Come out and let me see who I am talking to, *por favor*?"

Then behind them came another voice – a voice that spoke better Spanish. "I got them under my rifle, Jim. Walk out and get those saddle-bags. The first one that moves gets a bullet from my Winchester!"

Discretion screamed to de la Vega. He wanted to look behind him but he knew the slightest movement might bring guns booming. This required logic – and the proper unguarded moment.

"All right, Juan," the first man said.

He came out of the shadows now. He was about thirty feet away. He did not carry a rifle. But he had a six-shooter in his fist.

Don Enrique de la Vega's first impression was that this man was very tall. And that was the last idea he had in the world.

For at this moment, his man on his right lost his nerve. He wheeled his horse, gun rising, a terrible scream in his throat.

"This is a trap, *Senor*! They know about the dope –!"

Don Enrique de la Vega pulled his gun. He had no other choice.

But Jim Parker's bullet tore out the Don's brain. Jim shot from a crouched position, heavy Colt kicking his fist – and he shot with deliberateness, cold and icy and sure.

This man was scum, nothing more. Across Jim Parker's memory flashed the blurred, swift image of a woman – a young woman. A woman who'd once been beautiful, responsive to life, smiling and gay.

The dope smuggled into the United States by this man – and others of his low coyote ilk – had made her a living skeleton.

Jaw frozen, eyes ice, he'd placed his shot accurately. Although shooting at a human and not a coyote, he had less compunction about killing the human.

Don Enrique de la Vega's horse reared, pawing air with his fore-hoofs. Don Enrique de la Vega's body thudded into the dust ten feet from Jim's worn boots.

But already Jim had taken his mind and attention away from the dead Don, for a bullet had ripped through his shirt. Dimly he realized it had grazed his right ribs.

His second bullet smashed into the gunman's chest. It drove him from saddle, spilling him. Jim swung his smoking gun in a short arc to cover the third rider. But already the man's saddle was empty.

Jim whirled, staring through the dust. He saw the dim form of Juan Ferdin. The Mexican *rurale* stood on one knee, gun sagging, head down. Fear tore through Jim.

"Juan! They – get you, *amigo*?"

"My – eyes, Jim!"

Juan Ferdin raised his head, rubbing his eyes. The moonlight showed his ghostly smile. "Bullet hit that boulder there. Threw granite dust into both my eyes –"

Jim suddenly breathed easier.

"There's blood, Jim. On your shirt –"

For the first time, Jim became aware of his throbbing ribs.

"Don't think it broke my ribs," he said.

Juan Ferdin got to his feet. "I'm getting my canteen – Going to wash out my eyes –"

"I'll look over these stiffs," Jim said.

His gun and that of Juan Ferdin had extracted deadly toll. All three Mexican smugglers were dead. Perhaps the Circle N riders were close enough to have heard the gunfire. For a long moment his slitted eyes swept across the dark bed of igneous rock.

Nothing moved out there.

He caught the three Mexican horses and tied them to a live-oak tree. Later on they would come back for them ... if he and Juan Ferdin lived through this night.

He picked up the saddle-bags thrown from Don Enrique de la Vega's cayuse when the horse had fallen over his bridle-reins.

Jim tossed Juan Ferdin the saddle-bags. "I guess this is the junk," he said. "The whole dirty deal makes me so sick at heart I don't even care to open a saddle-bag."

Juan Ferdin tossed the bags over the back of his saddle. His long supple fingers tied it down with the saddle-strings. "Couldn't be anything else, Jim. What'll we do with these carcasses?"

Jim shrugged. "Far as I'm concerned, the buzzards can have them."

But Ferdin shook his head violently. "That we cannot do, Jim. They are the sons of good mothers, just as you and me. Somewhere in some little Mexican *pueblo* an aged mother weeps for a wayward son. And they are the children of God, too – like you and me."

"We'll send a crew out from Bravo with a wagon," Jim said.

Juan Ferdin chuckled. "I have two *rurales*

watching Hank Worthington. Two more watch his so-called medicine wagon. But the girl Martha is free to ride out of Bravo. We have to catch her in the act of taking the dope to her father."

Jim had lived like a hunted coyote the last week. Most of the time he'd been with *Rurale* Juan Ferdin in Old Mexico laying the groundwork for this raid.

He crossed the Rio Grande into the United States but a few times. One time he'd waylaid Matt Smith in the Texas brush.

He'd come in behind the grizzled Texan, gun in his fist. Their conversation had been brief but to the point.

Matt Smith knew about stolen Circle N cattle being driven south. And he knew they were being rustled by Carter Davis and Widespan Nelson.

"Bob Wiley used to ride with them, too, Parker. But your bullet took that o'nery son out of the deal, thank Moses!"

"How come you get wise?"

"Jus' noticed Circle N cows was disappearin'. An' I had a hunch they wasn't dryin' that fast from the drouth. So ... I kept my rump in my saddle, an' did some night ridin'."

"Does Clara Davis know?"

"I don't know for sure. Sometimes I suspect she does an' other times I think she don't. But Clara Davis is not only beautiful, Parker – she's got plenty of brains. And she keeps certain things to herself. But she's been in a saddle a lot lately like that night you jumped her."

"She could louse this whole thing up, Matt. She find out and jump Carter and Carter get word south to this Enrique de la Vega – and no more dope up the trail until things quieted down. And we got to get this de la Vega gent. He's the dirtiest skunk in the deal. He's the one taking dope north out of Mexico."

"He more important to you and this *rurale* than Carter Davis?"

"I think so. Without de la Vega, Carter Davis'd have no dope."

"I'll keep an eye on Clara, Jim. But I know one thing – she's been watchin' Nelson bunch them cattle on that mesa. Hades, I think she's wise, Parker."

Jim said slowly, "You'd better tell her all, eh?"

Matt Smith's seamed face showed bleak despair. "But she might warn her brother. Blood is thicker than *aqua*, you know."

Jim realized full well the terrible dilemma facing Clara Davis, once she knew for sure her brother stole Circle N cattle and traded them for dirty dope. And he'd said only, "I'll have to leave that to you, Smith. You know her better than I do."

Two days later, Matt Smith had ridden south across the Rio Grande into Old Mexico, Jim saw him through his field-glasses from a high butte.

"She came to me yesterday," Matt Smith said sourly. "She told me she was sure Carter and Widespan were chousin' Circle N cattle south."

Jim's heart sank. "What'd you tell her?"

"I told her I'd known it for some time. But I didn't tell her what I'd seen that night I trailed them into Mexico –"

"Didn't tell her they were swapping cattle for dope, eh?"

"No."

"That's good, Matt. What does she plan to do?"

"I told her to say nothing to Nelson or her brother. Stick close to the ranch house and not ride out to gather suspicion. Told her that when they went to move the next herd the Circle N boys an' me would head them off."

"She agreed to that?"

"Yes."

"Best thing you could've done," Jim'd said.

"When they move the next herd, I'll trail in behind them. I'll have to do it alone, Parker. Nobody on the ranch I can trust."

Now Jim became aware of Juan Ferdin's piercing black eyes studying him. And the *rurale* said gently in Spanish. "You are thinking of the girl – Davis is *hermana*, Senor?"

"*Si, Juan, si* ..."

Twenty-One

Once the stolen Circle N herd was south of the Rio Grande, trodding the soil of Old Mexico, the tension ran out of Carter Davis. The Mexican government paid little if any attention to this northern end of Mexico.

Widespan Nelson rode close. "Cripes, these cows are boogery, Boss. Never seen a herd so danged tetchy. One old steer just charged my hoss."

Davis glanced at the moon. "Moon-mad. Seen 'em that way one night on a trail-herd into Dodge. Whole herd went moon-mad. Stampeded an' took us six days or so to re-gather the critters."

Davis wished the cattle would settle down to a walk. But they kept trotting, jostling each other, horns clashing. He rode through the centre of the herd, hoping to slow it down, and a steer charged him, long horns down. Davis leaped his horse to one side. His doubled *riata* whacked down. The steer snorted, pivoted, swung to charge again, then thought better.

Davis fell back to tail the drags. He glanced at the cloud of dust hanging behind them, wishing they were on the lava bed. There would be no dust there on that flinty surface.

He wished this drive was over. He'd be glad when the gaunt form of Don Enrique de la Vega would come out of the moonlight. And there would be Martha, too, ready to take the dope-filled saddle-bags to Bravo town. And he and Widespan would head northwest, leaving Circle N forever – to the point along the Rio Grande where his bullet would crash through the back of Widespan's head!

He thought briefly of his sister.

He had no remorse about leaving Clara. They'd never been close, as an only brother and an only sister should be. She'd get along all right without him.

Better, in fact. With him gone, Circle N cattle would not be rustled. He glanced at the sky. Not a cloud in sight. Circle N would be doomed completely unless rain came soon. And it had to be lots of rain.

He was getting out at the right moment.

Now the lead steers were on the dark lava bed. Igneous rock crunched under their wild hoofs. Carter Davis glanced at the low ridge of hills to the west. The herd would pass along the edge of those flinty hills. And beyond the toe of the hills would be de la Vega and his men.

The drive was practically over.

Widespan Nelson swung in from his left. "Well, we got 'em on the lava bed, Boss. But this is the ringiest herd I've ever druv south. One big noise and –"

Widespan Nelson stopped speaking, mouth flapping open. For from the head of the herd had come a single, roaring pistol-report. It smashed across the backs of the cattle, pounding in their ears.

Carter Davis' voice was a bellowing roar. "That

drunken de la Vega! Full of *tequila*, the fool! He'll stampede this herd –"

Now another gun spouted flame into the moonlight. Gun-roar beat back at them. Already the lead cattle terrified and snorting, had whirled, heading away from this red booming terror – starting to run north toward the Rio Grande and home Circle N range.

"They're stampedin'!" Widespan Nelson screamed. "We gotta get out of here –"

The guns kept on booming, but now their sound did not reach Davis or Nelson. What they heard now was the angry muttering of terrified cattle pivoting back on them, horns clashing, hoofs jarring the earth. The stampede started in a second or two.

Davis heard a man holler, "You ride the east side of the herd, Juan! I'll take the west flank!"

The words bellowed across the cattle. Davis thought, I know that voice, and the answer was outlined in flame on his brain: *Jim Parker*! This was no attempt by de la Vega to stampede and hijack this herd!

This was Jim Parker – and some other rider!

Widespan Nelson had whirled his horse. Now he was low in saddle, streaking east to escape the horns of the lunging, bawling cattle.

Nelson was heading for open prairie. The fool! The western hills were the closest! Once in them, a man would be safe – but time was the essence, and already he'd wasted much of it!

Carter Davis spun his black horse, feeding him the vicious Mexican spurs. The sharp rowels tore into the bronc, bringing a squeal of pain, and blood.

And the horse, ears back, headed for the safety of the hills, running tail out.

Now Carter Davis saw a lone rider, black under moonlight, heading along the west flank of the running herd. That would be Jim Parker!

Davis raised his .45. He had little hopes of hitting the fast-moving rider. The distance was far. The moonlight made for uncertain aim. He let the hammer fall, the heavy gun kicking up, smoke trailing from its long barrel. And his heart leaped.

For Jim Parker's horse went down in a lunging, sliding fall. Then the cattle, swarming in, hid the horse and rider from view. And Carter Davis realized, with terrified heart, he'd hesitated too long to get out of the cattle's path.

For the stampede was on him.

Jim Parker watched from the side of the hill, sick at heart. Davis' lucky bullet had hammered into the fork of Jim's saddle. The blow had come with sledge-hammer hardness, knocking his bronc off-stride. Then the animal, having lost his footing, stumbled over a small boulder, going down in a skidding, squealing heap.

Hurriedly Jim had kicked boots free of stirrups, flying out of the saddle to land on his belly. He'd got quickly to his feet. Gun in hand, he'd run up the slope, working to gain altitude. Then, he'd stopped, breath frozen, staring at Carter Davis.

For the man was trapped in the mad stampede.

Seven hundred head of crazed steers, long horns down, slobbering, insane animals, lunging for home-range, the lava bed trembling under their pounding bovine hoofs. And, caught in its middle, was Carter Davis and his horse.

It lasted but a moment, no longer.

Jim saw mad horns lift the heavy horse in the air and carry him a short distance. Then the horse was gone, disappearing into the mass of sweaty, lumbering backs.

The lunging steers had thrown Carter Davis from saddle. He came down screaming, landing flush on the sharp points of a terrified steer. The steer had tossed him skyward again, much as a fighting bull tosses a gored matador.

Jim heard his death-filled final scream.

Then Davis was out of sight, down on the lava, hoofs cutting, pounding, killing. And Jim could see him no more.

Shakily, Jim went to his horse, pistol in hand. Across the herd he saw jagged, red gunflame. Juan Ferdin was shooting it out with Widespan Nelson. Jim found his saddle, knees shaky.

Across the herd, the gunfire suddenly stopped. Now the last of the steers thundered by, tails up, bawling in rage. Within a minute, the herd was gone, only a black splotch moving north across the lava, heading for the Rio Grande.

Jim finally found his voice. "Juan!" he hollered.

There was only silence. Fear tugged at Jim Parker. Juan Ferdin and Widespan Nelson had both gone down!

Then fear left him. "Over here, Jim. He got me in the shoulder. I'm over by this big boulder, fella."

"Nelson?"

"Dead as he'll ever be, Jim. Davis get away?"

Jim moved his horse out onto the lava. To get to Juan Ferdin he had to ride past the mangled, torn thing that had been Carter Davis. He did not look down. He was sick at heart.

He found Juan Ferdin sitting with his back against the boulder. The tough *rurale* had already ripped off his old shirt. He held his bandana against the bullet-hole in his left shoulder.

"The bullet went straight through, Jim." The *rurale* spat the words through pain-clenched thin lips.

"Can you move your arm?"

Juan Ferdin gingerly lifted his arm. He clenched his fist, let his arm drop.

"Then no bones are broken," Jim said. Suddenly he rose to his tall height, gun in his fist, staring to the north. Juan Ferdin, too, had got to his boots, back against the boulder, gun in his hand. Three riders moved out of the moonlight toward them.

Then a voice called, "This is Matt Smith, men."

Jim's gun sagged. Juan Ferdin let his length slide again to the ground. Ferdin said, "Clara Davis must be with him."

"The other looks like a woman, too," Jim said.

Matt Smith led the horse bearing Martha Worthington. Martha's hands were tied to the saddle-horn.

"Ran across her back yonder," Smith said, dismounting. "Reckon she was ridin' over to pick up the dope."

Jim spoke to Clara Davis. "What are you doing here?"

Matt Smith answered. "She wouldn't let me ride out of the rancho alone." His next words came hesitantly. "Carter? Where is he?"

Jim pointed silently at the dim form lying on the black lava.

Smith asked, "You – killed him?"

Jim looked at Clara Davis. Her eyes bore down on him. Her lips trembled but she sat poker-straight in her saddle, hands clenching the saddle's fork.

Jim shook his head. "Juan and I fired a few shots to turn the cattle north again. But they stampeded. And Carter was caught in the middle –"

Clara turned her horse toward the lava bed. Jim caught her reins. "Please," he pleaded.

"He's my brother," she said stiffly.

She rode away into the moonlight. They watched her dismount and kneel beside the mangled figure out there on the lava bed.

Jim's heart was heavy.

Matt Smith squatted beside Juan Ferdin and studied the *rurale's* shoulder. Martha Worthington suddenly made a gurgling sound. Jim noticed for the first time she was gagged.

Jim told him about the shoot-out with Don Enrique de la Vega and his gang. Matt Smith got to his feet, slowly rubbing his rough hands together.

"We'll get this female and Ferdin into Cardenas. Ferdin to see the doctor, the girl to jail. Then we'll head across to Bravo to see how *rurales* came out there. We got lots of work to do."

Matt Smith helped Juan Ferdin into saddle. But Jim's eyes were on the pathetic figure kneeling there on the lava bed.

He heard Juan Ferdin say, "We're ready to move, Jim."

"I'll wait," Jim said. He walked out on the lava bed. Clara Davis walked slowly toward him.

Jim waited for her.

Her hat lay on her back, held by the chin-strap.

Moonlight shot golden glory from her red hair. She stopped. She lifted her eyes and looked at him.

"It was for the best, Jim. He'd die in a few months behind bars. He had a wild sort of freedom about him –"

Jim could only nod.

"It was best he died as he did. And I am glad you did not kill him." Her voice broke.

Jim tried to speak. He couldn't. His throat was too full. He felt her hand reach out and grasp his. Her fingers were cold. He took both her hands in his.

"You're wounded, Jim. I want you to stay on Circle N until you are well. Will you promise me that, please, Jim Parker?"

Jim finally found his voice. "The pleasure, Clara, will be all mine," he said huskily.

WILDERNESS

GIANT SPECIAL EDITION: HAWKEN FURY
by David Thompson

Tough mountain men, proud Indians, and an America that was wild and free! It's twice the authentic frontier action and adventure during America's Black Powder Days!

AMERICA 1836

Although it took immense courage for frontiersmen like Nathaniel King to venture into the vast territories west of the Mississippi River, the freedom those bold adventures won in the unexplored region was worth the struggle.

THE HOME OF THE BRAVE

But when an old sweetheart from the East came searching for him, King learned that sometimes the deadliest foe could appear to be a trusted friend. And if he wasn't careful, the life he had worked so hard to build might be stolen from him and traded away for a few pieces of gold.

_3291-0 $4.50 US/$5.50 CAN

LEISURE BOOKS
ATTN: Order Department
276 5th Avenue, New York, NY 10001

Please add $1.50 for shipping and handling for the first book and $.35 for each book thereafter. N.Y.S. and N.Y.C. residents, please add appropriate sales tax. No cash, stamps, or C.O.D.s. All orders shipped within 6 weeks via postal service book rate. Canadian orders require $2.00 extra postage. It must also be paid in U.S. dollars through a U.S. banking facility.

Name _____

Address _____

City _____ State _____ Zip _____

I have enclosed $_____ in payment for the checked book(s). Payment <u>must</u> accompany all orders. ☐ Please send a free catalog.

WHEN AMERICA WAS REALLY FREE!

WILDERNESS

By David Thompson

Tough mountain men, proud Indians, and an America that was wild and free—authentic frontier adventure during America's Black Powder Days.

#10: Blackfoot Massacre. After facing all the dangers the wild could offer, Nate King never expected trouble from a missionary bent on converting hostile Indians. But then the Reverend John Burke is trapped in perilous Blackfoot territory, Nate has to save him—or he'll bear the brand of a coward until the day he dies.

_3318-6 $3.50 US/$4.50 CAN

#11: Northwest Passage. When Nate agrees to lead a seemingly innocent group of pioneers, he makes a mistake that might be his last. For the members of the Banner party have a secret they do not want revealed, and they are more than willing to kill to keep it hidden.

_3343-7 $3.50 US/$4.50 CAN

#12: Apache Blood. When Nate and his family travel to the southern Rockies, bloodthirsty Apache warriors kidnap his wife and son. With the help of his friend Shakespeare McNair, Nate will save his loved ones—or pay the ultimate price.

_3374-7 $3.50 US/$4.50 CAN

LEISURE BOOKS
ATTN: Order Department
276 5th Avenue, New York, NY 10001

Please add $1.50 for shipping and handling for the first book and $.35 for each book thereafter. PA., N.Y.S. and N.Y.C. residents, please add appropriate sales tax. No cash, stamps, or C.O.D.s. All orders shipped within 6 weeks via postal service book rate. Canadian orders require $2.00 extra postage and must be paid in U.S. dollars through a U.S. banking facility.

Name _____

Address _____

City _____ State _____ Zip _____

I have enclosed $_____in payment for the checked book(s).

Payment <u>must</u> accompany all orders.☐ Please send a free catalog.

GORDON D. SHIRREFFS

Two Classic Westerns
In One Rip-roaring Volume!
A $7.00 Value For Only 4.50!

"These Westerns are written by the hand of a master!"
—New York *Times*

LAST TRAIN FROM GUN HILL/THE BORDER GUIDON
__3361-5 $4.50

BARRANCA/JACK OF SPADES
__3384-4 $4.50

BRASADA/BLOOD JUSTICE
__3410-7 $4.50

LEISURE BOOKS
ATTN: Order Department
276 5th Avenue, New York, NY 10001

Please add $1.50 for shipping and handling for the first book and $.35 for each book thereafter. PA., N.Y.S. and N.Y.C. residents, please add appropriate sales tax. No cash, stamps, or C.O.D.s. All orders shipped within 6 weeks via postal service book rate. Canadian orders require $2.00 extra postage and must be paid in U.S. dollars through a U.S. banking facility.

Name _____
Address _____
City _____ State _____ Zip _____
I have enclosed $_____in payment for the checked book(s).
Payment <u>must</u> accompany all orders.☐ Please send a free catalog.

CHEYENNE

JUDD COLE

Follow the adventures of Touch the Sky as he searches for a world he can call his own!

#1: Arrow Keeper. Born Indian, raised white, Touch the Sky longs to find his place among his own people. But he will need a warrior's courage, strength, and skill to battle the enemies who would rather see him die than call him brother.

_3312-7 $3.50 US/$4.50 CAN

#2: Death Chant. Feared and despised by his tribe, Touch the Sky must prove his loyalty to the Cheyenne before they will accept him. And when the death chant arises, he knows if he fails he will not die alone.

_3337-2 $3.50 US/$4.50 CAN

LEISURE BOOKS
ATTN: Order Department
276 5th Avenue, New York, NY 10001

Please add $1.50 for shipping and handling for the first book and $.35 for each book thereafter. PA., N.Y.S. and N.Y.C. residents, please add appropriate sales tax. No cash, stamps, or C.O.D.s. All orders shipped within 6 weeks via postal service book rate. Canadian orders require $2.00 extra postage and must be paid in U.S. dollars through a U.S. banking facility.

Name _____

Address _____

City _____ State _____ Zip _____

I have enclosed $_____ in payment for the checked book(s).
Payment <u>must</u> accompany all orders. ☐ Please send a free catalog.

SPEND YOUR LEISURE MOMENTS WITH US.

Hundreds of exciting titles to choose from—something for everyone's taste in fine books: breathtaking historical romance, chilling horror, spine-tingling suspense, taut medical thrillers, involving mysteries, action-packed men's adventure and wild Westerns.

SEND FOR A FREE CATALOGUE TODAY!

Leisure Books
Attn: Customer Service Department
276 5th Avenue. New York. NY 10001